THE WHYTE
HARTE

THE WHYTE HARTE

P.C. DOHERTY

St. Martin's Press

New York

In memory of
Colonel Gilland Corbett, D.F.C.
killed in Vietnam 1967.

Library of Congress Cataloging-in-Publication Data

Doherty, P. C.
        The Whyte Harte / P. C. Doherty.
                p.   cm.
        ISBN 0-312-02318-9
        1. Great Britain—History—House of Lancaster, 1399–1461—
Fiction.
        2. Richard II, King of England, 1367–1400—Fiction.   I. Title.
        PR6054.037W48   1988
        823′.914—dc19   88-17670
                                                               CIP

First published in Great Britain by Robert Hale Limited.

First U.S. Edition

10 9 8 7 6 5 4 3 2 1

PART ONE
The Whyte Harte

1

I have always been a liar. I must try hard to tell the truth. I have taken a vow to be honest but I find it difficult to keep a straight face, even as I write these words. Just think, Matthew Jankyn, Oxford scholar, soldier, veteran of Agincourt, confidant of kings and rebels! Well I know the truth. And what is that? Jankyn is a spy. Jankyn is a coward and, above all, Jankyn is a liar. I look back on my life and search hard for the truth. Jankyn amidst the mud, shit and corpses of Northern France. Jankyn in secret chambers, in shadows, in hamlets, in palaces. Jankyn in cold rooms, wet and dishevelled. Jankyn wrapped in silken sheets with soft-fleshed, white-skinned, perfumed girls. But, always, Jankyn the liar.

It was not always like this. I was a child once, innocent and quiet, smiling at all, and disapproving of no one. Perhaps that is when it started, not with a king who refused to die, but with a mother who died too early, too soon, buried and forgotten in a forlorn, derelict cemetery of Newport, a small village in Shropshire. I was born there. My father was well to do. An educated man of few words and no past. He worked for the Coate family. Lords of the manor, which included Newport, a host of other little villages and all the land in between them. A hard man my father. He drove my mother into an early grave, or so the village gossips muttered. He wanted sons and got them, but they only died, scraps of flesh baptised, shrouded and buried. Finally there was me, mewing weakly, the runt of the litter, only this time it was my mother who died. She never stopped bleeding after my birth, caught a fever and was dead within six months of my baptism. My father hired a wet nurse, who fed and raised me and noisily served him in bed. She was the only parent I had. My father neglected me, apart from a gruff word or the occasional kick or blow.

I grew up rather sickly, fully determined to win my father's approval. I failed to do that. Instead, I was educated. I was thin and short but, in the words of the local priest, 'The good God had given me a brain'. Silly bastard! What did he know? My father swindled him. As a steward, my father controlled the Coate estate and consequently the priest's house and glebe. The church was my father's meeting-place, not the sanctuary with its great oak altar and marble steps hidden by the chancel screen and rood loft. My father left the sanctuary alone and used the huge vaulting nave where he exercised his power and office of steward, sitting in his heavy carved chair behind a long polished bench. Here the villagers came to present their accounts at Michaelmas and midsummer. My father was stern but, in the main, fair. He only kept back a small portion of their rents for himself but the old priest was a different matter. My father did not like priests. I never knew why but when the villagers brought their tithes, my father always pocketed some of them. He also forced the fellow to provide me with the rudiments of education and I learnt avidly. I mastered Latin, a little Greek, courtly French and even some history, most of it wrong but at least it gave me some idea of a wider world and more exciting events. It also comforted me for the village children treated me as if I were some strange animal or marauding beast. They did not like me, with my shock of black hair, thin white face and clever green eyes which, they stupidly maintained, reminded them of a weasel rather than a boy. I had my revenge. I used to plot and follow them and when they broke into an orchard or tried to take fat carp or juicy perch from the manor pool, I would tell my father and listen gleefully to the details of their punishment. After all, I did them no wrong except try to make friends, only to be driven off.

On one occasion, in my twelfth or thirteenth summer, I fell into one of their traps. They encouraged a village wench, high-bosomed and wide-hipped, to look coyly at me during Sunday Mass. Even then, at that tender age, I found I responded quickly to any girl or woman who favoured me. This was the first time. The wench repeated the performance the following week and began to wait for me when I finished my lessons with the old mumbling priest. I remember her as if it were yesterday, standing in the sunlight of a summer day, wanting to talk to me or ask my help with some minor rustic problem. I responded. One evening, full of courage, I followed her into a cornfield, up along a hedge into a small copse at the top of a hill. I began to fondle and kiss her, desperately trying to push my hands up into her thick fustian skirt, but she laughed and teased me and I grew red-faced and strident as both my lust and my resentment grew. Suddenly the copse came alive with village children who laughed, pointing their dirty fingers at me and calling out rude names. I stood, white-faced, hands clenched, the scalding tears running down my face as the girl burst into peals of raucous mocking laughter while the children ran off, their cruel jibes and insults carried back on the soft evening breeze. Since then I have rarely cried or trusted any woman, except one, but that is another story.

In my fourteenth summer the priest informed my father that he had taught me all he could and I was packed off to the monastery school at the abbey of Lilleshall. Lilleshall was an Augustinian monastery about three miles from Newport. In my lonely expeditions into the countryside I had often seen its towering church soaring above the trees and watched the monks and lay brothers going about their business in the outlying granges or fields. I never dreamt I would spend some of my life there but that fool of a parish priest informed my father that I had completed the 'Ars Minor' of Donatius and it was time I moved on to greater things. My father listened, nodded his thanks, and within two weeks I was on my way to Lilleshall.

I was neither pleased nor sad to leave home, just indifferent. I sat behind my father on his huge chestnut horse which had seen better days as a destrier of Lord William Coate and been bought by my father at a low price, while all my possessions were loaded on to a sumpter pony. When we reached the abbey, my father had a few words with the novice-master, a thin, ascetic man with a hatchet face and steel-grey hair. He listened politely enough to my father's words, accepted two clinking leather pouches, stared at me and muttered his thanks. My father did not say goodbye but gently tapped me on the shoulder and shoved me towards the waiting novice-master. I was then in my fourteenth summer and committed to spend four years at Lilleshall.

I may have moaned about my life in Newport but at least it was comfortable. My father had owned a two-storied building with a hall, parlour, kitchen and buttery over wide deep cellars. On the first floor were bedrooms with soft feathered mattresses, bolsters and thick woollen blankets. There was a garden containing a small orchard, pear and apple trees and rectangular flower beds, all ringed by a high wall. Let me put this right. My father looked after me. Food was never scarce, a sup of wine or almond milk in the morning, quince marmalade, fruit preserve, fresh cooked meat and warm baked bread, but Lilleshall was different. I was frightened by the huge, airless church, the stonework rising above me with no evident support, it always seemed as if it was about to crash about our heads. There was a tympanum above the entrance with Christ in judgement staring down at me, the saints held in one hand while on His left, grotesque devils with faces of monks and the bodies of women hurried the damned to the ever-flickering stone flames of Hell.

There were other boys in the abbey, some were scholars, others novices. We were all equally miserable. Everything I remember about the place was cold. The church, the library, the cloisters and the long, draughty dorter where we slept in wooden beds, made no more comfortable by thin straw mattresses which would have disgraced a peasant's hovel. Our day was ruled by the dreary routine of the abbey, the horarium; up before dawn and down in our sandals and habits to the ice-cold church to sing Matins to a God who, if He had any sense, would have been fast asleep. The only warm places in the abbey were the calderium (or drying room) and the infirmary. I tried to feign sickness but the cold-hearted novice-master hunted me down and threw me out whether I was sick or not.

After Prime or morning prayers, we had watered ale and dry bread before the day's tasks began. In spring and autumn it would mean hard labour in the outfields of the abbey, but usually it was cleaning the piggery or the lavatory. The novice-master always ensured that I was assigned to such tasks – the bastard. I can never really trust a monk since my four years at Lilleshall. The rest of the day, however, was spent in study and schooling broken by prayer and a meal of boiled cabbage or lettuce and old salt-pickled meat, garnished with onions, shallots or leeks. Our lessons took place in the library, a long, narrow room by the cloisters with desks at right angles with the walls so we had the light from the pointed horn-glazed windows. At first it was the basics; I was given a penner, a belt with its own ink-horn and a sheaf of pens, then taught how to clean parchment by rubbing the coarse vellum smoothly with a rounded pumice stone. After this we graduated to the trivium and quadrivium; the books being removed from their heavy wooden carved aumbries or cupboards and brought to be chained to our benches.

These books were my release. My escape. I read the writings of Jerome and the fathers. The *Monologion* of Anselm, the *Policraticus* of John of Salisbury. Yet, praised

be God, there was more. Each heavy, leather-bound
volume contained other words stitched into it. The
revoluntionary theories of Marsilius of Padua and the
strange utterances of a Leicestershire priest, John
Wycliffe, who taught that wicked priests or rulers should
not be obeyed. I thought of the novice-master and the
gaunt, severe prior and heartily agreed with Wycliffe
whoever he was. I knew nothing of him then and so could
not imagine how his teachings would bring me within an
inch of the rope and a strangling death in St Giles market
in London. But enough of this, I hurry on. At Lilleshall I
was only concerned with surviving each brutal, cold day
and books and study provided the escape.

I portrayed myself as an avid student to Brother
Christopher, the dotard of a librarian who was only too
willing to admit me to his sanctum. I combed each volume
for material to read and valued the treasures I found.
Legends about Arthur, portions of Boccaccio's *Decameron*,
and the sainted Chaucer, so recently dead. The
Augustinians admired his writings and I greedily read *The
Astrolobe* and, above all, *The Patient Griselda*. A tale about a
saintly wife who, stupid bitch, allowed her husband to beat
her. I remembered the girl at Newport and the hot,
scalding tears her mockery had provoked and read the tale
whenever I was tired or fatigued. My desire to study and
the quick absorption of all I learnt commended me to the
brothers who relaxed their discipline, though I was
virtually shunned by my fellows for being too studious. I
did not care, biting my lip when I was not invited to find
the shinbone of an ox, to go skating on the frozen pond, or
be involved in their raucous music when, on feast days,
they relaxed with the gittern or rotte.

On these holy days we were given a rest from our duties
and allowed to rest. The others, as I have said, played
music, rolled dice, or went walking. I returned to the
library to read and dream about a life of luxury or the
coming meal. We ate well on feast days, mustard and

brawn, fresh-spiced soups and herb-strewn pot-roasts with
a cup of full-bodied wine and sliced, roasted apples. After
such a meal I would return to my dreams of women, trying
to remember the soft brownness of the girl in Newport or
the smooth-limbed bodies of curving dancing girls which
were drawn with resplendent colour and vigour in the
corners and margins of some of the manuscripts I studied.
The monks who had drawn them had added tails, scales,
the heads of horses and the faces of monkeys. I did not
care, for their bodies were still marble-white, smooth, and
they fevered my imagination and plagued my dreams.

The days, months, seasons passed; all marked and
registered by the horarium of the abbey and the liturgy of
the church; the 'Puer Natus' sung on misty Christmas-day
mornings, the 'Resurrexit sicut dixit' of Easter and the
dirges for the dead in November. The outside world, my
world, rarely intervened. My father sent me money, the
occasional pound, and visited me once. But, even then, I
knew, secretly realised that my youth was dead. The real
world, the cruel, mouth-yawning, hungry world made
itself felt. Ricardus Rex. King Richard II, blond-haired,
blue-eyed, imperious and tyrannical, was, ironically, the
first to disturb my life. Lilleshall was a quiet island in the
swirling, blood-frothed politics of the time but the news
came through in my first year at the abbey. Pedlars,
messengers and chapmen brought us fragments of
information which joined together and seeped into our
lives. Richard the King was gone. He had travelled across
the western ocean to Ireland to crush the wild tribes and,
in his absence, Henry of Lancaster, his long-banished
cousin, had returned like a thief breaking into an empty
house. Henry landed in Yorkshire, bravely claiming that
he had come to save his own inheritance but the barons,
the powerful, silk-garbed earls had joined him and poured
honeyed poison into his ear. How he, like his cousin, King
Richard, was the grandson of the mighty King Edward III
and so had a better claim to the throne, much better than

the childless, childish Richard, or his weak cousin, Edmund, the Earl of March. Henry listened to them and claimed the throne of England. His troops, swollen on every side by the armies of the Percies, the great northern barons, poured south like some ravenous torrent and trapped the hapless Richard in Wales.

Henry's army invaded the monastery for a few days, its cloistered stillness broken by their high northern voices and the clash of booted spurs. The abbey was full of them; knights in half-armour, their foam-flecked destriers grazed on the abbey lawns while their men-at-arms invaded the kitchen. I watched a group of the latter, short, burly men in steel-rimmed hats, boiled leather jackets with stout, brown leggings pushed into dusty battered boots. Their eyes were red-rimmed, cold and hostile, their unshaven faces cruel, though they moved with a swagger and pride I envied. I wished I was with them and, of course, failed to appreciate that one day I would be, in the most terrible of circumstances. Then they were gone, the quiet air still ringing with catcalls and their strong northern words which burred the air and stung your ear. They were hunting the King, who was fleeing like the Whyte Harte of his emblem, and they brought him to bay in the castle of Flint. Richard was handed over to his captors, hurried to London, deposed and hustled north to his secret death. The countryside was rife with rumours that perhaps the King, the Lord's anointed, could not die and so Richard was free, riding a pale, bright stallion through the green, dark woods of England. Yet the rumours meant nothing to me. Strange! Like a swimmer I ignored the rising ripples which would later swamp me.

The new King, the brown-berried, bearded Henry IV, soon had troubles of his own which disturbed the life of the monastery. His problems began in Wales among the mist and tortuous politics of that mysterious, divided country. The Welsh Marcher barons, who supported Henry in his bid for the throne, now believed they could encroach on the rights of the Welsh princelings and annex their river meadows and rich valley lands. The greater predator amongst these was Grey of Ruthin who began his own private war against the Welsh lord, Owen Glendower, a spark which fanned up into a fierce blaze, for Glendower resisted, checked Grey and brought all Wales into open revolt against its English king.

The Welsh pushed the English back and followed them into the border counties of Hereford, Gloucester and Shropshire. Our prior had to levy troops and sent urgent requests for help against bands of marauding Welsh who ravaged the surrounding countryside, leaving columns of smoke which rose above the trees to hang in black clouds against the summer-blue sky. Yet the Welsh did not attack us and the King sent his own son, Prince Henry, to drive the rebels back up their valleys and into the forests or high mountains. However, Henry IV's problems did not end there. Fresh rumours reached the abbey that the flaxen-haired Richard II, in costly robes of black velvet, riding a richly caparisoned sorrel, had been seen in countless places, always preceded by a smooth-skinned, pure white hart which bore a blazing cross between its antlers. Brother Christopher told me these were rumours spread by wandering friars who had always loved the former king and resented Henry's usurpation.

Nevertheless, the rumours were rife and believed by the powerful Percy faction, led by their general, Hotspur. He now openly acknowledged that his former support of the usurper, Henry of Lancaster, was mistaken and vowed he would act to redress the wrong. He did, in the hot boiling summer of 1403. His troops once more marched south, hurrying to join up with Glendower, who would come out of Wales to join him. The Welsh prince never arrived and King Henry and his warlike heir trapped the rebels at Shrewsbury and utterly destroyed them. Hotspur was killed by an archer and his troops melted away like snow under the sun. The rebel leaders were dragged by the heels into Shrewsbury town and hanged like gutted pigs in the market place.

Some of the rebels brought the news to Lilleshall. I was working in the outfields the morning they came. At first they were simply puffballs of dust but, as they drew nearer, racing along the track which served as a road between the fields of golden corn, I could see they were defeated, harassed men. Their horses were blown and covered in heavy white lines of sweaty foam, their riders dishevelled, bloody and scarred. They stopped to draw water at the well to refresh their horses, shouting strident commands and looking fearfully back down the track. Then they were gone and, in a short while, their pursuers appeared, brusque, hard-faced men wearing the red, gold and blue of the royal livery. I think they caught their prey, for one of the lay brothers later reported seeing black-faced corpses swinging from elm trees outside the village of Donnington. So, King Henry was safe and the scene was now ready for me. I did not know it, I ignored the rumours that King Richard was still alive, his sacred white hart still padding softly through the green woods of England, ready to draw hundreds to their death.

2

In the January of 1404, a few months after King Henry's victory at Shrewsbury, my father made one of his rare visits to the monastery. He came alone across the black, frost-hardened countryside and, for the first time ever, seemed pleased to see me. He sat slumped in the paved

room of the guestmaster, warming numb fingers over a
brazier, and smiled as I came in. I felt a twinge of
compassion for he looked tired and worried but I did not
ask how he was. It was too late. You cannot expect, can
you, flames and warmth from dead coals?

'Matthew,' he murmured. 'It is good to see you.' He
nodded towards the silent guestmaster. 'I understand you
are doing very well. In fact, the monks can no longer teach
you and that is why I am here.' He looked down and
shuffled his feet. 'I have,' he almost whispered, 'always
done the best for you. Your mother would have wanted
this.' He looked at me beseechingly but I just stared back.
After seventeen years he referred to her but still I gave no
response. 'You are,' he rushed to continue, 'to leave here in
late summer and go to Exeter Hall at Oxford University.'
He smiled wearily. 'My son,' he exclaimed, 'at Oxford!'
Then I did smile back. I was to be free of the abbey and far
from my father. I knew what the theologians meant by
heavenly bliss. Little did I know it was to mark my descent
into hell.

The months passed. My father returned with money,
robes, a horse, a sumpter pony and mouthfuls of advice. I
ignored the latter and took the rest and was free of the
abbey by August, making my way across the lush,
summer-green freshness of the Cotswolds towards
Oxford. It was a pleasant rural scene made all the more
beautiful by a sense of complete freedom which sang like
wine in my head. I stopped at a village with an ale-stake
house and ate and drank what I wanted. Then I seduced
the slattern who worked there, taking her time and again
in a ruined, deserted byre which served as a stable. After
that my blood cooled and I travelled more apprehensively
as I crossed the main roads which stretched north. Once
again there were troops trudging through the dust, spears
and billhooks slung across their shoulders, their steel
helmets doffed and their boiled leather jackets open to
afford some relief from the hordes of flies and the heavy

summer heat. Long rows, columns of foot and archers whilst behind them trundled carts piled high under barrels, stores and weapons. I asked one of the many outriders what was happening and he stared at me strangely. 'Have you not heard?' he asked, wiping sweat-grimed lips, greedily grabbing the water-bag I passed him. 'No,' I muttered. 'I have been away.' The rider rinsed out his mouth, spat and took another long drink. 'It's Northumberland. Percy again. Hotspur's father. He's returned from exile announcing that Richard II is free and should be restored to his throne. We are going north to kill him and, once and for all, we will finish this business.' He handed back the water-bag, nodded and galloped off. I sat and waited for a gap in the column and crossed on my way.

Strange wasn't it that even then the Whyte Harte made its appearance, crossing my path? I should have seen it as an omen but I was too stupid, too concerned with immediate affairs. I continued on my journey. I had been worried about the dangers of the road, from marauders and outlaws, but I went unscathed. Perhaps it was the presence of soldiers in the neighbourhood or the many scaffolds and gibbets I passed, each with its load of blackened, maggot-ridden corpses. On the fourth day after leaving Lilleshall I crossed the river into Oxford and made my way down the busy high road towards Carfax, then round into Broad Street and into the Turl where Exeter Hall stood, a three-storied house with a warren of rooms which served as my home for the next six years.

I suppose everyone knows Oxford as a place of learning. A peaceful island in the middle of the hurly-burly of the times. If you do, dismiss it as nonsense, the jabberings of people who really should know better. It is a dirty place. The city is built round nine colleges or halls with other buildings, churches and a myriad of ale-houses. The centre, Carfax, stank like a sewer because of the great runnel down its centre full of ordure, shit and animal corpses. Broad Street had piggeries with the swine rooting for food amongst the rubbish (ever since I saw a pig nosing at the swollen belly of a dead mongrel, I have never been able to eat bacon). Admittedly it was not all filth. Catte Street, full of scriveners and parchment sellers, was attractive with the house and shop fronts carved and sharply painted in white, pink and solid black. Nevertheless, the city was offensive and the university was no better. Exeter Hall, founded by Bishop Stapleton of Exeter, was a large building with a warren of rooms. On the floor level was a huge hall, forty feet wide, built over deep stone cellars where provisions were stored. Around this were kitchens, buttery, counting-offices and the chambers of the regent who supervised the Hall and exacted fivepence a week from me for bed and food. None of these amounted to much. I shared a garret room with three other fellows. We each had a battered trunk for our possessions and a wooden bed with a mattress which had more sacking than straw. The food was meagre and never enough and I had to buy pies, bread and ale from the market. My father sent me sufficient monies so I never starved, the same cannot be said of my companions and I constantly supplied them with food and pennies. Poor bastard churls! I never felt sorry for them. It is just that other people's suffering interferes with my own pleasure.

If I had become immersed in Oxford I might have stayed there for life. The course was long enough. I began in the Michaelmas term of 1404 and saw a comfortable life ahead for me. Four years studying for the Bachelor of Arts, three years more for the Master's and then another eight to ten years depending on whether I chose medicine, law or theology. Small wonder that many left with nothing. Not that I should complain, I was one of them. Our studies were based on the Trivium; Grammar, Rhetoric and Logic; followed by the Quadrivium; Arithmetic, Geometry, Music, I am sorry but I have forgotten the fourth. In fact, I can remember little of my studies. I attended two lectures a day and ploughed through works such as *Coeli et Mundi* (*Of Heaven and Earth*); Aquinas' *Summa* and Aristotle's minor works. God, how they bored me. Logic, however, was different. I excelled at it and attended every disputation, waiting to take the chair and present my own arguments, enjoying the clash of words and the subtle probings of clever minds. After four years I could have entered for my Bachelor's degree and obeyed the university statute which said I should spend a few days in the Schools, (the faculty building) and dispute any three questions in Philosophy and Logic. But, alas, I could not abide dry books and futile theological debate, so I turned to other matters.

I did not have many friends but I joined in the revelry, the drinking and endless games of dice and chance. I attended bear-baiting in St Giles. Mummers' plays in the market-place and, of course, the furious forays between the different nations at Oxford, taking special delight in provoking the French, Scots and Germans, whilst keeping an eye on the university proctors as well as the bailiffs from the town. The latter were the most dangerous. Riots between town and gown were common and, in Edward III's time, had broken out into civil war with students killed and the Halls put to the torch. Every year since then, on the anniversary of the riot, the Mayor of Oxford went to the university church of St Mary to do repentance and ask forgiveness for the town for their errors against the university. It may have allayed the wounded ghosts of the slain students but did little to improve relations between the townspeople and the university.

You must not think I was the merry student of legend, lecherous and carefree, but neither was I a chancery clerk with a lofty moral tone to my life and words. In fact, most of the time I was bored, taking my father's money and drifting like some leaf on a sluggish river. Once the freshness of arriving in Oxford disappeared I felt I was back in Lilleshall and so moved into defiance. Ovid's *De arte Amandi* was forbidden, so I read it. The church looked

down on Marsilius of Padua so he became my hero, and
Archbishop Arundel, that fiery old fanatic, was hot against
Wycliffe and the Lollards, so I became interested in them.
Wycliffe, a Leicestershire priest and theologian, had
attacked the church some three decades earlier. None had
escaped his bitter pen or acid tongue: pope, bishop or
priest. The sacraments, the mass, all were attacked with
equal venom. He had eventually been banned, driven back
to his country parish, but his followers, the poor priests
dressed in russet gowns, spread his teaching around the
countryside. They preached the primacy of scripture, the
poverty of Christ and attacked the wealth and pomp of the
church.

Richard II had left them alone, nay, even supported
them. Of course, there is no proof of that, except Richard's
first wife, the beloved Anne of Bohemia, came from a
country tainted with similar heresies. John Montague, Earl
of Salisbury, and Richard's most fervent supporter, was
certainly a Lollard. He protected them and, when Henry of
Lancaster was ready to strike off his head for supporting
King Richard, Montague refused the ministrations of a
chaplain, saying he trusted to God and his own prayers. The
Lollards found favour in Oxford, as did the emblem of the
Whyte Harte and the cause of Richard. Men persisted in
saying he was still alive. There were rumours that he was in
Scotland sheltered by Henry's enemies and, so widespread
were these rumours, they forced Henry and his Parliaments
to act. William Searle, Richard II's chamberlain, went to the
scaffold for saying Richard still lived and, in 1406, the King
was petitioned to pass a statute against those who claimed
King Richard was alive in Scotland. The troops I had seen
marching north to challenge old Northumberland won a
victory but the old Earl escaped to continue his campaign
against Henry of Lancaster and give credence to the
rumour that Richard was still alive. He continued to plague
Henry until royal troops trapped and killed him at Bramham on the wild Yorkshire moors in 1408.

I must admit I loved such intrigue. I was against the church for it was authority; against the King for he was a father while the vision of the Whyte Harte and a mysterious, undying king appealed to my bored, tired brain. I once heard a story, years later, about mythical beasts which decoy hunters to their deaths in the darkness of deep forests. The Whyte Harte of Richard II was like that and, like a fool, I blundered after it. I did not really care for the Lollards or their theology which I dismissed as illogical. If God is all powerful and He wants to shelter beneath bread and wine, then so be it. The only important thing is, do you believe it? No, the Lollards were a distraction, a flirtation with danger and, like any coward, I enjoyed it. The King retaliated against the muttering of heretics by decreeing they should burn and his old Chancellor, Archbishop Arundel, turned his full fury against the university, snouting out heresy like a rat does food. Oh, the game was a good one. I posed as a radical reformer and, God knows, the church in Oxford needed reforming. At nearby Littlemore Priory, the Prioress sold church property, invited her men friends in for a romp and wore her habit like any courtesan: her veil high on her head and gold rings on her fingers. She even persisted in keeping a menagerie of wild animals, squirrels, monkeys and dogs who ran wild through the priory and disrupted divine service. The canons at Bicester were no better, living the life of luxury with thirty servants to look after eleven silk-garbed priests. I joined in the general criticism, totally ignoring the good, poor priests or my own lechery and greed. I rejoiced in the epithet 'Lollard' and postured and posed as a radical reformer. The regent of our Hall, John Scawsby, sought an interview and warned me to be careful, but I laughed in his face.

'Do what you will,' I taunted, ignoring the angry flush which suffused his face. 'Tell me where I am wrong and, if not, leave me alone.'

Scawsby gulped back his anger and studied my face.

'You are an angry man, Master Jankyn,' he replied. 'You are also a fool to taunt me.'

'If the cap fits,' I quipped, 'wear it!'

'You may have to one day,' he almost shouted.

'Sufficient for the day is the evil thereof,' I retorted, misquoting scripture and, turning on my heel, walked out.

I did rue the day and so proved stupid Scawsby a prophet. My father constantly sent me money and letters, the former I spent, the latter I threw away but, in the December of 1410, both stopped. I did not query it for bad weather had made the roads impassable with heavy drifts of snow and thick sheets of ice. Yuletide came and went in a flurry of snowstorms. Oxford was covered in white, making the buildings stark and black against its brilliance. I dug into my own pocket for monies but by Twelfth Night I was desperate and sought an interview with the cretinous Scawsby. He almost seemed to have been waiting for me in his charcoal-warmed chamber. He was wrapped in a number of dirty old robes, a cup of mulled wine between his fingers. He did not ask me to sit but stared smugly at me as I haltingly made my request for help. I watched his small, hard eyes, two piss-holes in his snow-white face and realised something was wrong. He heard me out, nodded and began to search amongst the bits of parchment which littered his desk.

'I meant to send for you, Jankyn,' he began. 'I had an important letter from Lord Coates.' He searched again. 'Ah!' he exclaimed, picking it up from the table. 'Here it is. It's addressed to me so I cannot show you it, but it contains bad news.' He stared up at me, his face full of hypocritical concern. 'It would appear,' he began smoothly, 'your father is dead. He was stupid enough to become involved in some conspiracy on the Welsh March. A group of fanatics, supporters of the deposed King Richard, plotted rebellion, were caught and killed.'

I stared back, rigid with shock. First, I had never thought of my father dying. He was always there and, so I thought, always would be, like the sun or moon. As for being a supporter of the dead Richard? I thought hard. My father had never discussed anything with me, though I knew he was friendly with farmers who lived in Cheshire and had provided men for Richard's own bodyguard, the 'Cheshire archers' who packed Richard's court and overawed any Parliament, boldly flaunting the King's own insignia, the Whyte Harte. I almost smiled. How alike my father and I were and how curious that the Whyte Harte had once more touched my life.

'Do you want details?' Scawsby hopefully interrupted.

'Yes, yes,' I replied wearily. 'How did he die?'

'The conspiracy was organised by ex-members of Richard's Cheshire archers,' Scawsby replied. 'They lifted the black banner of revolt, openly wearing the Whyte Harte emblem, proclaiming that Richard was alive and the rightful king. They tried to seize Ludlow Castle but were trapped and scattered, your father was killed in the rout.'

I thought of my father lying in the cold marshy ground around Ludlow. 'His body?' I asked.

'Taken and buried,' Scawsby replied.

'Where?'

'Newport, a pauper's grave!'

Now I knew there was more. Some dreadful vision, just out of sight, and Scawsby was intent on bringing me to view it.

'A pauper's grave,' he repeated firmly. 'Your father died an attainted traitor. His land and chattels are forfeit to the crown. That is why you have no money, will have no money!' He almost snorted. 'Indeed you could be in danger. Son of a traitor, your Lollard sympathies are well known!'

I stood shocked, still listening to that malicious, vindictive half-man drone on. I was finished at Oxford and I knew that the ivory tower I had lived in since I was a child was now shattered. I ignored Scawsby and turned to go.

'You are to be out of this Hall within a day!' he shouted

after me. 'So what do you think of that? Is sufficient for the
day still the evil thereof?'

I turned. 'You did ask,' I replied, 'what I thought of your
words, so I will show you.' I unbuttoned my codpiece and
urinated on the straw-covered floor. Scawsby watched the
hot piss steam up and jumped squealing to his feet, but I
was gone, my fear hidden behind peals of raucous,
mocking laughter.

3

I did leave Exeter Hall within the day. My few belongings,
clothes, books and penner, all bundled into a parcel. I sold
the books and used the money for food while I begged
favours from friends. I slept on floors and in outhouses,
always moving on as I outstayed my welcome or the
university authorities, now alerted about my situation,
issued bans against me and used pressure on those who
might have helped. It was the same when I tried to seek
employment. Oxford was full of starving clerks and I had
no trade nor letters of accreditation. Slowly I slipped down
the ladder into the black mire of poverty. I began to collect
rags to protect my body against the freezing cold and
joined the other outcasts under the town wall sheltering in
crude, straw-thatched hovels, begging or stealing food.
That winter was hard and merciless; riders froze in the
saddle, the old just died, and any child or babe was lucky to
survive into the cold, wet spring. I ate dog flesh, raw
vegetables and putrid, discarded meat; my belly turned to
water, I caught a fever and spent days in some damp, leaky

hut shivering and shaking in my delirium. In my dreams, I met and cursed my father, saw the white, elegant hart lope over the green fields of Lilleshall, turning to beckon me to follow it, its curving white neck, perfect head and amber eyes tempting me into the cool, green forests of the night. I did not pursue it but, in my fevered state, stood my ground for something warned of death if I did.

The fever passed and I awoke, bearded and weak, but hungry enough to rise and look for something to eat. I was lucky, a drunkard in Broad Street spilled his purse and I quickly collected the pennies, pushing the man aside and glaring around like some savage wolf. No one stopped me. I grabbed my ill-gotten gains and fled, or rather stumbled, into Aldgate and the Blue Boar Inn to gorge myself sick on baked herring strewn with sugar, a dish of eels, spiced minced chicken, hot apples and pears, their age disguised beneath a layer of sugared almond cream, all of it swilled down with tankards of rich brown ale. It was a feast. A meal which saved my life but I should not have gone for I met Edmund Luttrell. I do not know if he just joined me or was there when I arrived but, half-asleep, belly swollen, I looked up and saw his thin, cruel face staring down at me. His black hood was pulled over his cropped head, hiding his clipped ears and shadowing his ice-blue eyes. Dressed in black, swathed in a threadbare cloak which concealed his tanned leggings and faded crumpled jerkin, he looked like some ruffled crow, his unblinking stare just as intent and predatory. I felt good so I nodded, he smiled, showing his yellow, broken teeth, and sat down beside me at the trestle table.

We made light conversation before he introduced himself, Edmund Luttrell, defrocked priest, former Oxford cleric, once a thief (hence the clipped ears), but now in search of fresh employment. He was a glib talker, replenishing my tankard with ale as he watched me closely. I told him my story and he listened compassionately, nodding at appropriate places and making sympathetic noises. He seemed interested in my father's rebellion and, fishing in his large tattered purse, passed a piece of worn cloth across to me. It was a badge of the Whyte Harte, the silver now faded but still distinct, it knelt with a small crown round its slender neck and its doleful eyes sought mine like a vision from my fevered brain. I shivered slightly and handed it back.

'Where does it come from?'

'Bramham Moor,' Luttrell replied. 'I was there when the old Earl of Northumberland was trapped by the sheriffs' levies. A terrible carnage,' he muttered, 'caught out there on the moor. On our right and back were marsh and on the other archers and soldiers of the local levies. We fought under the standard of the Percies and the Whyte Harte of Richard, for Northumberland told us that the King was still alive in Scotland.' He stopped to drain his cup. 'Anyway, we were defeated. Northumberland was cut down with all who stood with him.'

'And you?' I asked.

'Gone,' Luttrell smiled in reply. 'I fled when the royal troops closed in. After that I left rebellions and politics and turned back to thieving.'

We continued to talk into the night. Luttrell was a rogue, a villain, but a likeable one. A man of no principles and dead dreams, he represented cheerful anarchy in my sorrowful disordered state. We became friends, he obtained cheap lodgings for me and soon I joined him in his thieving forays. Nothing important at first, just filching from stalls, shop fronts, the trays of pedlars and chapmen. Gradually we became more ambitious. Loaded dice followed by checkstones, a game of chance based on a board of black and white squares, we would roll stones inviting the witless to choose a colour. If they chose white, then we would choose black. Of course, we always won, for the board was loaded. In one half of the board the white squares were slightly lower than the rest, in the other, the black, and we would roll the pebbles depending on which

colour our stupid client chose. After a while people
became suspicious so we turned to housebreaking.

On the feast of Corpus Christi 1411, many of the
townspeople were out along High Street and Broad Street
of Oxford, watching the priests in gorgeous red and gold
copes carry a golden monstrance containing the sacred
host through the city. The privilege of carrying the
blue-gold, jewel-encrusted canopy was always entrusted to
four leading citizens. Of course, their families and servants
came to watch and so many of the leading merchants'
homes along Christ Church meadows were left vacant.
Edmund found out which aldermen were carrying the
canopy and selected our prey. A spacious three-storied
building, black-timbered with painted brickwork, it stood
in its own grounds and looked deserted when we
approached just after noon on a hot summer's day. We
broke in through a side door and began to ransack the
place, looking for coins and small items of value. We
feverishly filled our bags and stopped suddenly as we
heard a sound from upstairs. Luttrell motioned me to be
quiet, drew a long, thin knife from his belt and gently
tiptoed upstairs. I followed just as quietly. There were
sounds of screams and squeals coming from one room. We
gently pushed open the door and saw an elderly man
enjoying the body of a young woman who was wrapped
around him, long hair trailing, mouth open, gasping in
pleasure. Luttrell and I grinned at each other and
continued our thievery.

It was a good haul and encouraged us to do more. We
became rich on the proceeds, able to afford more
luxurious lodgings and all the dress and trappings of
young courtiers. We also became too bold, too rash. One
evening in November, I think it was just after the feast of
All Souls, Luttrell and I were in the Blue Boar tavern in
Aldersgate. We'd had a profitable day picking pockets in St
Giles' market and were drinking heavily, Luttrell regaling
me with stories about his past life. Opposite us was a large,

florid-faced man, white-haired and well dressed beneath his velvet cloak. He was with some pretty young doxy and was attempting to undo the lacing of her gorgeous, well filled bodice. Perhaps distracted by the noise we were making, he began to watch us. At first I thought it was no more than simple curiosity but the intent way he was staring at Luttrell began to disturb me. Suddenly he rose, walked slowly over and grasped Luttrell by the wrist.

'The ring, Master thief!' he shouted.

Luttrell smiled up drunkenly. 'Yes,' he asked blearily, 'what about it?'

'It's mine, or rather my wife's,' came the cutting reply, 'stolen from my house last Corpus Christi!' His voice rolled round the large, dingy room and even the dogs, nosing for scraps amongst the dirty straw, raised their heads expectantly. Luttrell's eyes focused as he realised the sudden danger we were in.

'Is that your wife?' he asked, pointing to the red-cheeked girl, sitting open-mouthed at this sudden interruption.

'Never mind that!' the man snapped. 'You are a thief or a receiver of stolen goods. I think the city bailiffs will want to talk to you.' He grasped Luttrell by both wrists, so I rose and pushed him away.

I can still remember clearly what happened next, almost as if it occurred yesterday rather than years ago. The man fell back, a trestle table checked his fall and he charged forward. He stopped suddenly, hands outstretched, eyes staring, his mouth open in surprise and I saw Luttrell withdraw his long, bloodied knife from the man's stomach only to plunge it in again like a spoon into hot treacle. The man fell away, blood spurting in scalding streams from his belly, a thin line of blood seeping from his lips. There was a moment's silence, broken as the girl began to scream, loud and clear, rousing the tavern to life, men jumped to their feet and tried to take us. Luttrell, now sober, rolled his cloak a round his left arm and menaced them with his knife. I drew mine and we slowly edged to the door. Then we were free in the cold, sobering night, whilst behind shouts of 'Harrow! Harrow!' raised the hue and cry against us. We ran to the end of the lane, sobbing with fright and excitement. I turned and ran towards Carfax, thinking Luttrell was beside me, but he must have turned and fled down Aldersgate, hoping to reach Christ Church meadows and the outskirts of the city. I knew instinctively that escape route was out of the question and continued up to Carfax.

Behind me I could hear shouting and running feet so I fled down dark, twisting alleyways, my breath coming in noisy bursts, the cold air catching my throat, nose and eyes and making them stream. I slipped on dirt and crashed jarringly to the ground but rose and limpingly continued my flight. I turned, twisted and stopped, but the sound of pursuit still followed me like the distant baying of hounds. I was not going to escape and now knew there was only one way out. I fled on, now determined to win the race against certain death. I knew Oxford well and soon found myself in front of the university church of St Mary's. The main door was locked but a small, side door was invitingly open. I slipped into the darkness, sweating, trembling with fright, my chest heaving with exertion. A figure loomed up before me. I jumped, clutched at my knife and whispered hoarsely, 'Who is it? Who are you?' A tinder was struck, once, twice, and a candle flared into life revealing in its circle of light a round, smiling face beneath a mop of snow-white hair.

'Father Benedict,' came the soft reply. 'Rector of this church, and who are you?'

'Matthew Jankyn!' I gasped in reply, 'ex-student, ex-thief and accomplice to murder. I claim sanctuary!'

The priest nodded and beckoned me to follow him up the stone-paved nave through the chancel screen into the spacious sanctuary. It was pitch dark except for a pool of light thrown by the priest's candle and the red, winking vigil lamp above the altar. The priest lit a candle on the high altar and took me over to a small recess on the right of the sanctuary containing a stool and a straw-filled mattress.

'This is where you will be staying,' Father Benedict quietly commented. 'I will give you some bread and a little watered wine. If you leave the church, you will be arrested, even killed on the spot. In forty days you must purge your guilt and go. Now come and swear to this!' He led me back to the altar, its marble surface covered by a green, gold-fringed cloth, a silver cross lay above the sanctuary stone which held the sacred relics. He made me put my hand above the cross and swear that I would observe the rules of sanctuary. I did so, fully aware in that candle-flickering church of how low ·I had fallen: an outlaw, a wolf's-head, driven from society, every man's hand against me. I felt self-pity, but also a savage determination to survive, whatever the cost, whatever the price.

My stay in sanctuary was comfortable enough. The next morning Father Benedict returned with bread and a stoup of watered wine. 'You are, Master Jankyn, in considerable trouble,' he said sadly, sitting down on the stool next to the straw-filled mattress. 'The man you killed was Adam de Banastre, merchant, friend of the university, patron and benefactor of the poor and a leading burgess of this city.'

'I did not kill him,' I muttered.

'What?'

'I did not kill de Banastre,' I replied firmly. 'I broke into his house, took his jewels, but I did not kill this great benefactor when he was drinking with his whore. Luttrell did that! I was there but I did not stab the man!'

Father Benedict shook his head. 'You are an accomplice and you will hang.' With this he got up and walked away, leaving me in a black fit of depression.

I knew he was a Job's comforter, who must have listened attentively to many such stories. St Mary's was famous for its right of sanctuary. In the small alcove where I sheltered, the wall was covered with dates and writings of those who had fled there. Most were names, but the more educated (and there were depressingly many) had left some statements about their self-proclaimed innocence. Yet, they were gone and I knew that within forty days, so must I. I could escape, hand myself over to the bailiffs or abjure the realm. The latter would be the safer. I would publicly declare my guilt, purge it and proclaim that I would leave the King's realm within forty days. This would mean walking to the nearest port, cross in hand, and wading into the sea, begging that some compassionate captain would take me aboard and ship me to foreign ports. In theory this was the law, in practice I knew I would be lucky to get out of Oxford alive.

Father Benedict confirmed my worst fears. A week after I entered sanctuary, he came to tell me that Luttrell had been taken and tried before the King's Justices of Oyer and Terminer. He had been found guilty and was now swinging, black-faced, hands tied behind his back, on a special scaffold in Aldersgate. I felt sorry for the man. He had been a rogue, a villain, but an honest friend, now he was dead. I quietly grieved for him whilst silently plotting my own salvation. I knew the city was against me. The church was guarded by city bailiffs and whenever I looked down the nave, I could always see through the half-open doors some guard or official in silent vigil over me. I never left the church. If I wanted to clear my bowels or bladder then I used a small garderobe in the sacristy, a small recess behind a door where the sewer pipe and its terrible stench were regularly cleaned by rain water diverted from the roof.

It was the sacristy which gave me a vague idea of how to escape. There were cloaks, hoods, vestments and all the paraphernalia of the clergy. Why could I not take some? Disguise myself and escape? My determination grew. Soon the forty days would be up and the bailiffs, not to mention de Banastre's friends and relatives, would be waiting for me. I decided to escape on a Sunday after midday Mass

when the incense-filled church emptied its crowd of
worshippers and Father Benedict and his colleagues
departed for their weekly banquet in the priest's house. It
was now Advent, the time of preparation for Christmas,
and the churches were usually full. On that particular
Sunday, I stayed in my recess, well away from the
congregation, watching the priest celebrate Mass, going
through the majestic ritual of calling the God-Man back
from heaven before distributing Him under the appear-
ances of bread and wine to the faithful. The choir intoned
the solemn liturgical chorus, the censers swung and clouds
of incense rose like prayers to the spacious, intricately
carved roof. I watched every movement, heard each
prayer, marking the developing stages of the Mass. Then it
was over. The priests left in solemn procession, the
congregation dispersed and the church was left silent,
except for me and an ever-vigilant God. I decided I had to
go. The guards would be lax, Father Benedict and his
colleagues involved in their own pleasure, it would be dusk
before he returned with my meagre evening meal.

I left the recess, walked to the sacristy and took a cloak
from a huge cupboard. I wrapped it about myself before
crossing to the chest where the sacred vessels were stored. I
took one of the huge brass candlesticks and prised open
the lock, wrenching back the clasp so roughly that it would
never be used again. Inside, in red velvet-lined boxes were
the sacred cups, chalices and monstrances. I took out a
pyx, a small, silver-chased container used by priests to take
the viaticum, or sacred host to the dying, and a thick, silken
cope stiff with ornate embroidery and precious jewels. I
put this round my shoulders, pulled up the hood of my
cloak and picked up the pyx. I now looked like any
dedicated priest taking the sacrament to some sick par-
ishioner. I confidently left the sacristy, crossed the sanctuary, and walked down the nave. There was a guard on
duty at the main door but, when he saw me approaching,
shrouded in cope and hood, head bowed over the pyx as I

intoned the 'Anima Christi', he not only let me pass but
knelt and bowed in deference. Outside, the sharp, bright
sunlight dazzled my eyes but I stumbled on, glad to be free
of the oppressive building, secretly rejoicing in the clean
air and sense of freedom.

I had no clear plan except to be free of Oxford and
make my way east to live in London. I thought I would
succeed. The streets were empty, I turned into Broad
Street, the quickest route out of the city leading to heavily
wooded forests where I could hide if any pursuit was
organised. I passed my own Hall and continued walking,
head bowed, eyes lowered. In fact, that was my undoing
for I walked right into a group of people. Quick apologies
were made, I lifted my head to reply and found myself
staring into Scawsby's white, stodgy face. He gasped in
astonishment and shouted, 'Jankyn! It's Jankyn! He's
escaping disguised as a priest!' I stood and yelled before I
recovered my wits. I dropped the pyx and drove my fist
straight into his mouth, so hard that I bruised my knuckles
and sent a jarring pain along my arm. In the confusion I
dropped both cloak and cope and fled.

Once again, the sound of 'Harrow! Harrow!' echoed
along the narrow street, raising the hue and cry against
me. I cursed as I ran for the city was now coming to life as
the afternoon drew to a close. I could already hear shouts
and the patter of feet behind me. I fled, my muscles heavy
and aching from my enforced stay in sanctuary. My face
and body were covered in sweat, my breath coming in
anxious gulps of cold air. I was running blind, like a rat
trapped in a sewer pipe. I turned down alleys, often
slipping and twisting on the offal-filled runnels. Perhaps it
was the panic, lack of food and sleep, but I became
fevered, the people I passed were like shadows from a
nightmare. I pushed past them. On the other hand, certain
scenes remain clear like pictures on a stained-glass
window. I ran through Carfax and saw Luttrell's body still
swinging by its neck from the low-slung gallows. His head

was grotesquely twisted to one side, his mouth sagged open, and as the corpse stirred in the wind, it seemed as if he was grinning at me, inviting me to join him.

I saw a beggar, with blind white eyes crouching in a piss-washed corner, a small mongrel licking the suppurating sores on his bare, bony legs. A red-haired bawd opened her fat lips and smiled, showing yellowing stumps through carmine-painted lips. I ran on sobbing with terror, ever conscious of the shouts and footsteps behind me. I thought I saw my father at the end of a dark narrow street; he stood there calling, beckoning me to join him, he turned and went, a graceful, dainty white hart moving slowly behind him. A dream. A phantasm. I fled on up Catte Street, past the illuminators and parchment-sellers,, down an alleyway which ran behind the shops and houses. Still the sound of pursuit followed me. I could not go on. My heart banged like a kettle-drum. My legs were too heavy.

I crouched against a plaster wall which separated the alley from a private garden of a large three-storied house which rose above me. Like an animal waiting to be taken, I just squatted there, head bowed, arms folded, almost glad that soon it would be over. A gate opened, and there stood an old man, soberly dressed in a long russet surcoat, a fur-trimmed cap pressed over his head with a few white hairs struggling out. He looked at me, eyes narrowing, lips pursed.

'In nomine boni Christi,' I blurted out! 'Miserere mei,' – 'In the name of good Christ, have pity on me!' I later learnt the Latin saved my life though I will never know why I used it. The old man grasped me by the shoulder with one claw-like hand, pulling me through the gate which banged behind us. We just stood there silent as my pursuers rounded the alley and pounded noisily past the place where I had crouched.

4

The garden we stood in was a long rectangle, a few bare
trees on each side of raised beds separated from the
winding path by carefully stacked bricks.

'Flowers, vegetables and herbs,' the man said softly,
watching me gaze around. 'The trees bear apples
sometimes. Do you like apples?' he asked anxiously. I
looked into his brown, wrinkled face, the smiling lips and
innocent cornflower-blue eyes and burst out laughing.
Here I was, a fugitive, and my saviour was asking if I liked
apples! The old man waited for me to stop laughing and,
taking me gently by the arm, led me to the back door of the
house. We were met by a dark-haired woman, young and
possibly pretty if it had not been for her arrogant brown
eyes and pouting mouth.

'Who is this, Father?' she asked testily, looking me up
and down as a lord would a peasant.

'He is a friend, Mathilda,' he replied good-humouredly,
'an old friend who has just called in.'

'Then he needs to wash and change his clothes,' the
woman replied. 'Besides,' she continued suspiciously, 'he
has no cloak, pack or trunk.'

'He was set upon by thieves,' the old man smoothly
replied. 'Isn't that correct?' he asked, turning to me. I
gulped and muttered that it was and the woman swept
away, the green, tightly-fitting dress she wore emphasising
the movement of her hips. The old man watched her go,
turned and sighed. 'Mathilda is not as cross as she looks,'
he explained. 'Only circumstances and the times, oh the

times, have made her like that.'

'She is your daughter,' I asked.

'Oh no! No!' the old man replied. 'My daughter-in-law,' his voice faltered. 'My only son's widow.' He stared into the distance as if sadly contemplating some tragic event. 'Come,' he added briskly. 'Come into the house.' He led me through the passageway into a paved hall or solar.

A pleasant, whitewashed room with clean straw and herbs on the floor, sweet-smelling bracken in the rafters and a long, scrubbed trestle table with benches down each side. There were shelves with pewter mugs and cups, barrels on wooden supports, some broached, others not, two heavy cupboards with intricately carved panels and iron handles and, underneath them, baskets of dried herbs. The old man scooped his hand into one of these and sprinkled the two fiery braziers which warmed the room before beckoning me to sit on one side of the table. He sat facing me as Mathilda bustled into the room, frowning at me as she filled two jugs of ale and put trenchers on the table stacked with fresh-cut bread, cheese and rather sour wizened apples. As soon as she was gone, the old man introduced himself as Thomas Sturmey, stationer; a trader in parchment and vellum, benefactor of the poor, an important member of the town guild with his own livery and a special place in church. Thomas said it all wryly, like a man who had gained the world but kept his soul by finding it had all turned to dust in his mouth.

Of course, he questioned me and I told him everything from the moment I left Lilleshall to fleeing from sanctuary at St Mary's. He heard me out, nodding and picking at crumbs on his trencher. 'Tell me,' he said, 'tell me the truth on one thing. Did you kill the alderman?'

'Before God and His Mother,' I replied firmly, 'I did not, nor did I seek his death.'

'Good,' Thomas murmured. 'Good.'

'Now, you must tell me one thing,' I said. 'Why did you help me?'

Sturmey stared at the table, cleared his throat and eventually answered. 'My son,' he explained. 'My son, Robert. He studied law at Balliol. He was a good student, Master Jankyn, and a good man. He loved life and beauty. He was a brilliant scholar and won the attention of John Montague, Earl of Salisbury, Richard II's chief minister, a patron of learning. Anyway,' he continued wearily. 'Robert was invited to court in the summer of 1398 just before Richard's expedition to Ireland. Well, you know how King Richard favoured handsome clever young men. When Robert returned to Oxford, he was Richard's man, body and soul. He sported the Whyte Harte as if it were his own emblem and talked constantly of entering the King's service. When Henry of Lancaster landed at Ravenspur and later deposed Richard, Robert fell into a fit of black depression. He cursed Lancaster and all his house. I did my best to help, I arranged his marriage to Mathilda but still he continued to speak against the new king, openly flaunting his emblem of the Whyte Harte and proclaiming in the Schools that Henry was a knave and a usurper.' Sturmey fell silent and I just sat there, resting, sipping the dark, brown London ale. I did not insist that he tell me why he protected me for I was fascinated; once more the Whyte Harte had entered my life. I shivered as I remembered the fevered dream I had seen when fleeing from St Mary's.

'Matters stayed as they were,' Sturmey continued, 'until the summer of 1402 when Robert disappeared, returning a few weeks later very excited. King Richard, he proclaimed, was not dead. He had not been murdered by Henry's men at Pontefract. No, it was an impostor who had been displayed in a lead coffin and buried at Kings Langley. I tried to reason with him but my son was adamant: Richard was not dead but had escaped. He was alive at Stirling protected by the Scottish court. Robert also talked about conspiracies and mentioned the Welsh and northern lords. I dismissed it as nonsense, so did Mathilda.

Richard II was dead. Allegiance to the Whyte Harte was foolish. Then the crisis came like a summer storm, sudden and black across a clear sky. The Percies rose in rebellion, allying with Glendower in Wales, and openly proclaiming that Henry IV was a usurper and that Richard was alive.'

Sturmey stopped speaking and stared at me. 'What I dreaded happened, Robert disappeared. I knew he had gone to join the rebels. The rest you know. Henry utterly defeated the Percies at Shrewsbury. Robert was killed fleeing from the battle. I later discovered that he reached the village of Market Drayton, going from house to house looking for help, but no one gave him shelter.' Sturmey's voice faltered. 'Henry of Lancaster's soldiers caught up with him and a few others just outside the village and cut him down.' He looked up, his eyes shimmering with tears. 'You see, Master Jankyn, that is why I helped you. I know what it is like to be a fugitive from the law. Every day in my dreams I join my son in that dusty, merciless village, going from door to door, banging with my fist, asking them for the love of God to shelter my beloved son. When I saw you crouched against the wall,' he said, his voice almost a whisper, 'speaking to me in Latin, asking for help, I thought you were my son back from the dead.'

Sturmey gulped, as if to stifle a sob, and rubbed his face with his hands.

'I am sorry,' I said, 'very sorry for what you have told me. Perhaps,' I added slowly, 'I should go now. It will soon be dark and I'll be able to slip out of the city.' Sturmey brought his head up sharply.

'No,' he replied, sending my hopes soaring. 'You shall stay, you can hide here. I have need of a trained clerk, and I am sure,' he added shrewdly, 'I can trust you. There is a room at the top of the house. It is yours. Mathilda will not mind, despite her sour looks she is a good woman and has been a true daughter to me since my son's death. You will stay, will you not?'

I grinned. 'Where else can I go?' I replied. 'I have no

business except a meeting with the hangman which I would prefer to forget!'

Sturmey smiled. 'Good,' he remarked. 'Good. Then you shall stay here!'

Tired and exhausted, I would have left the matter there but I thought it was time to confront my own anxious dreams. 'Tell me,' I said, 'the Whyte Harte, the stories about Richard still being alive, are they true? Time and again in my life I have had encounters with men who believe in Richard II, cling to his memory and sport his emblem. My father, Luttrell, and now your son. What is it? Why do people insist on saying that a king, who was deposed and murdered at Pontefract some twelve years ago, is still alive?'

I was surprised at Sturmey's reaction. His mouth opened and shut like a landed carp, his face drained of blood and he became almost furtive, his eyes darting from side to side. 'I do not really know,' he replied evasively, licking his lips. 'I agree it is just a rumour. It still is, but men whisper about it in secret corners and groups. There are messengers to and from Scotland to visit the King. Someone drew a white hart on the gates of Windsor Castle, Henry's favourite residence, but,' he added harshly, 'these are just rumours, nothing more, nothing less.'

I nodded and let the matter rest though I had noticed that Sturmey had referred to Richard as 'the King', a title he denied to Henry of Lancaster. There was more to Sturmey than I thought and I decided to learn more. I needed something to use against him should he change his mind and inform the authorities. Yes, I trusted no one, not because I hated my fellow man but simply because I had no illusions about myself. After all, why trust others when you don't even trust yourself? Yet, God forgive me, I now know Sturmey was the one person I have met, in my long and complicated life, who was the nearest to being a saint anyone could meet this side of heaven.

Sturmey looked after me and protected me as if I were a

favoured son. His home was a spacious though simple affair. A paved hall, kitchen, buttery and offices occupied the ground floor. Here, Sturmey conducted business, storing his goods in stone cellars seven feet deep beneath the hall and, in fine weather, kept a booth or stall in front of the house where he sold vellum, parchment, ink, dyes, pumice-stones, wax and pens. On the first floor was the solar, a huge room of whitewashed walls covered in tapestries and drapes depicting scenes from classical history in red, gold, blues and purples. The furniture, tables, chairs, cupboards and stools were of gleaming polished oak and there was even horn and glass in the windows. On the second floor were small rooms or garrets beneath the roof. Sturmey gave me the largest of these as a chamber, together with a trestle bed, feather-filled mattress, bolster, sheets and thick woollen drapes to keep me warm at night. He also provided me with some of his dead son's clothes, for we must have been of the same height. He and his daughter-in-law had more spacious chambers near the solar yet, as I have said, he treated me like a son.

We dined and talked together but, when visitors were present, I kept to my own chamber. I did not dare to go out. At night, I had constant nightmares about being hunted once more through the streets and runnels of Oxford. I paid my host by working for him, checking bills, stores, writing letters, keeping accounts, even scraping the vellum and preparing the parchment he would sell at his booth. Mathilda tended to ignore me except for a sly look or open frown, though I know she was pleased to have a young man in the house. She took more care of her appearance, her hair was well groomed and her dresses emphasised her full breasts, hips and long legs. Sometimes I made her laugh and her face changed, becoming soft and young when it was wreathed in smiles. I felt I was safe with her for I knew she was devoted to her father-in-law. 'The old innocent,' she called him. She was right, men like good

Sturmey are very few. One of the great advantages about being a villain is that you can easily recognise other villains and on rare occasions, recognise a truly good man.

We talked about everything, philosophy, politics and, of course, theology, and it was here that I discovered Sturmey's secret. I always suspected there was one; mysterious strangers visited him at night; there was no cross or other religious emblem in the house and he talked scathingly about pilgrimages, relics and the scandal of the Great Schism. This was the crisis facing the Papacy at the time; three popes, each claiming to be the spiritual leader of Christianity, spent most of their time issuing bills of excommunicaiton against one another. Sturmey was well read; he knew the works of Marsilius of Padua, Ockham and, of course, Wycliffe. I found him once in the solar reading the heretic's banned translation of the Bible and realised he was a Lollard, a heretic. In a way I was glad. I had found Sturmey's secret and felt safer because of it. I showed I was sympathetic and was gradually drawn into his circle, joining him when he met his mysterious visitors, fellow Lollards, hedge priests and occasionally men of substance, merchants, even knights such as Sir Roger Acton of Tenbury in Worcestershire, a veteran of the Welsh war. I became dutiful and pious in my prayers, studying the scriptures, being moved by the spirit to bear witness, analysing the news of the heretical Hussite Movement in Bohemia.

All the time, like a predatory fox, I kept one eye open to see what would come next. I suppose I have a fine nose for mischief. I can smell it, like some sensitive rare perfume and I sensed there was more. For a start, the visitors to Sturmey's home had often been in the north, stronghold of the Percy faction – no real supporters of Henry of Lancaster. Secondly, a few had been into Scotland and, finally, they talked about a 'Master', their leader who knew all and planned everything. I questioned Sturmey about this but he was as evasive as his natural child-like innocence would let him. 'Tush, Jankyn!' he would exclaim, 'you know too much already. Why know more?'

Why indeed? Except my nose smelt something rotten, the sweet-sour smell of intrigue and I was becoming bored with being a prisoner in Catte Street. I was also alarmed that my protector, Sturmey, would, through his naivety, become involved in something which might attract the attention of the authorities and if Sturmey was taken then my own safety would be threatened.

I have always been totally dedicated to my own survival and became most anxious about what was happening. I shared my fears with Mathilda, pretending to be as dedicated a Lollard as her father-in-law but fearful that his innocence might lead us all into danger. After all, I pointed out, Archbishop Arundel was now hot against Lollards and energetically burning them in barrels at Smithfield. Mathilda dropped her sulky expression, listened carefully to me, promising to have words with her father-in-law.

The result was not what I expected. Much later, I think it was in December 1412, Sturmey sent for me. He met me in his counting-house, a small chamber off the main hall which smelt of candle-wax, parchment and leather. It was full of small brown trunks and caskets, grouped around a long table strewn with pieces of vellum, ink-horns, an abacus and broken pens.

'Come in, Jankyn,' he called. 'I wish to have words with you.'

I sat on a low, squat stool and Sturmey began.

'Matthew,' he said slowly. 'I have every confidence in you. You have been a dutiful son and servant. I am also pleased you have felt able to join us in prayer, but there is more and now is the time for you to know.' He stopped and cleared his throat before continuing. 'You have often heard us speak of "The Master" and you should know that this is none other than Sir John Oldcastle of Almery in Hertfordshire. Do you know him?'

The name did strike a chord in my memory but it was very vague so I shook my head. 'No,' I replied. 'I do not recognise the name.'

Sturmey seemed disappointed. 'He comes of good family, he is in his mid-thirties. Sir John has seen service against the Welsh and, in the summer of 1400, on the northern marches against the Scots. He is a patron of the arts and the new learning, a dedicated servant of the word of God. I tell you this because he will be here tonight and you will meet him.'

Sturmey evidently thought Oldcastle was very important, for the rest of the day was spent in preparation. He usually did without servants but, on that day, hired them to set the solar in order. Fresh rushes sprinkled with marjoram, rosemary and thyme were put down on the floor. Mock purple-gold tapestries were hung on the wall, the table was moved into the centre and four huge oak chairs placed about it. Braziers were put around the room to give warmth, pure beeswax candles and cresset torches were fixed in sconces along the wall, and silver salt-cellars, gilt-chased cups and spoons placed on the table. I did not see any of the preparations as I spent most of the day in my garret but when I came down I found the hall a blaze of colour and warmth, the silver pieces shimmering and winking in the light. The smell from the kitchens was mouth-watering as Mathilda supervised scullions in the roasting of herb-sweetened meats, such as pheasants, capons and lamb. Fresh tarts, meat pies, bowls of beef broth, quince tarts and dishes of sugared almonds, nuts and sweetened wafers were already on the table.

Mathilda was busying herself, supervising everything as if she were a queen. She certainly looked like one. Her hair, washed and shiny, was covered by a sparkling gauze net of small precious stones. She wore a velvet dress fringed with black lambswool and a froth of white lace at the neck and cuffs. A large gem on a thin silver chain was around her neck, a low slung, jewel-encrusted belt about her slim round waist. I told her she looked like Venus and quoted a verse from Ovid's *De arte Amandi* – *The Art of Loving.* She lowered her eyelids prettily, thanked me and, for the first time ever, I saw her blush.

Our visitor arrived well after dark. He came in the front door in a flurry of snowflakes, stamping and shouting greetings at Sturmey and Mathilda. He threw his heavy riding-cloak to the floor as if he owned the house and moved into the pool of light thrown by the hall's spluttering torches. Oldcastle was stout, of medium height with a sallow, fleshy face and a head as bald and shiny as a bauble. I suppose from the start I did not like him with his thin lips, cruel, beaked nose and razor-sharp eyes. Yes, Oldcastle was a deceiver, dancing and flirting amongst us, the most dangerous of men. A destroyer, a dark angel, a man of intense pride and bounding ambition. He would ruin, tarnish, blemish anything and anyone. I sensed it that night when I shook his soft, fleshy-white hand, caught his sharp eyes and saw him act the role of the great leader, the keeper of mysteries and deep secrets. Standing there in Sturmey's hall, booted and spurred, his face and head glistening like an angel's, his beringed hands fluttering in the air or constantly rubbing his long russet cloak made out of pure wool and lined with miniver. The shirt beneath was startling white cambric and I remember thinking that Oldcastle seemed as keen on the things of this world as on those of the next.

5

Oldcastle mesmerised both Sturmey and Mathilda, who stood squeaking with delight and adoration as he teased and laughed with them, a Herod amongst the Innocents. Mathilda, her eyes filled with pleasure, coy at the leery looks Oldcastle gave her, introduced me. He shook my hands, his face wreathed in a smile which somehow never reached his hard eyes and then he swept up the hall to the table, announcing he was starved enough to eat us all out of house and home. He nearly did, slurping the soup, his powerful hands and teeth tearing at the soft, hot, well spiced meats and all the time he talked. News from the shires, from the court, he was a spinner of tales and you could have caught spiders in the webs he wove. He was hot against the church, its corruption, luxury and open support of scandalous practices. He told us that even at the nearby tavern where he had stabled his horse, there was a man selling relics; the saddle on which Mary rode in the flight into Egypt, the foreskin of John the Baptist, one of Angel Gabriel's wing feathers and the hammer from St Joseph's workshop. Even I had to laugh at Oldcastle's description of the fraudster's antics and the absolute credulity of his customers. Oldcastle was particularly hot against the King, whom he contemptuously called Henry of Lancaster. 'A dropsy, pox-ridden old man,' he declared between mouthfuls of red meat. 'He can scarcely fart, never mind rule a kingdom! His brood of homicidal avaricious sons are no better. Young Harry, his self-proclaimed heir, can hardly wait for his father to die and so grab the crown. If he does, then the good God help us all!'

'But Prince Henry is your friend,' Sturmey timidly interrupted. 'You fought side by side in Wales.'

'Was my friend,' Oldcastle almost barked the reply. 'Until I saw him as a cold ruthless killer. A man of two natures is our young Prince. In London he runs wild with other young men of the court, totally devoted to the service of Venus and Mars. In public, however, he is the perfect prince dedicated to the crown and church. You have heard about Bardby?'

Sturmey was about to say he had but Oldcastle carried on.

'Bardby,' he began, 'was a tailor. One of us, a believer, whom the commons like to call Lollards.' He shot a conspiratorial look at me and Sturmey hastened to state that I, too, was a believer and could be trusted. Oldcastle smiled as if he found that difficult to believe and I realised he must know something about my past. 'Anyway,' Oldcastle continued, 'Bardby was arrested for heresy and tried before that old faggot from hell, Archbishop Arundel, found guilty and sentenced to be burnt in chains at Smithfield. Our good Prince Henry supervised the burning, sitting there on his horse, his belly full of stale London ale, his loins recently drained by some London whore. This paragon of princely perfection sat and watched the flames lick at poor Bardby's body. The screams were terrible. I was there, praying for it to be over, when Bardby, half burnt, stumbled from the fire. The prince dismounted and talked earnestly with him, encouraging him to recant. Bardby refused so our prince kicked the poor tailor back into the flames and watched him die!'

In the ensuing silence I saw Sturmey's and Mathilda's faces go pale for Bardby's fate was theirs if they were arrested and refused to recant.

'Poor Bardby, poor man,' Sturmey murmured.

'God will exact vengeance for his death,' Oldcastle interrupted. 'His persecutors are false, they have raised themselves to the throne and are as wicked as Ahab. God has weighed the House of Lancaster and found them wanting. They have no claim to the throne they sit on, Henry, the self-styled king, is already being punished for his usurpation. His body is rotting, his mind failing, even as his brood of sons yap at his heels begging him to die. When he does the crown should revert to the rightful line!'

'You mean to the Earl of March?' I abruptly asked. 'Richard II's designated successor, he has precedence in descent from Edward III.'

Oldcastle snorted. 'The Earl of March can go hang! Why

should the crown go to him when the rightful king,
Richard II, God's anointed, is still alive!' His words created
a still silence in the hall, broken only by the wind-whipping
flakes of snow against the window. I looked up and
thought I heard the gentle rustle of some fleet-footed
animal in the street outside; a gentle Whyte Harte passing
by, disguised against the snow, leaving a trail of crimson
prints in its wake, the blood of men who had died in its
cause.

'Richard II is dead,' Sturmey said hoarsely. 'Killed,
starved to death at Pontefract. Why do men say he is alive
and lead others like my son to their destruction?' His voice
almost broke with emotion. 'Why is it kings never die alone
but must take countless others with them?'

'Because Richard II is not dead,' Oldcastle replied
briskly. 'He escaped and fled to Scotland. He is there still.
When I served in the northern March I met prisoners who
had met him at Stirling. They described him accurately,
golden-haired, tall, white-skinned and regal. Richard
never died, that is why the Percies, whose lands lie just
south of the Scottish border, have never accepted Henry,
hence the constant rebellions in 1400, 1403 and 1408.
Even the friars, the Franciscans, constantly preach that
Henry has no claim to the throne while Richard is still
alive. Oh, Henry can kill such opponents and has, but the
whispers go on, the truth will not die.' Oldcastle leaned
across the table, his soft hand covering Sturmey's. 'Your
son did not die in vain,' Oldcastle continued softly. 'He
died a martyr for God's own cause and God will bring it to
fruition. Why do you think Henry of Lancaster rots and
frets away in his castles of Windsor, Westminster and
Eltham? Because he, for one, knows the truth!'

'And so who is buried at Kings Langley?' I interrupted
harshly, trying to throw off the spell woven by his sweet,
alluring words.

'An impostor!' Oldcastle retorted between deep gulps of
sack. 'A mummer, someone who looks like the King. God

knows, Richard II's good sire fathered enough bastards to fill a pew. After all,' he added bitterly, 'when the present usurper moved Richard's body from Pontefract to Kings Langley, all one could see were white pinched features, the face and head were shorn of their golden hair.'

I nodded and gazed at him steadily, one villain admiring another. Perhaps this disconcerted him for he produced proof which showed he was no bombastic drinker lying in his cups. He dug into the gold-filigreed wallet which swung from his belt and passed around a neatly folded piece of fresh parchment. Sturmey took it and read it, exclaiming in astonishment before passing it on to me. Written in Norman French, it began 'Richard, par la grâce de Dieu, Roi d'Angleterre' and continued to ask all his subjects, sheriffs and officers to give sustenance to his 'sujet loial, John Oldcastle.' The document was dated only two months earlier at Stirling in Scotland. I looked up, startled and amazed. The vellum was of good quality, the Norman French written in a clerkly hand and style and sealed with the King's own personal signet. I knew enough about the royal chancery to realise that if this was a forgery, then it was a very clever one.

Oldcastle preened himself like a barnyard cock, gulping from his cup, his eyes shining with enjoyment at our open-mouthed astonishment. 'A friar brought it to me a week ago,' he commented. 'He visited my manor at Almery and said he had met Richard at Stirling. I asked him to return and give Richard certain verbal messages which I made him commit to memory. The friar was successful, Richard granted him an audience, saying he would only come south if he was sure of support for, if Henry captured him, he would surely meet a secret and terrible death. The friar asked for proof that he could take back into England and Richard handed him this letter. The friar also gave me a detailed description which fitted Richard accurately, albeit he is now older and changed by adverse shifts in fortune.'

'Who is this friar?' I asked but Oldcastle winked and tapped his nose slyly with his finger.

'Did he send anything else?' asked Mathilda, who had sat, a wide-eyed listener to Oldcastle's revelations.

'Yes,' the knight replied and, delving once more into his purse, took out a piece of jet-black cloth and unrolled it on the table. It was made of costly silk about a foot square and bore the Whyte Harte emblem woven in white silk in the centre. The hind was sitting, its lovely neck circled by a gold crown, its slender beautiful face turned sorrowfully towards the onlooker. Above it, to the left, was a huge golden sun and around the borders of the cloth were red and white stars. Mathilda and Sturmey gasped in amazement at its beauty while I stared at the emblem like a thirsty man peers into a well of spring water. This was the motif which constantly touched my life and permeated my dreams; it seemed almost pointless to resist it. Oldcastle briskly leaned forward, whisked the cloth away and gazed around at us all.

'This,' he said carefully, 'is why I am here tonight. The people call us Lollards and traitors but all we want is the restoration of the rightful king; heretics but all we seek is a cleansing of the Temple. If we bring about a revolution which sweeps Richard back into power, the King would be only too pleased to accede to our demands for a radical reform of the Church.'

'And Henry of Lancaster and his brood of young vipers will just stand and let us take power?' I asked.

'No,' Oldcastle replied, 'but Henry of Lancaster returned from exile in 1399, a penniless adventurer with no claim to the throne, yet managed to seize it. Why cannot Richard, the rightful King, do just as well?' He leaned forward to refill his cup. 'After all, look at the country, heavily taxed, the coastal towns raided by French privateers and the nobles sullen at Henry's constant insistence on his rights.' Oldcastle wiped his greasy lips and fingers on a napkin. 'No,' he concluded. 'The time of deliverance is ripe and I need people like you to assist. Are you with me?' Of course, Sturmey and his daughter-in-law were totally taken in by his words.

Years later I can still remember that scene. Oldcastle sprawled like an emperor in his chair with old Sturmey and Mathilda vigorously nodding. I, too, gave my support. What else could I do? I was indebted to the family and hid my own misgivings. I wish, and still do, I had cut Oldcastle's throat on the spot and taken the consequences. The rest of the night was taken up with talk about details; numbers of supporters, the time to strike and what a golden time would dawn for us all when Richard came back into his own. I went to bed dizzy with wine and Oldcastle's words. I awoke late the next morning to find him gone but Sturmey and Mathilda were still excited at his speech and his glowing promises. I was wary of Oldcastle and tried to reason with both of them as we broke our fast on ale and pickings from the previous night's feast. They, however, were adamant and would hear nothing against him. Later in the day, after the hired servants had cleared up the hall, returning it to its usual sombre state, I went down to speak to Sturmey in his counting-house but, for such a mild man, he was remarkably obstinate. He saw the restoration of Richard and the attainment of his Lollard ideals as 'The Great Cause' and tried to dispel my doubts by referring to the letter we had all seen the previous night. Secretly, I think he was committed because he felt a debt to his son and a pact with the dead is always unbreakable.

I left him to continue the argument with Mathilda. She was in her bedroom folding clothes, storing them in a great trunk at the foot of the bed. She watched me strangely as I used all my logic and reasoning to dissuade her from Oldcastle's cause but she was as obstinate as her father-in-law and I felt she was teasing me. 'Why are you so concerned, Matthew?' she asked. 'Are you frightened of death?'

Of course I am terrified. After a life like mine, I am more than fearful of that dreadful, final audience with God. Yet I mocked her.

'Not death itself,' I jibed, 'but the death of a traitor. Do you know what it is like, Mathilda? To be down on your back, being dragged through the shit of London streets to the Elms at Tyburn? To be hanged by your neck till you are half dead in front of a gloating crowd, cut down, your heart and bowels plucked out before your head is struck off and your body quartered! Sweet God, Mathilda, Bardby's death would be nothing to such agonies!'

Mathilda just stared at me with those steady brown eyes. 'They would do that to me,' she replied thickly, 'to my body and you would not like that, Matthew?'

'No.'

'You have seen my body?' she teased.

I shook my head and stared as she rose and began to undo the clasps of her gown, her dress and petticoats falling in a pool of lace around her bare feet. She stood naked and proud and walked slowly over to me, loosening her hair until it fell like a veil around her face. She put her arms around my neck.

'Do you like my body, Matthew? Do you like it so much?'

I am afraid there are certain questions which defy words as answers and this was one of them. I stripped and made love to her, kissing her breasts, her neck, as she wrapped her long legs around me, gasping and crying, her body writhing under me until it was done and we both lay exhausted on the bed. She turned and smiled at me, running her hand along my chest.

'Well, Matthew, do you like my body?' she whispered.

'Of course,' I replied. 'I just never realised you liked me!'

She rolled away shrieking with laughter, her eyes crinkled, her breast heaving with giggles. I tried to kiss her but she pushed me away.

'Go, you fool!' she taunted. 'Go now, there will be other times.' There were. We met whenever we could.

I think the old man knew but he did not object, in his grieving mind I suspect he found it difficult to distinguish between me and his dead son. He continued in his commitment to Oldcastle's cause; strangers came and went, letters were received and despatched, money changed hands. Oldcastle never returned but his spirit dominated the house. This irked me. By January 1413 I had been thirteen months there, never venturing out except into the garden, and I began to feel it was becoming a prison. The harsh winter made it bearable but when spring came I felt a crushing depression at my enforced detention and wondered when I would be free.

In late March of the same year, Sturmey came into my chamber and excitedly shook me awake. 'Matthew! Matthew!' he almost shouted. 'The old king is dead. You are free, an amnesty and pardon have been proclaimed by the new king!'

I hurriedly rose from my bed, calmed him down and asked for all he knew. Apparently, one of his secret visitors the previous evening had brought the news. King Henry had been ill for months with a rotting disease which so disfigured his face he was repulsive to all who met him. He tried to reassert himself and made a visit to the shrine of St Edward the Confessor at Westminster where he fell into a deadly swoon and was carried into the Abbot's lodgings, to a room known as the Jerusalem chamber. The King recovered and asked where he was. On being told, the King resigned himself to death, for a soothsayer had informed him that he would die in Jerusalem. Henry turned his face to the wall and the watchers by his bed, thinking he was dead, covered his face with a cloth. His eldest son, Prince Henry, picked up the crown, but the old king revived and asked where it was. On being told the prince had taken it, he ordered both crown and son back to his bedside. Henry asked his son what right he had to the crown, seeing that he himself had none, to which the young prince had replied, 'As you have kept it by the sword, so will I as long as my life lasts!' The old king nodded, confessed his sins and died.

The new king, Henry V, had immediately ordered a proclamation to keep the peace, issuing an amnesty for all crimes committed during his father's reign. Sturmey was almost beside himself with excitement; the news showed that the Lollards had spies in the very heart of the royal household. Henry IV had died confessing his own guilt at seizing the throne (a vague reference, Sturmey believed, to Oldcastle's assertion that Richard was still alive) and now the new king had issued a pardon which would benefit me.

I was not so sanguine. There was no proof that the account of Henry's death was genuine. It could well be a moralising tale concocted by the Lollards. As for the pardon, well, that could wait for a while. I thanked Sturmey and waited for more proof. It came within days, Mathilda returned from the city, red-cheeked and breathless, to tell me there was a royal proclamation posted on the door of St Mary's church, offering pardon and amnesty for all crimes committed in Henry IV's reign. I thanked her in the only way I could and soon she was red-cheeked and breathless again as I made love to her on her great, empty, silken bed.

The next day I went out, confident that the beard I had grown over the last few months, together with the dye in my hair, would strengthen people's forgetfulness of events now over a year old. I found I had nothing to fear and boldly walked around the city, rejoicing in my sense of freedom and revelling in all I saw; the striped awnings of the booths in the market-place, the noise and bustle of taverns, the fire-eater calling for custom, the mangy bear angry at the pock-marked dogs which baited it. There was a freshness about everything, the women in their tight-fitting dresses, breasts pushing and jutting at the fabric; the students in hoods and gowns strolling arm in arm through the crowds, a supercilious look on their faces, even the poor, the beggars, the cripples seemed welcome companions. I wandered amongst them all, drinking their experiences like one does a good wine. I visited the Blue Boar and sat on the very bench where Luttrell and I had sat the night the murder took place. I wandered out up to Carfax and saw the scaffold. A fresh corpse now dangled there and it turned and twisted in the sharp spring breeze and my panic returned. I thought I saw someone staring at me and, pulling my cloak around me, I hurried back to Catte Street and the security of Sturmey's home.

Of course, I went out again, glad to be free, though this made me more anxious about Sturmey and his ties with Oldcastle. The latter had eventually gone to ground and I began to think wistfully all his plans and strategies were bombast but Sturmey changed all that. I remember coming back late one afternoon, surprised to see the booth and stall in front of his house had been cleared and stacked away. I found the old merchant in the buttery gulping a cup of sack under the anxious gaze of Mathilda. Sturmey blurted out his news. Oldcastle had been arrested after proclamations regarding his heresies had been posted at Cooling Castle in Kent and elsewhere. The pompous knight had tried to defend himself, both before Parliament and the King, but to no avail. He had been found guilty of heresy and handed over to the secular arm for punishment. The new King, Henry V, tried to show clemency and Oldcastle was sent to the Tower for forty days in order to consider his wrongs and so recant. Of course, Oldcastle refused and it looked as if he was destined to die at Smithfield. God knows why he had made such a display of himself, drawing attention to his heretical views. Perhaps he hoped to create a sensation whilst relying on his former friendship with the King to save him. Or, in retrospect, the King's spies had been more effective than we thought and Oldcastle had been arrested for his plotting against the King but arraigned on the less sensitive charge.

We received this news early in September 1413, there

was a touch of autumn in the air and Mathilda, dressed in a simple smock and with her hair tied back, was already collecting apples in the small garden orchard. We wanted Sturmey to wait awhile but the old man refused to listen and the number of secret meetings to his house increased. I attended some of these and became alarmed at the treasonable talk which ensued. Men came from all over England, openly disporting the Whyte Harte and cursing King Henry in language which would have sent us all to the scaffold.

At the beginning of October, Sturmey approached me and asked if I would accompany him to London, on certain 'secret business'. I tried to evade this, pointing out that Mathilda would be left on her own, but the old merchant openly ridiculed my excuses, maintaining Mathilda would be more than safe by herself and virtually pleading with me to join him. I reluctantly agreed, we made our farewells to Mathilda and rode east, our baggage slung over two sumpter ponies.

6

I was glad to be free of Oxford, back in the countryside, enjoying the warm autumnal sun, the cool breeze and the glorious banquet of colour as summer died in a blaze of yellow, purple and orange. The harvest was ripe and the villages we passed through were all busy collecting and storing the crops. Sturmey was quiet, lost in his own thoughts, and would not be drawn on his 'great secret'. So we journeyed east, stopping at wayside inns until we reached the great northern road which took us south to Bishopsgate and into London.

I must admit that entering the capital cleared all former fears from my mind by overlaying them with others. At first, London terrified me. I had an inkling of what was to happen when we joined the carts trundling into the city loaded with produce, fruit, wheat, rye, oats, slaughtered meats, penned geese and chickens. The noise was deafening as the great dray horses plodded slowly, the wheels of the cart rumbling like distant thunder, raising high clouds of dust. The air was filled with strange oaths, sudden quarrels and the crack of whips and the jingle of harness as people fought their way along the highway. We passed the great stone walls of the city, entering London by Bishopsgate and made our way south to Cheapside, past the Priory of St Mary's Spital, Portsoken Ward on our right, a huddle of tenements and open spaces where weavers did business by stretching fresh cloth on tenters to dry. After that, I lost all sense of direction as Sturmey led me through a maze of streets cobbled and slippery with a sewer running down the middle., There were huge gaps and holes in the roads, some were filled with bundles of broom and woodchip, but many were pot-holes, traps for the unwary like myself.

Oxford was busy but London hums continually like an overturned beehive; filthy, crowded, clamorous and opulent. Narrow streets, dirty, greasy and dangerous run like rabbit-warrens in every direction. They are dark with the houses packed next to each other, the upper stories gilted and gabled, jutting out to block the sunlight, built according to fancy and convenience rather than any set plan. There were houses with ground floors of stone supporting carved beams, houses of half-timber painted black and pink with whitewashed plaster; here and there a building of red brick or the tented sloping roof of a great hall. There were stalls and booths, shop fronts lowered and hanging by chains and all around the constant din of tradesmen: 'Hot pheasant!' 'Strawberry ripe!' 'Cherry on the branch!' 'Ribs of tasty beef!' or 'Rushes green!' Tradesmen plucked at our arms trying to inveigle us into giving them our custom and, when we refused, let us go with strange oaths or cries of 'Go by Cokke!'

The press was so great, we eventually gave up riding and, dismounting, gathered the reins in our hands and led our horses through the crowd. I was still astonished at the different people I saw. Lords, young gallants in thick doublets with fiercely padded shoulders and high waists, the sleeves puffed out in concoctions of velvet, damask and satin, their legs covered in tight multi-coloured hose which emphasised the shape of the calf and the grandeur of the codpiece. Their hats were fur-trimmed and clasped with jewels, their shoes pointed, so ornate that in other circumstances I would have laughed at such frippery. Their ladies were equally splendid, rich tapestried dresses, low, square-cut at the breast and gathered at the waist with cinctures of silk, velvet-tipped with precious pendants or jewel-studded leather tags. Their head-dresses were ornate and laced with clouds of fair linen, their eyebrows and forehead hair severely plucked to give their faces a monk-like appearance.

These gorgeous persons rubbed shoulders with lawyers in silk hoods and striped coats, bawds in scarlet gowns, mocking imitations of the great ladies; peasants in grey and russet clothes, some stooped beneath great burdens, shouting 'Way! Way!' I wanted to ask Sturmey questions but the bustle and noise was far too great and he was busy fighting a path through the crowd. We made our way into Cheapside. The vast crowded trading-area of London: shops and stalls filled with produce of every kind, piled high like honey in a beehive. In the distance, the spires of churches: Holy Trinity Priory, St Andrew Undershaft and, above them all, the massive building of St Paul's, its huge tower packed with relics (so Sturmey told me), such as the stone Jesus used to ascend into heaven. The whole edifice was crowned with a huge copper-gilt weathercock. Cheapside was as busy as any of the streets; Cornhill, the grain market, was crowded with long bread-carts from Stratford-atte-Bowe which sold penny loaves, two ounces heavier than the standard London loaf. The only thing we stopped to stare at was 'The Tun', a huge water-reservoir half-way up the street which stored water, brought into it through elmwood pipes from Tyburn stream. On top of the Tun was an iron cage where, Sturmey told me, the night-walkers, rioters from the previous night, fornicating clerics and drunks were placed by the night watch. Nearby was a wooden platform just as high, with the stocks and pillories. One bore a cook with a stinking pie he had tried to sell slung round his neck, his agonies worsened by a crowd of urchins busy slinging horse manure at him.

Gradually, we made our way down a series of side streets past houses fair and foul, skirting the Poultry where the stench of offal from the slaughterhouses made me feel nauseous, and into Farringdon ward and the great, dusty, stinking cattle-market of Smithfield. We crossed the execution ground which stood within hailing distance of the great porch of St Bartholomew's Church and hospital. I looked at the blackened, stone pillar and thick chains and shuddered, the sight dispelling the magic of London. If we failed, if we were caught, then Oldcastle's stupid treasons would bring us here to burn in great iron-bound barrels. In a side street near Smithfield, Sturmey stopped to stable our horses in a tavern called 'The Wrestler-in-the-Hoop'. Sturmey seemed to know the huge, balding inn-keeper who assured him that our horses would be safe. Sturmey refused the ale and a dish of spiced eels but accepted the offer of a groom to carry our bundles a little further to a nearby parchment-seller's house. Its shutters were lowered to form a stall while inside, the shop was draped in good sturdy buckram, and full of rolls of parchment, inkhorns, clamps, pastes, wax, paints and pens. A small, rat-faced man in a greasy robe bustled forward to greet us with squeaks of joy. Sturmey introduced me to John Taylor and I groaned inwardly as I looked at Taylor's lank, rat-tailed hair, watery eyes and yellow buck teeth. If this was the quality of Sturmey's allies then it did not augur well for the future. My gloom deepened when Taylor led us past a screen into his small wainscotted hall and introduced Thomas Burton, a young, shifty-eyed man with a limp, a soft handshake and a large gravy stain down the front of his green fustian jerkin.

Once introductions were made, Taylor's pert, surprisingly pretty wife served us with a simple meal and then led us up to a small chamber to rest from our journey. The following evening, Sturmey and I met Oldcastle's group of conspirators: Taylor, Burton, the keeper of the Wrestler-in-the-Hoop, a carpenter, John Burgate, and a wealthy draper from Dunstable called Richard Morley, and I watched in growing horror as they unfolded their plan for freeing Oldcastle from the Tower. I immediately objected, saying it was a fortress and could not be stormed. Taylor heard me out and smilingly shook his head.

'No, no, Master Jankyn, we do not intend to storm the Tower. Many people have escaped from the fortress, a Welsh prince during the reign of Henry IV, Roger Mortimer during Edward II's reign, and now Oldcastle. He is in a tower overlooking the river. We have already smuggled in rope, the window is large enough for Oldcastle to get through. It is simply a matter of Oldcastle lowering himself unobserved into a waiting boat.' He smiled, his yellow teeth jutting out. 'We are known in London,' he continued, 'so we hope you, Master Sturmey, and Burton will man the boat.'

'When?' Sturmey asked.

'Tomorrow night, we have already hired a skiff and an expert river-man to take you there. You will go?'

The rest of the group stared at me as I hid my panic, desperately seeking a way out of the madcap scheme.

Sturmey spoke up. 'Of course, he will go.' He turned his

innocent blue eyes to me. 'You will, won't you, Matthew?' I smiled and nodded, quietly cursing myself as a witless knave.

Late the following afternoon, I joined Sturmey and Burton and we travelled by foot to Westminster. The journey was long and hot and Sturmey would not let me stop to view the sights. Instead we pushed by people, past the shops of the goldsmiths of Cheapside with their precious metals, ornaments and jewellery, down towards Thames Street, a busy thoroughfare of cookshops, drapers and other merchants which ran from the west of the city right down to the Tower. I saw little for I was too taken up with my own dread fear which turned like some sharp knife in my bowels. I knew we were to hire a boat and travel downstream to some appointed place off the Tower. There, we would wait until dusk when, Oldcastle had confided to friends who had visited him, the escape would take place.

We eventually reached Westminster, Henry III's beautiful abbey, a veritable poem to God, a breathtaking vision of towers, trellised, carved stone, pillars and buttresses, its great glass windows catching the weak sun and sending it back in rays of coloured lights. Beside the Abbey, equally impressive, were the buildings of Westminster Palace dominated by the Great Hall, the hub of government where the King's Courts of Common Pleas, the Exchequer and King's Bench were in session. The wide steps leading up to the Hall were thronged with royal serjeants, lawyers and judges in their red gowns trimmed with white fur, as well as a string of felons being led away to Newgate or to the Tun, preceded by musicians playing mocking tunes on drums, pipes and trumpets. We skirted the throng, passed the Clock Tower and went under an ornate stone arch down some steps to the river wharf.

The quay was crowded with men seeking a boat to take them down river or across to the delights of Southwark and the air was full of the usual cries for boatmen, 'Wagge!

Wagge! Go we hence!' The watermen paid little heed to
that, concentrating on the wealthy few, as Sturmey
muttered, 'The richer the gown, the better the fee!' We
stood there for a while, I watching the turbulent
dirt-swollen waters with considerable trepidation, Sturmey
and Burton looking for the boatmen they had hired to
make contact with them. Burton carried a white cloth in his
right hand, the sign established by Taylor for the
watermen to recognise our party. At last, a grizzled-haired
man with a brown, leathery face and a cast in his left eye
came up and snapped at us to follow him down the steps to
where a tilt boat with a leather awning sat rocking against
its rope. We clambered in, the boatman followed, he
ordered us to sit down, and he cast off, and soon he and his
companion were rowing us hard down the river.

The journey was not smooth, we were against the tide
and the water was choppy. I felt sick and queasy and tried
to divert my mind by taking in the sights. The river was
busy, small boats like ours plied up and down, scudding
across like restless water-flies. Now and again, the stately
barges of the great glided past us back to Westminster or
Greenwich, floating pavilions of carved wood, ornate
prows gilded with gold, resplendent with multi-coloured
banners and the rich liveries of oarsmen and servants. I
felt jealous of their luxurious calm and angry that I was
sitting in a leaking skiff scudding down river to play the
traitor. All along the river bank, I saw further signs of
London's wealth, a forest of masts, tackle and cranes as
ships from Genoa, Venice and the Baltic disgorged their
stores and took on more. We passed great warehouses, the
green fields and pleasant gardens of the Temple, the ruins
of Savoy Palace burnt by the rebel peasant army at the
beginning of Richard's reign, then we were round the arch
of the river and heading for London Bridge, a wondrous
stone edifice, its nineteen arches spanning the Thames. A
small village in itself, so Sturmey pointed out, with its
shops, houses and chapel. We pulled through the arches,

our small skiff nosing its way through the thundering, spraying water, the boatmen cursing and praying that we would not be dashed against the stone pier. I wished we would and so end our dreadful journey but we were through, pulling past the steelyard and on to St Catherine's Wharf.

I looked back through the dusk to London Bridge and saw long poles bearing the decaying heads of traitors, my terror increasing when I saw the white looming turrets of the Tower. We did not stop but continued on until the boatmen brought their craft into a wharf just below Wapping. Here we would turn and use the tide to travel slowly back upstream to take up our appointed position. Burton, that whey-faced bastard, that turd of Janus, must have detected my fear, for he took great delight in pointing through the dusk to a row of scaffolds which bore the corpses of pirates sentenced to hang there for three turns of the tide. I cursed him softly, while the boatmen rowed slowly upstream until we were directly opposite the main wharf-gate of the Tower. We sat and waited, the boatmen gently touching the water with their oars, drawing against the current so that we stayed roughly in the appointed position.

Sturmey had two torches lit and placed in holders on both prow and stern so, to any suspicious onlooker, we looked like fishermen trying to supplement our supper with a late catch. Darkness fell, the river traffic became minimal and I began to ache with cold and tension. I heard a splash from the far bank but dismissed it as a matter of little importance until a wet, bearded face appeared over the side of the boat, the water glistening on its bald head. Sturmey gave a low cry of pleasure and hastened to pull the soaking Oldcastle into the boat, wrapped him in cloaks and ordered the boatmen to pull for Temple Wharf.

The journey back was uneventful, we arrived just below the Temple gardens and spent the night in the hovel of one of the boatmen who were Lollards and privy to

Oldcastle's escape. The next day we returned to Smithfield and a gathering of the whole coven. Oldcastle joined us, shaved, rested and quite recovered from his recent ordeal. He was the same arrogant, bumptious man, fully confident that what he was doing was right. There was one slight alteration, he was now consumed with malice towards the new King and openly stated that his imprisonment in the Tower was not for any heretical belief but because he knew Richard II was alive and that King Henry was a usurper. He did not convince me. I know a liar when I see one. Nonetheless, I did nothing to dissuade Sturmey from any further madcap endeavours.

Oldcastle was now intent on fomenting rebellion. He borrowed money to fashion badges of the Whyte Harte and asked his fellow conspirators to distribute these throughout the capital and the surrounding countryside. Arms were bought and stored in various cellars throughout Smithfield, brigandines, helmets, battle-axes, jacks and sallets for archers, bows, arrows, swords and clubs. Certain gentleman, including Sir Roger Acton, Sir Thomas Talbot and various London squires, young men of doubtful background, visited Taylor's house where Oldcastle wove before their eyes a beautiful tapestry for the future. He showed them Richard's letter, confided that other messages, more confidential had been received and hinted there was more to come. Richard was in Stirling! Richard had moved to the border and was assured of the support of the northern lords! With such rumours Oldcastle fanned the flames of revolt, pouring scorn on Henry V's attempts to placate his barons, pointing out that the new king was so desperate for support he was granting pardons, amnesty and restitution to the sons of those nobles his father had executed, so anxious was he to stamp out any aid for Richard and the cause of the Whyte Harte.

7

In December 1413 King Henry V certainly seemed aware of the growing rumours about Richard II's still being alive and did his best to settle the matter by ordering that Richard's body be moved from Kings Langley to the tomb that the deposed King had prepared for himself in Westminster Abbey. The transference was conducted with every pomp and ceremony as if King Henry was not only making reparation for his father's deposition of Richard II but trying to silence the stories of the King's possible survival. Oldcastle presented it differently. Henry was panicking, trying to quell gossip by this mockery of a solemn removal of some impostor's body. I admit that I saw the logic of Oldcastle's arguments and so did the heavens for the country was covered by savage snow blizzards which buried animals, cut off villages and froze the capital silent. It was ideal weather for Oldcastle for now any pursuit or search for him had to be called off. We knew the King's men were looking for him and heard that the Constable of the Tower had been imprisoned for letting him escape while proclamations had been posted offering rewards for his capture, dead or alive.

In mid-December Oldcastle called a meeting of the leading conspirators in the hall of Taylor's house. I still remember the scene: Sturmey, now Oldcastle's most fanatical supporter, dour Sir Roger Acton, Burgate, Burton and Morley. The last named was an arrant fool, boasting he had bought new harness for his horse and two

pairs of gilt spurs for, when the revolt was successful, he
was to be a great lord in the land. They all sat around the
table with Oldcastle at its head. Even then I thought we
looked like chickens being entertained by the fox and
wished I was back in Catte Street with Mathilda, away from
all this stupidity. Since I had left Oxford, Mathilda had
been constantly in my thoughts and only this sustained my
support for Sturmey. If it had not been for her, I would
have been over the hills and away, putting as many miles as
possible between myself and Oldcastle's vision of the
Whyte Harte leading us all into fresh green fields and a
luxurious future. More like the gallows, I thought, but still
I sat fascinated that cold December evening as Oldcastle
unfurled his plans.

'I have intelligence,' he began, 'that our self-styled King,
his brother and court have moved to the royal manor of
Eltham in Kent where they will celebrate Christmas and
Twelfth Night festivities. They will be cut off by the deep
snow and a select group of us will enter the manor and
seize them.'

'How?' I interjected angrily. 'Just announce ourselves,
our true identity and purpose?'

Oldcastle smiled patronisingly. 'It will be Twelfth Night,
the court will be celebrating the festivities of Christmas.
They will put on plays, pageants, mummery and other
ridiculous frippery. This year, members of our group will
be the mummers and they will stage a play that the King
has never seen before. They will capture the court and
hold the manor until we arrive in force.'

Oldcastle's speech brought gasps of admiration from the
rest. I saw Burton smirk and I felt despair seep through
me like some evil humour. Oldcastle, however, now
carried away by his own oratory, silenced the babble with
one wave of his hand. 'We must,' he said, 'arrive in London
with considerable force. Our agents in the shires have
prepared the commons to rise. They will act as
commissioners of array and march the force south under

the banner of the Whyte Harte. The assembly post will be
the fields north-west of Temple Bar!'

Sweet Christ! They sat there like lambs before the wolf,
bleating their admiration at his feckless plan. I could have
thought up a thousand questions and ten thousand
problems but I was silent. The good God knows I should
have spoken out but I was lost in a fit of despair. Oldcastle
sat, his soft, oily skin gleaming in the candle-light, his small
shrewd eyes flickering from side to side greedily looking
for praise and approbation. He got none from me and
stared accusingly.

'What is wrong, Jankyn?' he almost hissed.

'Well,' I replied slowly, hoping to quell the hubbub
around me and so draw the attention of others. 'Once we
have seized the King. Who will sit on the empty throne?
Not,' I jibed, 'Sir John Oldcastle or the weak, feckless Earl
of March! So who?'

I caught Oldcastle's eyes and shivered. They were
agate-hard, smouldering with fury. I remember shivering
for I realised this arrogant man would never forgive my
jibe and was now hungry for my death. He dug his hand
beneath his cloak and drew out the silk cloth I had last seen
in Sturmey's house in Oxford and, with a flourish,
unrolled it, drawing gasps and small cries of admiration
from my colleagues when they saw the Whyte Harte
quietly resting on its eternal field of green silk. The silence
was dramatic. We gazed at the sacred emblem. It hung
glistening there in that darkened room like the Holy Grail
or the raised chalice at the climax of the Mass.

We each saw our visions; banners and pennants stirring
and snapping in the breeze, phalanxes of knights ablaze
with colour slowly moving across lush meadows to the
blood-thrilling cry of deep silver trumpets. 'The Whyte
Harte,' Oldcastle whispered breaking, yet, at the same
time, grasping the magic. 'The banner of the Whyte Harte
will be raised alongside the gold leopards and silver lilies.
His Grace, King Richard II, will ride south and he will sit

on the throne of the Confessor and once again wear his rightful crown.'

'You have seen him?' I persisted. 'You have seen King Richard?'

I think Oldcastle was going to lie but he caught my eyes and shook his head. 'No,' he mumbled. 'I have not, but my messengers have, the couriers to Scotland. They say he will march south as soon as we are ready.'

I saw his eyes flicker to the side and I knew he was a liar and it was then that I decided to betray him. I am a liar amongst liars, a veritable Prince of Earl or Liars, even the Lord Beelzebub must blush at what I say. Yet I have one virtue, one flower amongst the thorns, I can always recognise another liar!

The meeting broke up, the rest dispersed, babbling like brooks, giving themselves the grave airs and graces little pompous men assume when they think they are involved in matters of great importance. I slunk away, Judas-like, into the night and plotted to destroy their treason with my own. I knew their plans would go awry and we would all end up with our necks stretched at Tyburn. Sturmey, myself and Mathilda hung out like bait for the cruel yellow beaks of the ravens. I wandered down the frozen, rutted street, my cloak swathed about me, and stood in the narrow, shadowed door of some house, oblivious of the cold as my mind probed at what I knew, digging like a hoe down into rocky soil. I must have stood for an hour until, numb with cold, I returned to Taylor's home determined to betray my colleagues.

Sleep evaded me, I sought it but my mind was agitated, the humours of my body tossing it like the wind does autumn leaves. I dozed, sinking into phantasms about a Whyte Harte leading me to a dark threatening forest where my father, grey-faced and gaunt in a dusty, threadbare shroud, was waiting for me in the shadow of the trees. Eventually, I got up from the hard truckle bed and, ignoring the snores of my companions (for we shared a small attic room), opened my pannier bags and drew out the best raiment I had; cloak, hose, cambric shirt, jerkin and strong leather boots. I remember it was freezing cold, I washed in the dirty, icy water in the communal basin, dressed quickly and quietly made my way down the wooden stairs.

The shop was deserted and silent except for the snores of Taylor's two apprentices bundled in rags, fast asleep under one of the tables. I opened the door and slipped quietly into the grey, wintry morning. There was a light snow underfoot and the threat of more to come. A cutting breeze caught my face and snatched away my breath. I stopped and panicked. Should I return? Forget the matter? Flee now? I steadied myself against the dirty wattle-daub of the house and decided to go on.

I still remember that freezing morning. The ice-packed snow, white and virginal in some places, a filthy blackened mess in the centre of the street where it choked the sewers with their evil contents. Icicles hung like enormous silent tears from eaves and window ledges. Now and again, the silence was broken by huge cascades of snow slipping from the sloping roofs and crashing to the ground. The streets were deserted, quiet under the snow; the doors of the wealthy were festooned with evergreen boughs and sprigs of holly. I remembered it was Advent, soon Christ would be born again. A priest hurried by, his fat face still florid from a night's heavy drinking. I bought a hot pie from a baker's shop and bit into the delicious soft crust, relishing the juices which filled my mouth and dribbled down my chin. A beggar-woman caught my arm, white-faced, hollow-eyed, her bony fingers scrabbled at my elbow as she jabbered for alms in the name of the sweet Christ. A pitiable, ragged bundle mewed against her shoulder, I shook her off, so she tried a pathetic smile and offered her body. I put my hand to her hair, kissed her on the brow and slipped a few coins into her calloused hands. I hurried on, brushing aside her thanks. I have always hated

compassion and never practise it. A dangerous virtue
which clouds the mind and blunts its cutting edge.

The snow-crusted palace and abbey of Westminster came
into sight, their yellow brickwork and stained-glass windows
gleaming in the frosty air. The road was busier now: bailiffs,
resplendent in their robes of office, straight-backed and
almost strutting in their power and righteousness, led bands
of felons chained by the neck and ankle through the frozen
mud towards the courts. I cast them a pitying glance, long
lines of men, women and children already dead except for
judgement or execution. Their faces sallow and gaunt, their
clothes a collection of rags whipped by the biting wind, their
naked legs and feet scarred and cut by the rocks cruelly
hidden under the muddy slush. I knew we could all meet
such a fate if we followed Oldcastle's madcap venture. I
hastened on, past a line of filthy, loud-mouthed bawds who
were being brought from the Tun prison to be fined at the
courts for constantly sinning against the morals of the city.
As was customary, musicians playing fife, drums and
bagpipes, tried to drown their constant jeering and flood of
obscenities. It was an unequal contest for the bawds'
comments carried clear and far and, for a short while, were
directed solely at me as I roughly pushed my way past them.

I was soon on to the main route past Westminster, the
abbey church with its lofty towers and walls gleaming like a
palace from some troubadour's song and alongside it the
Great Hall of Westminster, the home and court of kings.
Its courtyard was a bustle of activity; pie-sellers, bakers,
eel-catchers bawled across the great open space around the
great clock tower, each trying to tempt the petitioners,
summoners, messengers, lawyers and their officials with
tasty, hot-spiced food to break their fast. Soldiers in steel
helmets, their leather jerkins covered with resplendent
surcoats bearing the golden leopards of England, tried to
clear these petty tradesmen away but they always swirled
back like some insistent wave of water. The courtyard was

really reserved for the lawyers and their worldly business, here they met clients to save them from merited punishment, circumvent wills, upset land titles and seize the property of minors, orphans and widows. I caught muttered phrases, the glint of stern eyes and even harder mouths, I was slightly fearful of the silken robes and hoods of the King's serjeants; the red and white of the judges and the more sober, though just as costly, striped robes of the lawyers and professional pleaders. The law is a marvellous thing, it is a pity it has so little to do with justice.

I forced my way through the press, past these hawks and falcons in human flesh and up the broad stone steps into the hall itself. Above me was the great vaulted hammer-beam roof, a soaring expansive vision of gilt-edged, intricately carved woodwork which dominated the long, cavernous hall. The stone walls on either side were covered in thick, costly tapestries woven on Flemish looms, a fanfare of resplendent colours rivalled by the pure stained glass in the huge windows. I could only gaze in awe at the majesty of the place, deaf to the hubbub of noise around me. It was like stepping from the dark of winter into a beautiful summer's day. The black coldness outside was transformed by a feast of colours, flickering cresset torches, row upon row of candelabra and small, capped glowing braziers. A detail in one of the windows caught my eye, a Whyte Harte, a gold circlet round its neck, rested on the evergreen, lily-strewn bank of a blue-tinted river. Its sad brown eyes seemed to reproach me and I looked hastily away.

The hall was busy, along its sides in cordoned alcoves sat the Court of Common Pleas and at the far end, marble steps led up to the Courts of King's Bench and the Exchequer. I searched around for an official, a steward or bailiff of the court, and espied a portly individual in tight hose and brown, puffed, quilted jacket walking slowly up and down, a white wand of office in his hand. He did not look up as I approached him but continued to strut like

some plump, ancient pigeon does along its shit-strewn
parapet.

'Excusez-moi,' I said, blocking his path. Small shrewd
eyes studied me intently, the small petulant mouth screwed
up in annoyance, but I could see my French and sober
dress had quelled a bitter rebuke. 'Excusez-moi,' I
repeated, 'mais J'ai des nouvelles pour li roys.'

'Qu'est-ce que?' he squeaked.

'Grande trahison de Sieur John Oldcastle.'

I saw the words 'Treason and Oldcastle' drain his florid
face, he studied me intently and raised the white wand.
The noise around us died for a while as two royal
serjeants-at-arms appeared as if from nowhere. I was glad
I still had my hood up to conceal my face. The King had
spies but so did Oldcastle. The royal official muttered to
the serjeants, flicked his fingers at me and walked down
the hall, enjoying the attention my little drama had caused.
I followed. I had no choice with an armed, burly soldier on
either side.

We left the hall by a side entrance and along a maze of
cold, white-washed passages. My mouth was dry and my
heart pounded like a drum. I felt faint, nauseous with fear
and panic and, not for the first time, wondered if I should
have come. We stopped outside a chamber. The official
knocked on the heavy, iron-studded door and went in. I
heard voices, the phrase 'Another one!' and the official,
tight-lipped, came out and virtually shoved me through
the half open door before slamming it behind me. The
room was well heated and lit with pure wax candles which
blazed from two sets of candelabra. Luxurious tapestries
hung on the wall and there were even carpets on the floor,
Smelling of resin, wax and some delicious, fragrant
perfumes. It might have been a woman's room but, of
course, such luxury could have only been that of a Bishop,
Henry Beaufort, half-brother to the King, financier to the
court, the protégé of Popes and the darling of the courts of
Europe. Beaufort! Priest, saint, scholar or satanist? I never

really knew, with his clever treacherous ways, beautiful
eyes and perfidious heart. If ever a man charmed his way
into heaven it would be Beaufort. An illegitimate grandson
of Edward III, Oxford scholar, bishop by the age of
twenty, and later translated to Winchester, the wealthiest
bishopric in the realm. I remember him sitting there that
long-gone cold winter's morning, almost slouching behind
the great oaken desk, his glittering bejewelled fingers
steepled before him as if in prayer. The dark angelic face
and sensual lips conveyed an almost God-like, humorous
sadness, except for the eyes, large and dark, steel-hard like
precious diamonds plucked from the earth's cave.

'Your name. Monsieur?' The English was mellow and
soft.

'Matthew Jankyn,' I stuttered. 'A former scholar, now
apprenticed to Master Sturmey, parchment-seller of
Oxford.'

Beaufort looked at me and smiled slightly as if he knew
the truth but could not be bothered to tell it. 'And your
business, Master Jankyn? You mentioned treason and
Oldcastle.' He played with a thin, wicked-edged knife used
for slitting vellum. 'The two usually go together for they
mean the same.' He let the knife drop on to the table with a
clatter. 'So tell me, Master Jankyn,' he continued sharply,
'tell me all you know and it might yet save you from
hanging!'

'I am no traitor,' I yelped.

'You know about treason, Master Jankyn, and,
according to a statute of my grandsire, King Edward III,
that makes you a traitor. So,' he smiled, 'tell me about this
treason.'

I did. At least as much as I could, deliberately glossing
over my earlier life though I think he almost knew. I told
him about Oldcastle: the meetings, the conspiracy,
Sturmey and the plot to kill the King and bring back
Richard. He interrupted me there, raising his saintly face.
He stared at me with his devil eyes and questioned me

about the Whyte Harte, Richard and the belief he was still alive. I could see he, too, was haunted by memories different from mine but just as cloying. Then he nodded and let me continue until I lapsed into silence. The bishop lounged in his chair and looked beyond me as if clearing something from his mind. He puckered his lips and dreamily considered what I told him.

'Are you a Lollard, Jankyn?' he asked.

'If you live with wolves,' I replied, 'you learn to howl!'

'Aye,' he smiled, 'and if you sleep with dogs, you should not complain about fleas! Are you a Lollard?' he repeated.

'I am nothing,' I replied.

Beaufort nodded and straightened in his chair. 'But you are a traitor, Master Jankyn. You will hang!'

I felt cold with dread under his soft voice and hard eyes.

'But I do not wish to hang.'

'True. True,' he murmured. 'And I will remember.'

'Sturmey!' I interjected.

Beaufort looked at me quizzically. 'Ah, yes,' he muttered. 'Your Lollard patron. Well,' he shrugged, 'he will have to take his chances.'

The Bishop stared at me. 'Well, Jankyn. You have your thirty pieces of silver, so you may go!' I did, trying to hide my fear and embarrassment and ignoring the soft, mocking laughter which followed me out of the door. Not that I really minded. I knew I was a coward and a liar, extremely sensitive about my own hide. What I minded was anyone else knowing.

I returned through the snow-silenced town to the inn and tried to ignore the comrades that I had just betrayed but the eyes are like mirrors which tell all and they may have sensed something was wrong. Sturmey did but he thought I was just a coward and needed comfort. I did but for a less obvious reason. Poor Sturmey. The world needs more men like him and fewer like me. I believe he saw Christ's blessed face in every sewer-rat, whether they scrabbled on two legs or four!

The greatest rat of them all, that steaming turd, Oldcastle, kept hurrying back and forth like some old gossip at the village well. He brought badges of the Whyte Harte, promised supplies and sometimes actually kept his promises. He told us that the commons in the surrounding shires and villages were ready to rise in revolt. Richard would be marching south, Albany, the Scottish regent, would also send armies to help us. important officials and some great Lords were with us. Plans were afoot. Our coven became a pack of hunting dogs straining at the leash. If only that were the truth! More like a bunch of rabbits mesmerised by the smiling, blood-stained face of a stoat.

8

Beaufort was certainly ready, and struck like lightning on a summer's day. Christmas came and went with all the forced gaiety of Yuletide. We exchanged gifts, read the scriptures and stuffed our bellies with roast capon, pork and slices of beef washed down with sack, ale and fine Rhenish wines. Sturmey gave me a copy of Chaucer's poem, 'Troilus and Cressida', beautifully written and richly bound. I guiltily accepted and handed over a silver cushion, emblazoned with a reclining Whyte Harte and a pair of soft kid gloves for Mathilda. Sturmey's gratitude was so touching that I tried to take the opportunity of counselling him against Oldcastle's rash schemes but he simply smiled and shook his head in amazement. I became angry and shouted at him but he simply patted me on the shoulder and shuffled away! The old, gentle fool! Did he really think Richard, our Whyte Harte, would come riding along Cheapside, banners flaring, trumpets braying to the ecstatic cries of the populace? And that Henry of Lancaster's brood of young falcons, killers all, would hand over both crown and throne! Beaufort did for that. As I said, and I apologise for wandering but old age and a bellyful of wine affect the wits, Beaufort did not deal in dreams. The court did go to Eltham but suddenly moved back to Windsor and on to Westminster; troops were moved into the capital, fresh warrants issued for Oldcastle's arrest and, late on Twelfth Night, there were sudden raids on the Wrestler-in-the-Hoop and other Lollard haunts. They took no prisoners, the bungling idiots, but it threw our coven into disarray until Oldcastle arrived with his web of lies and false reassurances. 'All is well,' he brayed, 'the King is in retreat and the planned uprising will go ahead.'

The fools believed him. On Monday, 8th January, we left for the appointed meeting place at St Giles. I forget the freezing snow-sudden village we moved on to. Others joined us there, gap-toothed, red-faced peasants, citizens and a few minor officials, all armed in a number of ways, with billhooks, hatchets, hoes and spades. Oldcastle distributed more weapons but I was dismayed at his 'army' and wondered whether it would be better if I promptly took to my heels but virtue, God damn it, made me stay. I could not leave Sturmey, who still regarded everything as a holy crusade. Oldcastle gave us his familiar speech and litany of assurances and that was the last I saw of him.

We were divided into sections, each under a captain who carried instructions about the assembly point. As we journeyed back to London, I was heartened when we were joined by other groups and even a number of knights such as Sir Thomas Talbot and Sir Roger Acton, though I mistrusted these ancient campaigners of the Welsh wars who rode up and down our straggling column, waving swords and uttering bloodthirsty oaths. I do believe they had taken one too many knocks on their unhelmeted heads.

The journey was cold. Above us the sky dreamed, showing the occasional faint star and a stale-cream moon between the drifting clouds. The snow was ice-packed beneath us and muffled our tramping feet as well as the creak and rattle of the carts carrying provender and other supplies. Fear and cold kept us silent, though we whispered reassurances to each other about how the city gates would be opened to us and how fresh fighting forces from Suffolk, Surrey, Kent and even far away Wiltshire, would soon be with us. Just before dawn we passed Beech Lane and were on the empty moonlit route to Cripplegate. I marched like any veteran bowman though I was secretly terrified, wondering when Beaufort and the King would strike. The road narrowed abruptly between clumps of trees and I sensed it was here the King would await us. The silence was almost unnatural; no owl hooted or vixen yapped. I thought I heard a horse neigh, the faint jingle of harness and there was a rush of air like birds fluttering madly about us and the arrows fell thick and fast. A fellow in front of me whirled round, his eyes wide in surprise, his hands clawing at the arrow in his throat as he coughed and choked on his blood. Others dropped like empty sacks, falling in blood-strewn heaps on the snow. Our column broke and fled into the white darkness as horsemen burst from the trees and charged in flurries of snow towards us.

Sturmey shivered and clung to me like a child. 'Matthew! Matthew!' he beseeched. 'We are betrayed, what shall we do?'

I know what I wanted to do. Flee! I turned and saw horsemen on all sides; torches had been lit and stuck spluttering in the snow, casting long shadows on the panic and death around us. At least the arrows had stopped falling, though lines of foot-soldiers and archers had now joined the horsemen. Some of my companions fought and

were cut down. The rest surrendered, throwing down
their arms and kneeling, hands outstretched, and begged
for mercy. A few didn't get it. I saw a group of archers cut
the throats of two men and a youth but a horseman rode
up and shouted at them to bind the prisoners. I looked
around. Sturmey still clung to my arm whimpering with
fear and any hope of flight was now gone. There was a
circle of steel around us. We stood there as in a dream, like
corn-stooks waiting for the harvester. The attack was so
surprising that the slow-witted just gaped.

A group of archers approached. Sturmey pulled away,
the soldiers laughing at his frightened expression and
pathetic whimpering. 'A fierce one here!' one of them
joked as he deftly emptied Sturmey's purse and removed
all valuables. The old man tried to protest but the fellow
knocked him to the ground and promptly pulled off his
leather boots and thick serge cloak. Sturmey was forced to
kneel and his hands were tied behind his back. They did
the same to me, purse, cloak, belt and boots were quickly
removed, and I joined Sturmey to shiver in the cold. The
trampled, muddy slush seeped through my hose, the
freezing cold numbed my legs. At last we were ordered to
rise and shoved into long lines and ropes were tied round
our necks. The knights, Talbot and Acton, had also been
captured, stripped, and placed back to back on an old nag.
They led our sad, sorry column as it was escorted by long
lines of royal archers through freezing winter night down
to the prisons of the capital.

The journey was like some dreadful phantasm of the
night. The cold muddy road cut our frozen feet, those who
stumbled almost choked on the noose around their necks
and were beaten until they struggled to their feet. The
shock of sudden defeat and capture was fading and many
moaned and cried in terror for their mothers, wives,
children and loved ones. The archers mocked them,
hardened veterans, they callously scrutinised us with their
dead, bright eyes, jeering and taunting us. The banners we

had so proudly carried were trailed through the slush at
the head of the column where musicians with fife, tambour
and bagpipes played some mockery of a dirge. I looked
around as we left these fateful woods: perhaps it was some
trick of half-light on the snow, but I could swear I saw a
Whyte Harte, regal head and neck uplifted, one leg
delicately raised. Yet, when I looked again, it was gone. I
cursed King Richard, Oldcastle and, if he had not been
stumbling in front of me, I would have vilified Sturmey
and his simple, mad dreams.

At the church of St Giles we stopped, penned in like
cattle for the slaughter. Sturmey was in a state of collapse
with exhaustion and I whispered comfort about Mathilda,
friends, anything to calm and conceal my own panic. I
wanted to scream for mercy, say I knew Beaufort,
anything to break the nightmare but I knew it was futile.
We stood there in rows, as a sickly day broke. It began to
snow lightly and we shivered. Some collapsed, strangling
themselves on their nooses. Their corpses were dragged
away and the ropes refastened.

Travellers into the city, merchants, traders, pedlars and
peasants from outlying farms, passed and gazed anxiously
at us until the soldiers urged them on. A group of
courtiers, hooded and cloaked, came to view us, their
magnificent horses snorting furiously in the wintry air as
their riders urged them down our lines with gilt-edged
spurs and soft, leather boots. Someone murmured that it
was the King, his brothers with the Mayor and leading
officials of the city. I did not see anyone, I did not care. I
listened to the muttered conversations and gathered that
Oldcastle had escaped and that our fair-weather friends in
the city had simply faded away.

As the bells of St Giles began to clang the hours of
Prime, our columns were reformed and led through
Cripplegate into the city and down Wood Street. Already a
crowd had gathered, not the ecstatic populace described in
Oldcastle's lies or Sturmey's dreams, but a jeering mob

who pelted us with rocks, mud, offal, even the stinking corpses of rats, cats and dogs. We endured the insults, my feet had lost all feeling and the cold encased me like a suit of armour, I was hungry and faint with exhaustion. We passed the corner of St Paul's into West Cheap, trudging by Eleanor's Cross, raised by Edward I in memory of his dear wife. This was a small, lightly decorated stone tower containing sculptured scenes from Christ's life. One of the images was a gilt-edged statue of the Virgin standing in rosy-cheeked tranquillity with her small child vaguely smiling at our cavalry. The sight of this comforting symbol only made me worse and I slumped into a resigned shuffle as we wound up West Cheap to the dark forbidding buildings of Newgate prison.

These were no more than a collection of towers and houses in the old city wall. It was a pestilential place for, on the far side of it, was the city ditch, the open latrine and cesspit of London. We were crowded into the huge forecourt of the prison and the chief gaoler and his minions appeared. John Bothelmans, royal serjeant and the custodian of the King's prisons, was a terrifying sight. Short, thick set, shrouded in a dirty, grimy, scarlet houppelande or cloak tied loosely around his middle, he aped the manners of a courtier. His fat, red face with its protruding eyes and fish-like mouth was covered in small buboes and warts but his sandy hair was crimped and curled like a courtesan. He minced along the rows of prisoners clicking the chains of office around his neck as he scornfully surveyed the remnants of Oldcastle's army. He smelt of a cloying perfume and simpered at any good-looking youth amongst the prisoners. He stopped before one near me and smiled, showing a row of jagged, blackened stumps. The young man simply stared back before spitting at his would-be admirer. Bothelmans reacted with fury. He wiped the spittle from his face and, bringing his hand up, he scored two gaping red wounds in the young prisoner's face. The fellow collapsed, shrieking with pain and holding the bloody mess of his face, while Bothelmans continued to kick him. I noticed that the gaoler had no left hand but a cruel, steel hook fastened to the stump of his arm. At last, the boy was silent and Bothelmans turned to scream at us. 'You are traitors!' his voice bellowed. 'Traitors taken in arms against the King. Heretics, destroyers of Holy Mother Church! You will hang or burn but, until then, you will be here.'

Bothelmans stalked off and his minions, a collection of rogues dressed in black rags and leather aprons, shepherded us away. As I said, Newgate was a cluster of dwellings but beneath each one were stone caverns covered with heavy wooden trapdoors. These were now opened and groups of us shoved down into each of them. I managed to join Sturmey's group and after the ropes on my wrists were cut, I was dropped into a deep black pit. Sturmey collapsed into a heap but I immediately looked around. Our cell was simply a stone cavern, wet mildewed walls, rotting black straw with chunks of light let in through the cracks and seams of the heavy trapdoor above us. I reckoned that about two hundred had been captured near St Giles and now we were broken into groups of fifteen. There were three other prisoners already there who laughed and jeered when they saw us, not that we minded. I looked at my colleagues in the dim light and realised that, apart from Sturmey, there was no one I knew or cared for. My companions were just little men, poor peasants whose grandiose dreams and religious aspirations were taking them to the scaffold.

The three other prisoners looked tough ruffians. One of them approached me, a small dark man with one ear missing, the bright red brand mark 'F' on his cheek proclaiming to the world that he was a forger. He introduced himself as Philip Repton, native of the parish of Taunton in Somerset, who had come to London to further, as he put it, his future and status.

'You evidently failed,' I caustically observed.

He grinned mischievously and shrugged. 'You seem to have done no better,' he replied, his grating voice still carrying the burr of better places and happier times. 'What brought you here?'

'Lollardy, treason and foiled rebellion,' I replied. 'We were foolish enough to follow Sir John Oldcastle and his dreams of deposing young Henry and bringing back Richard and the cause of the Whyte Harte.'

'I have heard of Oldcastle,' Repton muttered, 'a man with no wits though his cause may be right.' I did not press him further on the matter as Sturmey was beginning to revive. Repton helped me make him comfortable, showing me how to cut strips of cloth from our hose to bind around our frozen feet and where to stand when the buckets of food and water were lowered from the trapdoor. The water was brackish and the food was a mess of greasy fat and rotten vegetables. Our conditions were really no better. Men having to relieve themselves in corners, the stench of their sick bowels offensive and cloying.

By day the cold was intense while the dark brought new terrors, rats, as large as young puppies, came scrabbling in from the city ditch to fight us for scraps and, at times, for the flesh of our dead comrades. Three died in the first day, old men who simply lay down exhausted and weak from cold, starvation and shock. The rest were piteous, though braver souls reasserted themselves and helped the weak. Human goodness is the only thing that has ever surprised me for it happens in the most unlikely places and at the most unlikely times. It's quite frightening really, perhaps that is why I have always tried to avoid it.

Not that our suffering was drawn out. We were captured on Tuesday and by Friday, the King and Beaufort acted. Commissions of Oyer and Terminer were issued, these mockeries were to give us a fair trial and hang us. We had heard rumours of how the Duke of Clarence, the King's brother, had raided homes and churches in Smithfield and Westminster the day before our capture, how the King had known of all our plans through spies working in our covens and how he was furious that Oldcastle had escaped. We heard such tales from gaolers and priests who came to minister to us. I heard the rumour about spies and trembled; if my comrades knew my secret they would certainly kill me and this, more than anything else, prevented me from making any plea for help from that arrogant bastard, Beaufort. I also wondered if Mathilda knew and, if she did, would she help? I needed her but, at the same time, hoped she would have the wisdom not to attract attention to herself.

She did not and the King acted quickly. As I said, on the Friday following our defeat, the courts sat and on the previous Thursday evening, we had visitors looking for leaders of the revolt. The first we knew about this was when the huge trapdoor was thrown back and the yawning gap above us was ringed with flickering torches. I got up and moved beneath it, foolishly thinking it was food, drink, visitors, any shred of hope in my nightmare. Instead, I stared up into the fat, plump face of Burton, who grinned down at me. Beside him was Bothelmans and a figure wearing the silk hood and striped gown of a royal serjeant-at-law. The latter held a stuffed, spiced pomade to his nose to ward off the stench and evil humours of the cell. He lowered this and muttered to Burton. 'Point out the leaders,' and I knew that Burton was a spy, he had betrayed us which explained Beaufort's phrase. 'Another one,' which I had overheard the day I visited Westminster. I realised that my visit had been fruitless, and Beaufort would assuredly let me hang. Despite my weakness, I raged with pure terror at Burton, calling him 'whoreson', 'git' and every filthy epithet I knew. He simply smiled and pointed to me. 'He was a leader,' he observed. 'Matthew Jankyn,'

'Jankyn!' the lawyer said, peering down at me through the gloom. 'I think not, Master Burton. We want the real traitors.'

Burton's accusation and the lawyer's unexpected defence silenced me but the rogue was not finished. He grabbed a torch and held it to peer around the dungeon. He saw Sturmey and named him and three others. There was, as God is my witness, nothing I could do. Bothelmans lowered a ladder and a number of burly gaolers scrambled down and seized the selected victims. Sturmey was hauled, half unconscious, up the ladder and the rest, pleading and bleating, were also dragged out. The trapdoor slammed shut and I sat in the freezing darkness and, for the last time in my life, wept.

I sometimes wish God's justice was as quick as man's. Sturmey and thirty-five others were condemned at Westminster the following morning and taken back to different cells that afternoon. On Saturday, so I later learnt, they were brought back out, stripped of their remaining rags, tied to leather hides and dragged by horses through the city to the meadows near St Giles. There, carpenters had erected new pinewood scaffolds which could take three men at a time. The prisoners were hanged in batches and left as a warning to all rebels against Church and State. The following week, a fresh group were taken and tried but, as these were convicted Lollards and heretics, they were removed to Smithfield, chained in barrels and promptly burnt.

After that there was nothing. We were left to rot, the King and Beaufort seemingly satisfied that the revolt was crushed and the leaders executed. Some of my companions died of goal fever but I survived. My only virtue being that I was young, strong, and fear for my own safety kept a flicker of hope alive. Repton also helped. I suppose like attracts like. He knew I was a villain and no Lollard and so felt a bond with me. We exchanged stories and I was surprised to find he was a defrocked friar who had fled his community for the more alluring pursuits of wealth and women. An educated villain, his sharp wit and tart observations on life comforted me after Sturmey's

death. Once, sitting on my own, I began cursing Oldcastle
before moving on to Richard II and the cause of the Whyte
Harte.

'Oldcastle may have been right,' he observed.

'What do you mean?'

'Well,' Repton seated himself comfortably against a
piss-stained wall. 'I was a friar when Richard II was
deposed. Our order was very much in favour of the
deposed king and followed his fate closely. I was at the
Aylesford house when the dead Richard was supposedly
killed, brought to St Paul's, where he lay in state, before
being moved to Kings Langley in Hertfordshire for burial.
Yet the rumours persisted that the corpse really belonged
to Richard Maudelyn, a priest almost identical in
appearance to the dead King. Richard II, so these tales
went, was alive in Scotland. I knew of these stories but I
was not interested in them. I also heard there was a revolt
in the January of 1400, when several great lords rose in
rebellion saying they had the true Richard free from
prison and would put him back on the throne. The revolt
was crushed at Cirencester. The great lords lost their
heads which were put in sacks, their bodies were
quartered, salted and slung on poles to be taken back to
London.' Repton paused to clear his throat. 'It was that
revolt, they say, which made the old King order Richard's
death but the Franciscans refused to accept this. In 1402
several Franciscan houses became involved in a conspiracy
to raise men and bring them to a place in Oxfordshire to
meet Richard. The conspiracy was quelled and, for the
first time ever, two priests, brothers, Roger and Richard
Frisby, were executed.' Repton turned his face towards
me. 'Do you know, Jankyn, I never really thought about
this but why should King Henry of blessed memory kill
two priests for believing Richard II was still alive? What
did the King fear? Why did our Provincial Chapter, held in
1402, proclaim that any friar who mentioned Richard's
name would suffer life imprisonment?' Repton paused

again and stared at me before continuing. 'I found it even stranger when Richard Frisby was tried for treason before King's Bench. Henry IV insisted on being there in person and interrogated him. The interview became famous and was often quoted in our order. So,' Repton turned to me, 'what did that brother know?'

I listened but did not answer for I was surprised at what he had told me. Oldcastle was a villain but did that mean he was a liar? Once more the Whyte Harte was back, a shadow in the depths of my mind. That night I dreamed once more of my father standing in a forest, a Whyte Harte behind him. He beckoned me to join him but I woke sweating in my dismal cell.

9

The months passed. Summer came bringing the heat and humours of the city ditch into the prison. More of my companions died, their bowels turned to water. I thought Mathilda would come, write or make contact, but there was nothing. I was a forgotten man though poor Repton was not. In the summer of 1414, the Court of Gaol Delivery sat at Westminster and Repton was taken before it. He hoped for the best but received the worst. Three times convicted already, the sentence of death was pronounced against him. I sat with him the afternoon before he was hanged, he had tried to put on a brave face but, at length, he crumbled and wept. In the evening a priest came to shrive him, not one of your florid-cheeked, fat-bellied monks but an austere man with Christ in his face and compassion in his heart.

He took Repton to a corner of the cell and they sat there talking quietly. It was night before the priest left and he was back early in the morning with Bothelmans and the death escort. Before he left the gaoler asked if Repton wanted anything. Repton smiled. 'Yes,' he replied. 'Be certain that when you bury me, I lie on my back and not on my side.'

'Why?' Bothelmans asked, genuinely surprised. 'What difference does it make?'

'Ah,' replied Repton, 'if I sleep on my side, I have nightmares.' He winked at me and continued up the ladder. The trapdoor shut with a clang and another small part of my humanity died.

I stayed in that God-forsaken cell for a year. Twelve months of my life in a black pit with rats, dirt and my dead or dying comrades. Then, it must have been January 1415, almost the anniversary of the Lollard defeat outside St Giles' Field, I was suddenly moved from the pit to a comfortable cell above ground. A white-washed room with clean straw, a bed of sorts and one or two sticks of furniture. Oh, sacred God, it was pleasant to smell the air, rank though it was, and catch sight and sound of the city. The priests tell us hell awaits after death. Don't you beleive them! The Newgate pit and its torturers would have taxed the ingenuity of Satan. Within days of this move, I knew something was afoot. Bothelmans was deferential: better food was provided, drink, a soaking bath in an icy tub of water and a change of clothes. I was treated like a wealthy debtor, in prison, but treated well just in case better times came. I think it was Candlemas, the feast of the Purification of the Virgin, when the real change began. I was awakened early and shaved, my hair was cut and I was provided with another bath in the water-butt in the prison forecourt. While the barber tended me, I saw my face in a round metal disc and hardly recognised the long, furrowed face, lined eyes and hard mouth. I was no beauty to begin with, but my year in gaol had not improved my looks. Bothelmans brought me a pair of slightly scuffed brown boots, purple hose, a shirt of Holland cloth, a doublet of purple satin and a tawny cloak. These, too, had seen better days but when I asked Bothelmans where he had obtained them, he just sniggered and said their former owner no longer had any need of them.

About noon, dressed in a dead man's clothes and riding a cob which was almost lifeless, I was led by four royal archers out of Newgate and along Old Dean's Lane and, keeping the City lane on the left, we went down on to the main route to Westminster. I knew I was going there and half guessed who had summoned me. I really did not care. The fresh air, the first signs of early spring and the hustle and bustle of the crowd revived me. I was almost drunk and dizzy with the sight and the smells and gazed wildly around, drinking in everything I saw. The archers left me alone though they watched me curiously. They did not really care. Dressed in the red-gold surcoat of the royal household, their peacock-feathered arrows and deerskin quivers slung across their backs alongside their wicked, long yew bows, they all looked like brothers. They would have cut my throat without a second thought but, as their leader informed me in a terse, clipped sentence, they were to deliver me at Westminster.

I expected to be taken to the Great Hall but we stopped outside the chapel of St Stephen which lies on the river north of the Abbey. The leader ordered the rest to stay and, taking my arm, led me into the chapel. If Newgate was hell, then the chapel of St Stephen's was heaven. A two-storied chapel about ninety feet long and thirty feet wide, it smelt of sandalwood resin and fragrant incense. The windows were glazed in a wild variety of hues and every inch of the walls and woodwork was gilded or stencilled in brilliant colours with wall paintings under each of its huge windows. The fellow led me out along a winding whitewashed corridor and into the great painted chamber of the King's palace. A place of great beauty.

Oh! Sweet saints, I have seen in a day what others never glimpse in a lifetime. The chamber was covered with coloured, fire-glazed tiles, the ceiling boarded, painted and covered with studded intricately carved brasses. Every wall was draped in eye-catching paintings depicting warlike scenes from the Bible. On the north side was a huge fireplace filled with blazing logs, a man in purple robes sat slouched before it, his feet on a small stool while, beside the chair, was a half open leather trunk spilling rolls of parchment out on to the floor.

I recognised Beaufort but he did not stir. An official, gorgeously dressed and carrying a white wand, appeared. He imperiously dismissed the archer while beckoning me to follow him over to the fireplace. When I was near, the official turned and, wide-eyed with horror as if I had committed some sacrilege, hastily indicated I should kneel. I did until Beaufort's soft, liquid voice told me to sit, one elegant, leather boot kicking a stool towards me. I felt a little ridiculous, squatting there almost like a child at his father's feet but that is what Beaufort intended as he gazed at me with his clever dark eyes.

'Well, Master Jankyn, we meet again. Oh,' he delicately lifted one right hand, 'I am sorry it took so long.'

'A year,' I replied. 'A year, a lifetime in that stinking gaol and you promised me. You promised me that Sturmey ...'

'I promised you nothing,' Beaufort interrupted sharply. 'Not to you, Matthew Jankyn, son of an outlaw, former Oxford clerk and still wanted in that city for robbery, murder and for fleeing sanctuary, not to mention heresy, treason, consorting with traitors, conspiracy and open revolt against the King.' Beaufort plucked a thin scroll from the heap of documents beside the chair. 'It's all here, Jankyn,' he said softly, 'and there's more. Burton said you were a leader of the rebellion.'

'Burton is the turd of a liar!'

'Burton,' continued Beaufort smoothly, 'was our principal spy. He told us more than you did, Master

Jankyn, which made us all the more suspicious. We believed you were trying to keep a foot in either camp. Once the revolt was crushed, the King himself reviewed the case of every leader; when he came to yours, His Grace was insistent that you hang!' Beaufort looked at me sternly. 'I keep my word, Jankyn, I saved you but to do that I had to sacrifice Sturmey but not his daughter-in-law. You must know that a traitor's property is forfeit to the King. I made an exception in Mathilda's case. A great concession, Jankyn, when the woman herself was scarcely above suspicion.'

'So, what now my Lord?' I asked.

'Oh, do not be so obtrusive, Jankyn, the King has not forgotten or forgiven you. He has executed some of your coven but believes in clemency for the rest, except for you.'

Beaufort watched my face tense with fear and laughed softly. 'Do you really think you can commit robbery, murder and treason in this realm and then walk out of the King's palace scot-free? You must earn that freedom!' Beaufort clicked his fingers. 'Like any wolf's head, you must serve in the King's army in France. Our sovereign has ordered the French to hand over their crown and northern provinces as his rightful inheritance. The French, of course, will refuse and, before the year is out, there will be an English army in France. King Henry is offering an amnesty to all outlaws who agree to accept his peace and serve in his army. You, Master Jankyn, will only receive a pardon if you go to France. You are young, ruthless and could survive.'

I could hardly believe Beaufort. Me! An archer in France! The thought alone terrified me but it was freedom and who would make sure I went?

'Secondly,' Beaufort studied me closely, 'if you refuse or abscond, sentence of death will be passed against you and the known traitor, Mathilda Sturmey. In that case, Master Jankyn, France might be the safest place for you because I would certainly hunt you down!'

'And if I agree, my Lord?'

'If you stay, if you agree, a place in my household. A pension for services rendered.'

'What services?' I said softly.

'To bring me information, to track down Oldcastle, to destroy and bury the Whyte Harte and the legends which surround it.'

Ah, so there it was. The thread in my life. I gazed desperately at Beaufort. Would it never go away?

'My Lord,' I said, 'the Whyte Harte is nothing but rumours and stupid stories. A legend about a king who never dies.'

Beaufort shook his head. 'But it won't go away, Jankyn, and that is why I have saved you from the gallows. I have studied the few wretched facts I know about your life and you and the Whyte Harte seem intricately bound together. You will help me unravel the threads of this mystery.'

'But Richard II is dead,' I shouted. 'He lies buried in Westminster Abbey. His cause is really a phantasm. A lure for poor idiots like my father and Sturmey!'

Beaufort looked at me strangely. 'Is it?' he asked. 'Even now, great lords of this realm are plotting Richard's return.' He held up a hand to fend off my questions. 'Enough of that, you, Master Jankyn, are to go to France and when you return, I shall have work for you.'

So, I was released and became a yeoman archer in the Bishop's household. Naturally, I wanted to bolt like a rabbit to his warren but, there again, for the first time in years I was a free man, not skulking from the law or stealing for my bread. The Bishop's steward was waiting for me when I was dismissed and took me to a spacious inn further along the Thames where the Bishop had set up his household. An indenture was drawn up by some grumbling clerk in which I was promised to serve his Lordship in peace and war as his yeoman. In return I would be paid sixpence per day, provided with a bundle of faggots each day in winter, livery robes twice a year, a gallon of beer a week and as much meat from the kitchen as I could pierce on a long knife. The agreement was drawn up on a piece of smoothed vellum and then repeated. The parchment was cut with a special knife, I was given the bottom half with dark mutterings of how costly it would be if I lost it and wanted a re-issue.

So Jankyn became a yeoman, with gown, hood, hose, knife and belt supplied by the clerk of the Bishop's wardrobe, food by the clerk of the spicery and money by the treasurer. Ah, it was a grand, idle life, swaggering the streets and taking ale and the whores in Cock Lane. I visited there often, venting my lust on any who took my fancy. I did nothing irregular for I knew I was watched. I was given a garret along with three other men at the top of the inn and I am sure that Beaufort had one of them there to keep an eye on me. Yet I was no fool and gracefully accepted my situation as the best I would get. I was entrusted with small tasks, messages to other Lords, the purchase of provisions, playing my own small part in King Henry's planned invasion of France.

10

King Henry was intent on war for glory, plunder and the licence to kill as many people as he could. There were other reasons but I did not know them, in that soft early summer of 1415 as England prepared herself for war. France was ripe for plucking, like an orchard with its prize fruit shaken from the trees. Its King, Charles VI, was sinking into senile madness; his wife, Isabeau of Bavaria,

fat, gouty and promiscuous, did little to help. She presided
over her own court, cut off from her husband,
surrounding herself with animals and birds: swans, owls,
doves, dogs, leopards and her favourite, a monkey dressed
in grey, with a furred coat and red collar who was allowed
to climb and piss over everything. Her eldest son, Charles,
given his parentage, did not amount to much; stunted,
knock-kneed, vacuous and prone to fits of 'grand mal'.
The boy hated his mother who openly reciprocated. This
precious threesome, this unholy Trinity, were fought over
by two leading noble factions, led by the Dukes of
Burgundy and Armagnac. Neither of these let slip the
opportunity to butcher each other with the utmost
ferocity. Burgundy had the King's younger brother cut
down by assassins in the Rue Barbette in Paris. In turn, the
Armagnacs seized and tortured the Queen's principal
lover before having the poor unfortunate sewn in a sack
and thrown into the river Seine. Eventually the royal
family chose sides; the Dauphin sided with the Armagnacs
so Isabeau began secret negotiations with the Burgundians, openly proclaiming that her son was illegitimate and
so could not succeed to the throne of France.

Perhaps I have some of the facts wrong, for I was never
a keen student of French politics and the years have
dimmed my memory, but this was the gossip in Beaufort's
household that long, lost summer so many years ago. Our
puissant sovereign, Henry V, had now decided to
intervene in these unhappy affairs with claims that the
French crown, together with most of northern France, was
his and, if this was not conceded to him, he would cross
over to claim his own. Of course, many saw it simply as an
opportunity for plunder, the more cynical and wordly-wise
as Henry's attempt to unite the kingdom about him.
Beaufort, of course, knew the truth. One June day I was
summoned to his chambers where he was resting after
days of negotiations with Commons for more money for
the King's foreign adventures. I remember him, lounging

in a chair beside an open window to catch the refreshing breezes from the river. He looked like a young lord in his velvet hose, soft calf-skin boots and unlaced satin shirt. He told me to sit on a foot-stool and served me with wine, a light, refreshing Rhenish faintly spiced with herbs. We exchanged desultory conversation: Beaufort sat for a while gazing into his cup and I thought he had forgotten me. I coughed quietly, he turned and smiled. 'Do you know, Master Jankyn, why our King is off to France?'

I told him what I had heard but he laughed and shook his head.

'No,' he replied. 'None of these reasons, Henry is going to France to exorcise Richard from his mind. His father deposed Richard, took his crown and allegedly murdered him. A pure act of vandalism, Henry of Lancaster had no right to the throne for though Richard was childless, he had already designated his heir, Edmund Mortimer, Earl of March. Now, our peasant king was a favourite with Richard, who could have had him executed during the invasion of 1399 when Henry of Lancaster came back from exile to claim the throne. Instead, Richard showered the boy with presents and sent him back to his father. So, Jankyn, we have a king who owes his life and crown to Richard II, a ruler his own father deposed and cruelly imprisoned, a burden of guilt he now has to carry.' If I were king I thought, I would have no such burden but scruples are the luxury of the rich, so I kept my mouth closed and let Beaufort continue.

'Our King has never really accepted that he is King and the French have made matters worse. In 1396, three years before he was deposed, Richard II married Princess Isabelle, daughter of Charles VI of France. The girl was only a minor, a mere child, and when Richard was deposed the French demanded the return of both the princess and her dowry. The French added insult to injury. They said Henry had no right to the throne, nor did his son. They refused Isabelle's hand in marriage to the Prince of Wales, rejecting Henry and his sons as usurpers. When our present King claimed the throne of France, Charles VI's ministers hotly denied his claim, pointing out that he does not even have a rightful claim to the throne of England.' I thought Beaufort, in this pensive mood, was going to tell me something else, a darker, more mysterious secret, but he thought better of it and smiled quietly to himself. I sat, waiting for him to continue. He rose and leaned against the window embrasure, looking out across the city. 'You may wonder, Jankyn, why I am telling you all this. Some day you may know the full truth but, for the moment, a little will suffice. You are an educated villain steeped in the legends about Richard and the cause of the Whyte Harte. You are also alone and I can trust you, a little.' He turned his head and smiled. 'I have you watched, you have made no attempt to escape. Now I want to trust you with a mission!'

I quietly cursed. Such a mission would mean danger and I had been hoping that Beaufort was going to arrange my release from enforced military service. He seemed to read my thoughts. 'Jankyn, you are to go to France. I cannot release you from that but you are free until July, the second Sunday, when you must return here. I will have your task ready.' He then dismissed me.

I knew he had given me licence to leave and, before the day was out, I had commandeered one of the fastest horses from his stables and galloped as quickly as possible to Oxford. It must sound romantic, a wild gallop through the night to see the woman I loved. Nothing of the sort. I was a lack-lustre horseman and fell off at least three times and was only too willing to stop at inns to soothe the aching sores on both my thighs and arse. It was almost midsummer as I trailed through Tetworth and Wheatley to Oxford. The countryside was green, promising a full harvest. I passed churches, the dull clay-red houses of the peasants, walled manor houses and the occasional isolated friary. The roads were busy for this was the centre of the wool trade. Wagons, covered in leather sheets, transported it in bulk to friars and markets; occasionally, in villages I passed through, women rolled the fleeces on long trestle tables or combed them to supply yarn for the local weavers. Usually, I travelled alone, pleased to be in God's clean air and riding through countryside which reminded me of Newport and the green, empty fields of Shropshire. Sometimes, I rode with merchants, threadbare scholars or in the entourage of silk-clad lords and their gaily caparisoned retinues. After my falls, I did not hasten to Oxford but rode slowly, savouring my freedom and looking forward to meeting Mathilda.

I did not enter the city but stayed outside at a small inn, 'The Trout', sending an ostler in with a message for Mathilda. I did not wish to arrive unexpected, and to be truthful, had no real desire to be seen in a city where I had no friends and, possibly, still a few enemies. The ostler returned later in the day, bearing a message which he delivered by word of mouth that the lady would meet me in her garden that same evening. Oh, I acted like some callow youth alive with excitement: I combed my hair, put on a fresh cambric shirt, multi-coloured hose and a short gown of fustian, slashed at the sleeves with red taffeta to match the long, pointed shoes I had bought in London, aping the extravagant ways of my betters. Really, I should have known better. I arrived, in Oxford during a lovely dusk evening and rode to Catte Street where I dismounted and led my horse down the same alleyway I had hidden in so many years ago. I had no difficulty in finding the back gate of Sturmey's house and, after hobbling my horse, gently tapped on it. I waited for a while, heart thudding as I heard the patter of light feet before the gate swung open. Mathilda was there as beautiful as ever, dressed in a simple green dress, a chaplet of white flowers iced her hair. She smiled vaguely and beckoned me up along the smooth tile path covered with a fine, white sand which cut between the raised flower beds now a blaze of glory, the old herb garden still well stocked with comfrey, mint, alkanet and buckram. I followed Mathilda and she indicated that I should sit beside her on a bench of hardened turf covered with a russet cloak. I did so, slightly bewildered. Mathilda was welcoming but acted as if I had been gone for minutes rather than years. She sat beside me, head slightly bowed, hands in her lap, then she looked at me sideways, almost slyly, and I knew there was something wrong.

'Well, Father,' she said softly. 'Where have you been and how did the business go?' She touched my wrists, her fingers cold as icy water. My heart lurched and a chill crept up my spine. 'Do not fear, Father, Joan will bring some wine!'

Mathilda smiled and tossed her head. The girl was mad, she had lost her wits. I heard a sound behind me and Joan was there, an old woman with grey, straggly hair, a brown, crinkled face and sad, grey eyes. She handed me a cup of wine, turned to Mathilda and asked her to fetch a tray of sweetmeats from the buttery. Once she had gone, the old woman peered at me. 'Who are you, Sir?'

'A friend,' I wearily lied. 'I knew Mathilda and her father years ago. I heard about the tragedy to Sturmey on my return to this country, so I thought I would pay my respects, but I did not expect to find her witless!'

'Aye,' Joan replied. 'I was with Mathilda when Sir John Oldcastle and that creature, Burton, arrived with the news of her father-in-law's death. I am her old nurse and came to stay with her when the old man went off on his mad escapades.'

'Oldcastle? Burton?' I interrupted testily.

'Ah, yes,' the old woman sucked her toothless gums. 'They told Mathilda that Master Sturmey had been taken prisoner and betrayed like all of them had, by a close friend of Sturmey, a young man whom they had befriended.'

'Burton and Oldcastle?' I repeated in disbelief. The old woman nodded and I rose wearily.

'Will you not wait for Mathilda to return?' she asked.

'She lost her wits after Oldcastle and Burton visited her?'
I said.

'Aye,' Joan replied, 'within days. First she went quiet as if
in a trance, much as you see her now.' I nodded and,
hearing a sound from the house, walked down towards the
gate.

'Sir,' Joan cried. 'It is dark! Be careful!'

'Why should we, who come from the darkness, be
frightened of it?' I muttered and left, not waiting for any
answer.

I returned to London ten days before my agreed
meeting with Beaufort. I did not go to the Bishop's inn,
but took lodgings in Mark's Lane, from where I began my
own search. At first it was difficult because I arrived back
in London on the eve of the feast of St Peter and Paul, one
of the great feasts or pageants when the city mustered in
arms to show its strength. An important occasion,
especially when troops were pouring in to Blackheath and
Smithfield in preparation for the war with France. From
early morning the citizens were awake: women and
children trooping into the woods to cut fennel, hawthorn
and greenery to deck their doorways. Servants piled up
heaps of wood and coal and at night bonfires were lit and
lanterns hung out. The citizens feasted and danced in the
narrow streets, oblivious of the reeking pools of blood,
bone and rubbish deposited by the cooks serving the
tables. The guildsmen of the city gathered at their halls
smartly arrayed in their jackets and sallets, bows and
arrows. Under countless flickering torches, led by the
Mayor clad in purple-bright brigadines and seated on a
war horse, the city militia tramped through the streets of
London. It was not the night to begin my search,
Beaufort's household, not to mention to countless spies,
would be out and abroad.

The next morning, however, I began in earnest in the
dingy taverns amongst the docks and wharves of London.

I remembered the man I was looking for had once told me, in his cups, that he had been a sailor. At Galley Quay, near the Tower, I searched amongst the Venetian galleys disgorging bales of damask, velvet and spices and then west to the Wool Quay, amidst the grain ships, Flemish carvels, heavy-bottomed Hanseatic merchantmen and the fish-reeking weather-battered ships from Iceland. I crossed to the stairs of Southwark, visiting the rat-infested runnels and dingy little taverns, my evident youth, ugly face, as well as the cruel knife stuck in my belt, discouraging any would-be assailant. Still, I could find no trace of my quarry so I returned across the river to Thames Street, jostling the fishmongers bearing huge wooden panniers of salted stock fish as I made my way up to Crooked Lane, visiting 'The King's Head', 'The Bull' and on, past the stone-crofted mansions of the wine dealers who dwell around Vintners' Hall.

So it went on for days until I went to the place where, perhaps, I should have started, the open space of Smithfields. I reasoned I would not be recognised but still kept my face hidden in a cowl for this had once been a Lollard stronghold. The great open space was clear of its stalls and butchers' carts as the celebrations in the capital were still continuing. Threadbare mountebanks and tinkers danced and sang as they juggled knives or beat scruffy tabors while gaudily dressed girls and boys performed fire tricks or balanced themselves on swords thrust deep into the earth. I walked amongst them, past townspeople bright in their blue-gold livery and silver badges to a great wide platform in the centre. This rested on six great carts and, underneath a soaring but shaky scaffold, a troupe of actors were re-enacting the death of Thomas à Becket, the sainted Archbishop of Canterbury. A golden angel swinging down to minister to the dying 'Thomas' as the blood from concealed pigskins splashed across platforms to the 'Oohs' and 'Aahs' of the audience.

I stood and watched and was about to move away to the

Wrestler-in-the-Hoop when I saw my victim, half drunk, staring vacuously across the platform. I made my way slowly through the crowd, even stopping to see a perjured juryman, a whetstone around his neck, getting pelted with refuse in the stocks. Still I watched my quarry from the corner of my eye. I edged closer until I was behind him, leaned forward and whispered 'Burton!' The villain turned, a drunken smile on his face. It was still there when I drove my dagger into his soft, sagging belly, but, as he slumped unnoticed to the ground, he muttered a curse against me. I merely whispered 'From Mathilda,' before slipping away into the crowd.

I doubt if anyone missed Burton. There was no hue and cry, no proclamations or rewards offered. I often wondered if Beaufort knew. He looked at me strangely when I met him at his inn a few days later but did not refer to Burton's death. 'I must tell you,' he began, 'that I have seen His Grace, the King, and you, along with other attainted but pardoned criminals, must go to France. The King is determined, he will not change his mind.' Beaufort seemed nervous, so I sat there quietly, even though his words terrified me. 'However,' Beaufort said, 'I have a task for you. It is the Whyte Harte.' His words fell like a rain of pebbles in a pool of water. The ripples spread out and I was caught up. A dead king and a Whyte Harte walking in a forest of death where, from every rotten branch, a corpse swung, twisting by its neck. I was tired, tired of it all!

'My Lord, Richard II is dead. He died at Pontefract Castle.'

Beaufort rose, came over and looked me full in the face. 'Before God, Jankyn, if you repeated this to another man, I would deny it and send you gagged to a terrible death. The truth is that we do not know if Richard is truly dead. The King does not know. He is most anxious about the matter.'

'But,' I intervened, 'Richard's body was reinterred at Westminster!'

'I have said all I can for the moment,' the Bishop replied. 'The King is most concerned about the matter but he will let it rest until these French campaigns are finished.'

'That is why I have to go to France!' I burst out. 'King Henry does not wish to leave people like me at home. Oldcastle's dreams were not so madcap!'

'Yes, they were,' Beaufort quietly replied, 'even if Richard was still alive. What sort of king would he make now? We forget the tyrant he was, his arrogant ostentation. When he ruled, he was a killer of men, and sixteen years after his deposition he still lures men to their deaths, even now!' Beaufort stopped speaking and chewed nervously at his lower lip. Despite his urbanity, his cool cynical approach, he was agitated, hiding something.

'Even now, my Lord,' I repeated his words.

'Yes.' Beaufort walked over to a small chest and, lifting the lid, pulled out a roll of parchment. 'Richard, Earl of Cambridge, Henry Lord Scrope of Masham and Thomas Grey of Heaton are conspiring with both the Scots and the French. They plan to kill the King at Porchester Castle as he makes his way to Southampton. They intend to bring the Scots into the kingdom, restore Richard II and, so the French hope, make a lasting peace with France.' Beaufort smiled at my astonished face. 'Yes, the cause of the Whyte Harte! Your former leader, Oldcastle, is involved though we do not know his whereabouts. The leading conspirators are well watched and pose no problem to the King. The Scots believe Robert Umfraville, keeper of Roxborough Castle, will allow them into the kingdom. In fact, he will, but only to destroy them. The French, well,' Beaufort's voice trailed off as he stared at a point above my head. He shook himself and continued speaking. 'The only real doubt exists about Edmund, Earl of March.'

'Richard II's appointed heir?' I said softly.

'The same, and that is your task. The Earl of March is residing at the Bishop of Ely's inn in Holborn near Leveroune Lane. You are to go there, seek an interview and deliver this verbal message from me: "The Whyte Harte is gone, the King will sail to France but whatever happens, the King intends to exalt certain lords higher than Temple Bar".' Beaufort paused. 'You do understand?'

I nodded and Beaufort made me repeat the message until he was satisfied I had it by rote.

'Good,' the Bishop commented. 'I am not sure what March will do. He may walk away, act angrily or give you a name. If he does the latter, you are to kill the man he names while the English army is in France.'

I jumped up in amazement but Beaufort curtly told me to sit down. 'Come, come, Master Jankyn, a tender conscience in someone like you! Of course, the King wants you in France but not just for revenge. The man you will kill is a traitor. More so than you or Sturmey, and, if I am correct, he is a great lord and has been guilty of many unproven treasons. You will kill him and,' he waved a finger at me, 'in a way and at a time when no man can suspect a felony.'

I knew what the cunning bastard would have said and done if I had refused. So, never loath to lose an opportunity, I asked the obvious. 'If I accept?'

'If you accept, succeed and survive,' Beaufort replied smoothly. 'Then a free pardon for all crimes and past offences not known to the crown: the sentence of attainder passed against your father rescinded: the restoration of his estates and property: a permanent appointment in my household and a role in the capture of Oldcastle. Finally, an opportunity to establish the truth about the Whyte Harte.'

Some of these rewards had been offered before, Yet I accepted without demur. Beaufort gave me further instructions about how and where to join the King's army going to France. He told me we would not meet until my return and, extending his hand for me to kiss, briskly dismissed me.

That evening, I packed most of my belongings into a fardel. I was pleased with the turn of events and tried not to consider the flaws in Beaufort's silken promises; I had to go to France, fight a war and survive. I was no dreamer and knew that if I did not, Beaufort would have others waiting to carry out his bidding. A terrifying realisation also gripped me; if King Henry failed to return, since he had as yet no heir, who would be King? Was that why he was so concerned about the Earl of March?

The next morning I journeyed up to Holborn and the sumptuous inn of the Bishop of Ely. In my most arrogant manner, I kicked some petty official and told him I bore important messages for the Earl of March. The fellow, bowing and bobbing as if I were the Emperor of the Romans, showed me into a wooden-vaulted, luxurious long hall. At one end was a painted screen behind the raised dais on which was a long, polished oak table bearing a great, silver-filigreed salt cellar. I stayed near the door next to the large water-pitcher and a wooden lavarium which bore wash-bowls and frilly-edged napkins. I was admiring these when the Earl of March appeared, a tall, gangly, blond-haired man with watery blue eyes and the face of a tired horse. I bowed, not too low, and without introducing myself, gave Beaufort's message, word perfect. Well, the effect on the man was dramatic, his sallow face paled, he stuttered and spluttered before questioning me. 'Does the Duke of York know of this?' I smiled wanly in reply, knowing that the man I was to kill was Edmund Langley, uncle to the present King and a leading peer of the realm.

11

I never answered March's question but gracefully withdrew leaving the Earl rooted to the spot, whether through shock or amazement I did not wait to find out. I left the Bishop of Ely's Inn, returned to collect my fardel and proceeded immediately to Blackheath where the archers that Beaufort had hired to serve the King would be waiting. I introduced myself to John Druell, the master bowman and captain of the company, who looked me up and down in pure despair. 'Another gaol bird!' he muttered and told me to camp with the rest, a mixture of rogues and yokels, all eager to serve the King and become rich.

There was a smattering of professional archers, hard, grizzled men who openly mocked all newcomers and, sometimes, tried to use us like a cock does barnyard hens. I was no exception but I had a knife and I had help. As I have said on many an occasion, like attracts like. One of these professional killers, Nym, with a craggy face and fiery red nose, drove the others off. He befriended and protected me. An able, expert knifesman, a thief saved from the gallows many years ago, Nym grasped my white, unshaven chin in his calloused hand. 'Look,' he said. 'I don't know who you are or where you come from! I don't care but I'll protect you. All I ask is that you pick me up when I am drunk, safeguard my purse when there's something in it and make sure I don't drown in my own vomit!'

I looked at his villainous, friendly face, the red drunken nose and watery eyes, one with a cast in it so you were never sure where he was looking. I grinned and nodded. We became friends. Nym was a rogue and a fierce drinker but a good comrade, while he lived.

None, however, not even he, knew of my past life or my links with Beaufort. I acted the simpleton, green in every way, though I thought constantly about Edmund of York and how I was to kill him. The quartermaster visited our camp and gave us our arms: steel rounded hats, boiled leather jackets, thin boots, hose, belts, braces, daggers and, most important, bows of polished yew and buckets of cruel, goose-quilled arrows. I was already trained in archery but Druell treated us all like callow youths who knew nothing. We drilled for days, holding, aiming and loosing at the straw-filled butts. If we were successful there was nothing but, if we failed, Druell brought his supple cane across our backs and legs. Believe me, whatever they say, this is an efficient way of improving your archery.

We stayed outside London for weeks, only marching south at the end of July. By then, for the first time in years, I was a member of a group. A soldier equipped and trained to kill though I heartily wished I were elsewhere. We reached Southampton Water at the beginning of August and for the first time ever I saw the sea, the choppy, laced-top waves of the channel. It was a pity it was not the only time for I have come to dread the sea.

We camped outside Southampton while the rest of the army gathered; professionals, mercenaries in their boiled, leather jerkins: ploughboys in rags, some with old bows or the odd, creaking arbalest. There were others like us, the retainers of lords and great prelates. The captains, men from the royal household, drilled with a string of curses and iron-hard discipline. All the time the royal purveyors brought in carts piled high with stores: arrows, bows, dried meats, leather skins of wine, fodder and bedding for the destriers, horses and mules. I watched this like a dreamer observes his dreams, calm and detached, yet fully aware of the frenzy in the scenes he watches. I thought of Mathilda, the Whyte Harte, secretive Beaufort and my own mission to kill a duke, a peer of the realm.

I gossiped with my fellows collecting, like a gull does scraps of food, pieces of information about my intended victim and I began to see vaguely the threat he posed to any King. He was a waverer, a man who liked to please all parties, a plotter without the cunning or stamina to see his designs through to the end. A man of many parts, but true to no one. He had been Richard II's lieutenant but then went over to Henry of Lancaster; he served Henry IV but plotted against him only to panic, tell all and so send better men to the scaffold, an old man who had learnt nothing. He reminded me of Oldcastle. Nevertheless, I dismissed him from my mind for I had still to set eyes on him or any of our noble generals. So, I trained with the rest on the steep hills above Southampton Water while the port began to fill with ships, cogs, fat-bottomed merchantmen, galleys and other transports while warships patrolled the sea roads and entrances guarding against a sudden French attack. Not that the French would attack, they had yet to declare war. Ostensibly, King Henry was trying the way of peace but secretly baiting the garrulous, senile Charles VI and his equally stupid son, the Dauphin, into war. Henry succeeded. The Dauphin dismissed Henry's claims, echoing Beaufort's remarks that King Henry had little claim to the throne of England, never mind to that of France. The Dauphin continued his insults: Henry was a mere boy, and he added insult to injury by sending Henry a set of tennis balls with the advice that he should stay in England and play with them. Our bold, pursuant killer of a King sent the balls back with a letter that he would soon follow them to France to play a different game.

This declaration of war and the stories behind it swept the camp. I remember Nym squatting on the hill top: behind us the camp was now a muddy mess, the ground

softened and soaked by the heavy showers of rain which
had swelled the latrine pits till their rotten contents swilled
over into the camp. There were rats bigger than cats, the
bloody flux had broken out and the dead were now being
burnt in huge funeral pyres. On the cliff-top, however,
you could still smell the sea. Nym and I often went there
with a bag of apples and a wineskin filched from
somewhere. I recall sitting, jerkin unloosed, boots off,
Nym lying beside me, his scarlet nose flaring like a beacon
in the light sea breeze. We looked across the sea and he
came out with his usual pronouncement. 'It's going to be
war, Jankyn, war in France. We'll sweep in like a hot spoon
through soft cream, and then.'

'And then, what?' I dutifully asked.

Nym shrugged, slurped some wine and passed it to me. I
often refused. Nym's nose was a powerful warning against
the danger of drinking too much wine.

'Then,' he would reply slowly. 'There will be a great
battle and, if we win, France will be ours – for a while!'

'And if we lose?'

Nym laughed as he always did. 'Then, Jankyn, our
worries will be over for we'll be dead and past all cares!'

Nym was right, it was war. Royal heralds with trumpets
blowing under fluttering standards edged with black
proclaimed the news throughout the camp. Early in
August, King Henry joined us with his brothers and
leading generals. He had been delayed on his way south,
stopped at Porchester Castle where the plot mentioned by
Beaufort had come to light. There, Edmund, Earl of
March, admitted all he knew about the conspiracy but
loudly protested his own innocence. Henry, probably
advised by Beaufort, believed him but ordered the
immediate arrest of Earl Richard, Grey and Lord Scrope.
The traitors were questioned and confessed all before a
Commission of Peers hastily assembled at Porchester
castle. They were condemned to be hanged, drawn and
quartered but Henry commuted this to a simple beheading

and their heads were sent to be displayed on London
Bridge. So, the King kept his promise, they were certainly
exalted high in the kingdom. As far as I could, I felt sorry
for them. They, too, had been betrayed by the Whyte Harte
as well as by the Earl of March. I knew he had heeded
Beaufort's warnings and decided it was better to be a live
earl than a dead, would-be king. I wondered about Oldcastle's role in the plot but dismissed him from my mind, for
the time being he would have to wait in the shadows.

As I have said, King Henry arrived in the camp at
Southampton. It was the first time I had seen him. He did
not look a killer with his shaven head, monkish face and
long, miserable nose. Oh, but he was! He drenched France
in blood, and for what? Conquest? Plunder? If they tell you
these were his reasons, don't believe them. Henry was
haunted by the image of the Whyte Harte and the knowledge that he had no right to the throne. He went to France
to show he was king, to prove to the world he had won God's
favour. I don't think he did, otherwise he would not have
screamed from his deathbed at Meaux when the bloody flux
was rotting his corpse. 'Ah, Jesus, no! My lot is with Christ
and His saints!' But, that was for the future. When Henry
came into our camp at Southampton he looked like a young
Mars dressed in black, his predatory eyes scanning everything. His deep, mellow voice removing our present dis-
comforts as he painted a golden future: silver by the bucket,
heavy ransoms, open countryside and fat, luxurious towns
would be our playground. The troops cheered him. I was
quiet, Nym simply picked his nose and answered my questions by pointing out the Duke of York, a large, fat, red-
faced individual dressed in sable and furs. I studied him
well, taking careful note of the colours and insignia emblazoned on the small pennant a knight banneret carried
behind him. I must admit I did not take to York with his
morose, petulant mouth. This comforted me, although I
still could not decide how I was to kill him.

Once Henry had raised our spirits with fair words and

fresh provisions, we began embarkation. An awesome
sight. An entire army on the move from land to sea. First,
the supplies, carts and wagons disgorging their heaps into
boats which were rowed out to the waiting fleet. The
horses, on rafts or long barges, plunging and rearing
despite their blindfolds. Soldiers and sailors fought to
control them and paid for it with broken arms and legs and
staved-in skulls. After them, the men embarked. Some had
to wade out to the waiting lightweight cogs, others were
taken by boats. Finally, the King in a sumptuous barge
adorned with silks, velvet cloths and crowned by a huge
blue and gold standard. We huddled on deck and watched
him come aboard before stealing back to our rank,
rat-infested corners to be ill, vomit and squat in our own
excrement, the barefoot sailors mocking and jeering at us
as they scampered about the deck. Ropes were tied, cords
lashed down and chains hauled in. Sails were loosed under
a stream of oaths and orders, they billowed, sank and
billowed again, full and pompous as the fleet slowly turned
to make its way out into the open sea.

I hated the sea passage. The cog we were in pitched and
rose with each wave. The green, salty water poured
through the scuppers and soaked everything. Chilled, sick
and fearful, our only dream was to reach dry land and
pray that the warships protecting the fleet would drive off
the French. I cursed Beaufort and the ill chance which had
brought me to such a pass. I did not worry about future
battles, wounds or possible death: the French did not
trouble me or the Duke of York, against whom sentence of
death had been passed. All I wanted was to survive, to get
off that ship.

Eventually we did land, disembarking in a rushed chaos
of men, animals and supplies at Chef-des-Caux on the
Seine estuary. Our camp marshals made us stay in the
surrounding flat, monotonous fields while cavalry went
out to forage and look for enemy patrols. There were none
except the drenching rain which began to fall almost as

soon as we had landed. So, Henry issued his orders: we were to march north into Picardy, seize the town of Harfleur to secure our rear and communications with the fleet, and, with good fortune, entice the French into battle.

The march began in good order but the rain and the carts churned up the mud. The convoy became strung out like beads on a broken necklace. God knows what would have happened if the French had attacked but, fortunately, they did not and we reached the town of Harfleur. I will never forget it. A pox-ridden, heavily walled port which shut its gates at our approach. They greeted any envoys we sent with arrows, stones, excrement and the corpses of dead animals. They did more, refusing to acknowledge Henry as King, they displayed banners bearing crude paintings of a Whyte Harte, pierced in the neck and side with cruel barbs. I do not know the King's reactions but when I saw them I felt as if I were being pursued by a nightmare. The banners, crude taunts to our King, also seemed to deride and mock me with desertion and, quite understandably, cowardice. Memories of Sturmey, Mathilda, my father and the hundreds who died because of that emblem flooded back like water through a sluice. I had dreams, phantasms of the night, of standing before a threatening forest and watching an elegant Whyte Harte moving slowly towards it. Once, there had only been a distant figure there. I always thought it was my father but now there were more. Men, hanging and twirling by their necks but still alive, gesturing that I should join them. I always woke sweating and cursing. Nym thought I had the sickness and was concerned enough to move away from me. I never bothered to tell him about my dreams. I suppose everyone has his own private nightmares.

King Henry may well have been disturbed by the banners at Harfleur yet he showed little sign of it and launched a savage assault on the town; mines were dug beneath the walls, ladders and scaling machines put up against towers but nothing happened. So, the army squatted in its filth and waited for the town to fall. Food was short, rats were rife and more men died of the bloody flux than at the hands of the French. There was more. A huge French army was gathering, moving to push us back into the sea. King Henry, however, was adamant; victory was near. Harfleur would fall. It did not but waited for help to come and, when none appeared, surrendered. The King accepted the keys of the city, forbade plundering and, leaving a small token force, ordered us to resume our march. By then I had already decided on a way to kill Edmund of York. I had studied the old, fat duke slouched on his destrier before the siege lines, dressed in half-armour, mopping his bald brow. He was a wine-guzzler, constantly calling for his 'Stirrup-cup'. Sometimes, he was so drunk, I doubt he would have even recognised the enemy.

It was the wine which gave me the idea. Before we left Harfleur, I went into its market and bought crushed powders from an apothecary. I spoke French fluently and so made sure that he poured the right powders into two small leather pouches. Satisfied, I rejoined the camp, helping to hoist the sick aboard home-bound ships before I joined the rest for our mad dash towards Calais. The French were massing hordes of mounted cavalry under their constable d'Albret. Reports said they had over thirty thousand knights against our thousand: our real strength lying in six thousand bowmen and a few thousand foot. In addition, our forces were tired and weak from disease, yet still we had to drag our carts and three cannon through the mud of Normandy. King Henry now changed his tactics: he wanted to display his banner to the French, taunt the enemy and get back into Calais and then home to an English Christmas. Nym dismissed the whole plan as 'horse-shit', loudly farting when the camp marshals came to inform our group of the order of march. I agreed with Nym's sentiments though, perhaps, not the way he expressed them. We had little food and our weak stomachs had to digest wild berries and walnuts. Whenever I smell them now, years later, I'm back, drenched and sick in the mud of Normandy, plodding back to Calais.

Henry kept us going;. riding up and down the columns, urging us on with promises of huge rewards. He still kept up the pretence of being King of France, displaying the silver fleur-de-lis alongside the golden leopards of England. He forbade us to plunder but his newly found subjects just burnt what they could and fled at the first sight of our troops. Nym, the poor bastard, chose to ignore the King's order against plundering; he stole a pyx from a church and then ravished the soft, plump body of a woman. By good fortune, I was not there but, unfortunately for Nym, the priest was. He appealed direct to the King who heard the case, seated on horseback under a dripping tree. The camp marshals took Nym, drunk and still carrying the pyx, before him. The King heard the priest out, questioned Nym and, using the hilt of his sword as a cross, sentenced Nym to hang from a branch of the overhanging tree. A camp chaplain shrived him and Nym was hoisted up by his neck and left to swing slowly, his legs kicking furiously. The King sat and watched the poor sod while beside him, Edmund, Duke of York, tittered like a ninny. Perhaps it was that. I never really know for I am a coward and had done nothing to help Nym, but the sight of York giggling at the poor bastard's death-throes spurred me on. I rushed forward and, grabbing Nym by the heels, pulled him down. Nym died instantly and with some dignity though (and isn't it strange how one notices such things?) even in death, his nose remained red. The King, impassive, watched me stagger away from the now dangling corpse. 'Soldier,' he called out. 'Come here!' I went back and bent the knee warily before him. I was already regretting my impulsive action. The King, patting his horse's neck, leaned forward. 'Your name, soldier?' The voice was nasal, the English clipped with a strange French accent. 'I asked your name soldier?' he repeated testily.

'Matthew Jankyn, Sire.'

'Ah, Jankyn!'

I looked up and saw a gleam of recognition in the dark, obsidian eyes.

'This man was your friend?'

'A comrade Sire.'

'Then, Jankyn, his property is yours,' and, dismissing me with a wave of his hand, the King turned and rode away. York, his slack-jawed face gazing petulantly at me, followed suit. I realised how pleasant it was going to be to kill him. I stayed to bury Nym under the same tree he had died on. I took his weapons, spoons, coins and belt. I left the boots, they were not worth anything.

Our march continued and so did the rain. We were scarecrows, lonely men in a desolate rain-soaked land and only fear kept us moving. Our mounted scouts brought in news of a massive French army coming from the west, threatening to cut off our retreat across the river Somme. They were successful; we found the bridges destroyed and the corpses of some of our scouts bobbing face down in the reedy shallows while others swung by their necks from ruined bridges.

Although he never showed it, King Henry must have been frightened. We abandoned our baggage wagons. We were bereft of food and had not yet crossed the Somme. Reports were coming in of large French armies under the constable d'Albret, the Duke of Orleans, and the Duke of Alençon, pushing into Normandy, threatening to trap and surround us. We had to cross the river but every bridge was destroyed and each ford held by strong French forces. Looking back over a long and dangerous life, most of it spent intriguing or fighting the English warlords, I have come to the conclusion that the real quality of a good commander is luck and Henry certainly had that. By the middle of October, after marching up and down the Somme, we had reached the village of Nesle when the King learnt that a small ford near the village of Béthancourt was unguarded. Henry immediately despatched mounted men-at-arms to hold it and the column's pace quickened. We arrived there, I think it must have been about the 19th October, to find the causeway, or *pavé*, across the swamp destroyed. We filled in the gaps with timber and brushwood and poured across the river. Once on the other side, our mood lightened and our scouts brought back firm news. The French had set up headquarters at Peronne. Some of their commanders were trying to persuade the rest to let Henry reach Calais and go home to England with nothing, but the Dukes of Orleans and Alençon ignored Henry's offers of peace and wanted battle.

They sent heralds, preceded by trumpeters and standard-bearers, to inform us they would fight us before we reached Calais, that they were already haggling over a ransom of the King and his leading captains but could give no guarantees about what would happen to the poor bastards who trailed behind the great ones of England. We watched these French heralds enter and leave our camp on their gaily caparisoned horses and Henry deliberately fed us with the terms they had brought. We were tired, wet, starving and frightened. The French changed all that. If we fought then we would have to win. There would be no compromise. No clemency or mercy shown to us. Henry continued his march through the muddy, sodden fields of Normandy until we reached the small villages of Agincourt and Tramecourt, where we found the French had blocked our passage. Their left wing on the village of Tramecourt, their right bordered by a cluster of houses and farms at Agincourt.

I will not bore you with the military details of what happened next. We camped before the French on the night of 24th October, and on the 25th the camp marshals ordered us awake. We were given the first hot meal for days and then our captains began to organise us in accordance with the King's command. Late in the morning, protected on each flank by a small wood, our army advanced into a narrow gap. There were two wings, one under the Duke of York and the other under Lord Camoys. Between them were three blocks of men-at-arms and connecting each of these were bowmen formed in wedges. Every archer planted in the soft ground before him a sharp stake which he had been carrying for the last two days, and took off his left boot to get a firmer grip on the muddy soil. The King, riding a small grey mare and wearing the royal surcoat over his armour and a beautiful gold crown on his bascinet, passed along the front of our army, cheering us up with words of encouragement and pointing out that the position was ours and the French would ride to their deaths. He was right. The French formed up in three divisions their vanguard a blaze of colour and heraldic symbols. The massed chivalry of Europe advancing towards us, their horses halting and stumbling in the soft, muddy ground. By the time they reached us many of the horses were exhausted. Our ranks held firm although some of the men-at-arms wavered at the crashing of the horses against the stakes, their armed riders looming over us, beating the air with their swords, axes and morning-star maces. We held fast. The order was given 'Notch! Loose!' and thousands of arrows sped into the air and fell like a black sheet of death on the French cavalry. The great destriers stumbled and fell, spilling their riders on to the stakes or into the mud-soaked ground where they lay helpless. As one wave of horsemen was beaten off, we ran forward with axe, sword, leaden mallet or misericorde dagger to finish off the wounded. Many a fine, young gentleman cried, 'Ayez pitié, ayez pitié!' If they were rich, or we thought they were, we had pity but, if they were not, then their throats were cut and their bodies hastily plundered. I was green then. Ignorant of the value of ransoms, so I took what I could carry, then went back to the lines.

During the lull in the fighting, while both sides reformed, I decided to kill York. I stood in a wedge near the flank under his command and had glimpsed the fat duke, slouched on his destrier, helmet off, his skin a sheen of sweat. It was so simple. In my belongings piled at my feet was a small, leather flagon of wine I had filched. I unstoppered the cork, poured in the powder and slipped back through the lines to where the Duke was sitting. His entourage let me through without hindrance as I bawled, 'Wine! I bring wine for the Duke!' The cretin did not even bother to thank me but imperiously lowered his cup until I had filled it, then waved me away as he continued to study the enemy massing in the near distance. I obliged immediately. Looking back I think I was unkind. You really cannot expect someone you have just poisoned to thank you.

The French attacked again in magnificent battle array, their surcoats, banners and pennants seemed like a mass of steeled, gorgeous colours moving towards us. Again the orders were shouted and once more we loosed volley after volley. A day of wrath. A day of anger. God's vengeance falling on the French from the skies. Then, late in the afternoon, Henry gave the order for the two wings to close in and the slaughter began. The ground, damp as it was, could not absorb the blood. In places it was ankle deep. Other more terrible things happened. Henry thought that a new French force attacked our rear but it was only a group of desperate hotheads. Nevertheless, our King ordered the slaughter of all prisoners. The soldiers, canny lads, cried out in protest, so a company of royal archers did it. A pitiable sight, men begging for their lives, hands oustretched, then looking down in horror at the blood splashing from their slashed throats. A brave bully-boy was our good King Henry. I am glad I took no prisoners. I saw grown men weep at the ransoms they lost that day.

By early evening the French had fled. Their dead covered the ground like some rumpled, stained gorgeous carpet. Henry, who had fought vigorously in the thick of the fight, immediately instructed a Te Deum to be sung, the dead stripped and the plunder stacked up on wagons. During this, York's body was found, face down in the mud. Not a scratch on him. No suspicions were raised. He was a drunkard and common report had it that his heart simply failed him. There was little mourning after all, he wasn't missed and at least he died in the company of men more honourable than he.

The day after the battle, we left Agincourt and set off for Calais from where, after suitable celebrations, we embarked for England. An ecstatic welcome greeted us from Dover to London and, as we rode from Blackheath into the city, the entire populace turned out in gorgeous pageantry. Statues symbolising victory, gaily painted wooden towers, banners streaming, their gold tassels jerked by the stiff, cold breeze, trumpets blaring, splendid pavilions of many hues, cheering crowds and a chorus of beautiful maidens singing a victory paean. The conduit of Cheapside ran with wine. Oh, we came home in glory, but I remembered poor Sturmey who had thought such a welcome would greet our rebel force some two years earlier. How London would embrace both the Lollards and the cause of the Whyte Harte. I recalled his excitement and dismissed the cause of the Whyte Harte as childish nonsense. I had forgotten about Beaufort but, of course, he had not forgotten me.

12

The army broke up, the shire levies making their way out of London, the mercenaries flooding the fleshpots of Southwark. It was almost Christmas and the usual festivities were heightened by the news of King Henry's victory. The French prisoners who had survived the slaughter were led through the city to the Tower by their principal peer, Charles, Duke of Orleans. I thought his capture was a mere accident of war, forgetting the savage mêlée around his position. I later found that he too was linked to the legends and mystique surrounding the Whyte Harte.

Anyway, I dallied in the streets, taking lodgings in the narrow garret of a merchant's house off the Poultry. I enjoyed life: ale, soft women, the luxury of being a coward when others see you as a brave man, a strapping bowman, a noble archer, a veteran of Agincourt. Oh, I feasted, drank and wenched on my reputation. Sometimes, at night, I thought of my father, Sturmey, Mathilda, Nym and the Duke of York but I dismissed them from my mind. God knows it was cold that winter, even the meat hanging on the hinged flaps of the butchers' slabs froze hard as stone. I was tempted, like the prodigal son, to go back to the luxurious comfort of Beaufort's lodging but I resisted such thoughts. For the first time in years, I was a free man not a rebel, a Lollard or a wolf's head. However, I developed a pain in the small of my back, sharp, piercing, as if a thin slit knife kept penetrating my innards. I did not wish to consult a physician, a crowd of thieves in my opinion, who should have adorned every gallows in the country. I remember one in Oxford when I was a student: a fake, an illiterate quack. A woman had come to him asking for a cure for the fever, the fellow wrapped up some inscribed parchment in cloth of gold, told her to wear it, and charged her a fortune. She died but her family took the rogue to court where he was sentenced to ride bareback through the city to the sound of trumpets, the parchment and a whetstone around his neck. A public warning about the dangers of doctors.

Nevertheless, the pain became so intense, I decided to return to Beaufort's household. I almost crawled down a rat-infested runnel of a street to collapse in the courtyard of the Bishop's Inn. The steward recognised me with hails of welcome and pompously ordered servants to lift me, 'the hero of Agincourt,' to a room. The Bishop's doctor, a silent, bewizened creature, but more clean and honest than his fellows, came to see me in my small garret and rubbed an ointment into my back. In three days, the pain had disappeared and the doctor returned and sat clucking in wonderment at his achievement. I thought he was so surprised that I had recovered, I asked him what the ointment was.

'Oh,' he almost whispered with pleasure. 'I collected a good number of those beetles which in summer are found in ox dung. Also some crickets. You know, the sort which sing in the fields. I cut off the heads and wings of the crickets and put them, the beetles and some common cooking oil in a pot.' He stopped speaking and smiled deprecatingly. 'I covered the pot and left it for a day and a night in a lined oven before removing it to a fire. Once it was heated, I pounded the paste and made the ointment.' He beamed at me and shuffled away. I wished I hadn't asked him, but at least he didn't tell me to drink the stuff.

Of course, Beaufort arrived, smiling, secretive, wrapped in warm, costly robes against the cold. He looked content, almost smug and I remembered vague rumours about the Pope being willing to raise him to the cardinalate. He smiled.

'Hail the conquering victor, Master Jankyn! So you were successful?'

'The Duke of York is dead,' I replied.

'Ah, yes,' Beaufort pursed his lips and looked sadly at me. 'You know, he deserved to die. Edmund Langley, Duke of York, betrayed everyone and was involved once more in his stupid plots. The King was reluctant to destroy his own uncle, so you were given the task though,' Beaufort paused, 'I have no desire to know the details.'

Beaufort poured mulled wine from a pitcher into two

cups and handed one to me. He sipped from his before continuing. 'But you survived, Master Jankyn. Why did you not return immediately? The King and his army returned many days ago!'

I looked at that clever face, resenting the vague hint of authority in his persuasive voice. 'We made a bargain, my Lord? A pardon? Restoration of my father's property?'

'Ah, yes.' Beaufort pulled a small roll of parchment tied with a green ribbon from under his robe and tossed it to me. 'You will find everything there,' he continued. 'A charter of pardon and letters of restitution, all sewn on the one roll.' I picked it up and threw it on to my heap of belongings in the corner of the room. I did not want Beaufort to see my relief or joy. I was, for the first time in years, a free man, owning property and status. On reflection, I think people are right, virtue is its own reward.

Beaufort coughed. 'Of course,' he continued smoothly. 'I keep bargains and I do not have to remind you that part of this bargain is that, for a while at least, you serve in my household.' I looked at him and smiled, though my heart sank. Chained to Beaufort for the rest of my life but I quickened as Beaufort continued. 'You were a member of Oldcastle's coven, an associate of the conspiracy of the Whyte Harte?' He did not bother to pause for my reply. 'Is it not time we searched such rumours, Master Jankyn? Lifted the veil on legends which lured your father and so many of your friends to their deaths? And it still draws others, allows plotters, mischief-makers like York, the opportunity to stir the mud whenever they wish to cloud the waters.'

'But where do we begin?' I answered. 'The mud is deep and it seems there are many weeds. Why not let the matter rest? What does it matter now? King Richard went, some sixteen years ago. Our King was only a boy. Now he is the crowned prince, the victor of battles, the conqueror of France!'

Beaufort looked at me strangely. 'I have told you,' he replied. 'The King feels guilty about Richard.'

'Surely, that has now gone?'

'No, the King is determined on the truth.'

'So why choose me?' I asked.

'Ah!' Beaufort smiled. 'Because you know Oldcastle.' I remember gasping with shock as Beaufort sat and smiled secretively. He had hooked me like some lazy summer perch. Of course, I thought about Oldcastle and, when I did, cursed his evil soul. Sturmey and Mathilda were victims of his love of intrigue and conspiracy. If I had met him I would have killed him but I had given him up as dead. I put this to Beaufort who shook his head. 'No,' he replied. 'Oldcastle and the Whyte Harte are very much alive. We have reports about him in the north plotting with the Scottish regent, in the Midlands with other conspirators and on the Welsh March with the remnants of Glendower's army.' Beaufort's voice thrilled with subdued rage. 'And always the Whyte Harte. That accursed emblem is still daubed on tavern walls!'

'The same song,' I observed, 'but different singers. How is it you cannot track him down?'

Beaufort shrugged. 'It's like catching moonbeams or the rays of the sun,' he replied. 'It looks so obvious, so easy, but you never grasp anything!'

He reached into his voluminous pockets and drew out another scroll. 'This is all we know about Oldcastle. Read it. The physician says you are better. In days I expect you to begin your task, track this man down, Jankyn, and bring the Whyte Harte to bay!'

He left in a swirl of faint perfume and soft, velvet robes while I sat on my bed and thought about what he had said. I unrolled the parchment he had left but gazed at it lazily, my mind wandering along the past, recalling Oldcastle, feeding my hate with images of his face, fleshy lips and dangerous words.

For a while, I did not return to the document. I was tired

of intrigue, war, marching and great affairs and became immersed in the festivities leading up to Christmas, the season of misrule. Beaufort's household were given licence to mock and rejoice at the same time. A page was selected as a boy bishop, who presided over games, blessed Beaufort's retinue, allowing himself to be regaled with bread and wine while he presented us all with our Christmas liveries. I received £8 worth of the finest scarlet cloth as well as an allowance for clothes, wine and food. The weather was cold and hard so none of us wished to wander the streets but stayed indoors celebrating with mumming and gaming, dicing and the occasional banquet.

On the day after Christmas, Beaufort sent me a letter instructing me to prepare for my task, followed by a short interview in which he asked if I had read the scroll he had given me. When I replied no, he became irritable and ordered me to do so within days, stating he wanted me involved in the task of tracking down Oldcastle before Twelfth Night. I quietly cursed but agreed. From his scriptorium I collected pages of parchment, a pumice stone for cleaning, together with a little scraper for making equal surfaces. Once the parchment was ready, I ruled margins on either side. The weather was cold and foggy so I had to put the inkhorn in a hot basin so that the ink would dry more quickly on the parchment. I unrolled the manuscript Beaufort had given me and began the laborious task of copying it. I have that document today, blackened and greasy, though I can still remember the day I began to write on its soft, white, virginal surface. I thought my adventures had been extraordinary but the story I transcribed was as intricate and complex as any painting or tapestry from Bruges. It reads as follows:- *The full confession of William Swinderby, tailor in the town of Norwich, taken down by the clerk to the Mayor's court, John Mar, in the first year of the reign of King Henry V on the feast of All Souls* (I reckoned this to be 2nd November 1415, only a few weeks previously). *I, William Swinderby, on oath, swear that the story which I relate is true. I was a man of substance in the town of Norwich and owned a shop and tenement in Rottle Street. I was a mercer, married with two children. My life was a happy and prosperous one until I clashed with the parson of the local church over certain dues he claimed I owed him. He attempted to pursue his case in the courts and bribed the bailiffs to seize my property and chattels. In a fit of temper I slew him in his own churchyard one Sunday morning after Mass, and fled the town. For weeks I lived outside the town, begging and thieving until I was given refuge by a family belonging to the sect of the Lollards. Through these I got to know Sir John Oldcastle and became involved in his plot to cause rebellion against our Lord, the King, and restore Richard II who, Oldcastle boldly averred, was still alive and residing in Scotland. My skill in writing, as well as my determination to flee Norwich, made me a valuable accomplice to the knight. On his behalf I undertook a journey in the summer of 1412 to Scotland to deliver certain messages to King Richard II who was said to dwell in Stirling Castle.*

Sir John supplied me with money, arms, horses, a sumpter pony and the necessary letters of introduction. My journey north was an uneventful one. I did not believe that King Richard II was alive, thinking it was some mummery or masque staged by Oldcastle to satisfy the stupid and the gullible. However, in Scotland I found this to be different. I was met there by an officer of the Regent of that country, the Duke of Albany. I showed him the letters and warrants of safe conduct from Oldcastle and was allowed to continue unmolested. By August of that year, around the feast of the Assumption of the Blessed Virgin, I found myself in Stirling and sent letters to the Constable of the castle asking for an audience. He agreed and did not seem surprised when I informed him that I had been sent by Sir John to seek an audience with King Richard of England. He told me to return in a day and, when I did I was ushered into the great solar or hall of the castle and found the man claiming to be Richard waiting for me, seated in a great wooden chair on a dais at the far end of the room. He beckoned me to approach and I saw a man of about six foot in stature, dressed in a blue silk robe trimmed with white ermine fur.

His face was long and slender and framed by blond hair which fell down to his shoulders. He was seated almost in the shadows and it was hard to distinguish his features but the hand I kissed was soft, white and bore costly rings. When he spoke, the voice was fluent in French, but on finding I was unable to follow that language, he managed to converse in clipped, rather stammering English. At times he seemed to forget me, lapsing into silence, but I became convinced that this was no mummer or masque player but truly King Richard II of England.

He informed me that he had been freed from Pontefract Castle in the winter of 1400 some fourteen years previously and become involved in a plot to oust Henry IV and so win his own reinstatement. When that plot failed he had escaped north with friends and had been given shelter and sanctuary by the Scottish court. Since then, he claimed, he had constantly attempted to find friends and allies in England who would aid him in his restoration and the destruction of Henry of Lancaster and all his family. He believed that the cause of the Whyte Harte was just and supported by God. I was given a livery bearing the emblem of the Whyte Harte and sealed letters issued under his own privy seal. He also signed these letters and the signature (so I later discovered) was identical with that of Richard when he was king.

The day after my interview I travelled south, the documents hidden in a secret compartment of a trunk, and I took them to Oldcastle in London where he was sheltering at an inn called 'The Wrestler-in-the-Hoop'. I apologised to Sir John for not believing him, fully attesting to all who would hear that I had met King Richard, kissed his hand and brought his letters south for those still faithful to his cause. Oldcastle continued to use my services, sending me to different parts of the country; Leicester, Devon, the marches of Wales and Coventry in the Midlands. On these journeys I carried messages from Oldcastle in preparation for the great rising planned for January 1413.

I should have been at the meeting outside St Giles but a sudden snowstorm closed the roads and I remained trapped in St Albans unable to join Oldcastle's army. I was fortunate for the rebellion failed and Oldcastle and many of the leaders fled north, judging it was safer to remain concealed until the royal commissioners exhausted their fruitless task to track us all down. I fled back to Norwich in the hope that time had healed the injuries I had done there. Nonetheless, I remained in hiding until the summer of 1415 when Oldcastle sent me a letter, dated many weeks earlier, asking me to join him at Wenlock Abbey in Shropshire.

I was tired of hiding and, despite the failure of Oldcastle's rebellion in London, I rejoined my old leader. Oldcastle had been hiding at Wenlock during the months following the failure of the rebellion, the Prior was his close friend, a supporter of the Lollard cause and an adherent of Richard II, openly flaunting the banner of the Whyte Harte in the abbey church. Oldcastle did not seem dismayed or disillusioned by failure, claiming it was only a temporary setback for he still had the support of the great ones of the land. At first I thought this was bluff, a farrago of lies but then he sent me with letters to the Earl of Cambridge and Lord Scrope. I later found that these were involved in a conspiracy to kill the present king when he visited Porchester Castle on his way to join the army in France.

Once again Oldcastle's plot failed and others, including the Earl of Cambridge and Lord Scrope, were sent to the scaffold. I travelled back to Wenlock Abbey and openly reproached Oldcastle for his constant failures but Sir John simply smiled, claiming that he would finally succeed for nothing could stand against him. He hinted that he had no allegiance to any king or any church, asserting that his loyalty was to the old faith. I do believe he had dabbled in black magic and secret rites, though I was never sure of this. He used to leave the abbey at night, returning after dawn looking tired and dishevelled. I felt it better not to enquire though I heard rumours from peasants and lay brothers who worked in the abbey, that dark, secret rites were practised in the surrounding forests and wastelands. Perhaps my disagreement with Oldcastle became apparent. I found it difficult to talk to him and began refusing to carry any more messages. Eventually Oldcastle and I parted, he was affectionate in his farewells and generous in his parting gifts and I left him for Norwich.

Perhaps I should have been more careful. For years I had

wandered the country and never been molested by officers of the law but, on my return to Norwich, I was suddenly arrested, hauled before the magistrates' court and committed to the Justices' Assizes. When they arrived in the town on their circuit, I was taken before them, judged and condemned to death. It is only in the hope of saving my life and soul that I now make this confession.

I put Swinderby's confession down. It had astonished me, yet, at the same time, told me very little new. I was not surprised at Oldcastle's treachery and treason. He was no more a man of God than Beaufort but I was amazed at his ability to survive while sending others to the scaffold. Swinderby's confession stirred the black hatred I had for Oldcastle. The man was like some plague travelling from place to place up and down the country, destroying others and passing on. I had always believed he was evil and agreed with Swinderby's suspicion that he was a Satanist, involved in dark rites so popular in the deserted hamlets and villages of England despite the strictures and warnings of the priests.

I immediately went to Beaufort, curious about Swinderby's assertion that he had met Richard in Scotland. 'Is this the truth?' I asked. 'I knew Oldcastle always maintained that the deposed king had fled to the protection of the Scots. Oldcastle could also produce documents and letters despatched under Richard's seal but this is the first time I ever heard of anyone actually meeting him.'

Beaufort was taciturn. 'We do not know,' he replied. 'I have shown this document to the King. The Scottish Regent, the Duke of Albany, has often hinted to our envoys and diplomats that Richard is still alive but rarely shown in public, and usually refuses requests by visitors to view this Richard.'

'Do you think Swinderby is wrong?' I asked.

Beaufort shrugged. 'He could well be. Remember, Jankyn, you are a professional liar. A man will say anything to save his own skin.'

'But surely,' I persisted, 'Swinderby could be interrogated, put to the question?'

'Oh, no,' Beaufort answered. 'I doubt that very much. You see, the royal justices were not at all taken with his confession. There are certain details that Swinderby could not corroborate and no shred of proof to substantiate his story. Such reports came to the chancery many weeks afterwards and by then Swinderby was hanged, so his confession only poses more questions than it answers.'

For the first time ever Beaufort touched me, clasping my right hand in his. 'Jankyn,' he urged, 'there is a similarity between you and Oldcastle. You can both survive. You must track Oldcastle down! He knows the truth about Richard and the Whyte Harte.'

I remember Beaufort pausing, still holding my hand as if he wished to say something further. 'I need to find out,' he continued, 'what Oldcastle knows about the ghosts which haunt King Henry's mind. If you find him, perhaps I could exorcise these ghosts.'

13

Two days later I left the Bishop's house, took lodgings at the Craven Arms in Smithfield and began my search amongst Oldcastle's previous hiding places. I was healthy, well armed and carrying letters of protection from Bishop Beaufort so I feared nothing. I moved from tavern to tavern, dark and dingy, with their greasy tables and slop-strewn floors, but my questions drew blank stares or muttered curses. I gathered that Oldcastle was not as popular as he once had been. The Lollard cause was dead and all that remained were cruel memories. In the Smithfield and Southwark areas many families had lost men, husbands, fathers and brothers during that fatal rebellion. There was also a great deal of fear as the church continued its persecution of the Lollards, sending the most obdurate to die at the Elms or Smithfield.

I could find nothing. I must have spent two weeks searching the capital from Aldgate in the east to the stews of Southwark in the south and, despite the muttered curses and dark looks, I rashly thought no danger threatened and should really have known better. I had been travelling from Holborn into Cheapside after another exhausting and fruitless search in one of Oldcastle's old haunts. It was early in the morning and already the streets were crowded and busy. A general hubbub on all sides, men and women were crying their wares. 'Pies! Hot mutton pies!' 'Live eels!' 'Hot oatcakes!' 'Fresh herrings!' 'Fine meats!' Apprentices were busy taking down shutters, opening their shops and setting up little stalls, whilst their masters brought out their stock. I had some business to transact in Cheapside and came out to some woman's soft, persuasive voice trying to inveigle me into her shop. 'See here, Sir, fine lawn, good cambric and bone lace!' I smiled, shook my head and walked along Goldsmith Row past grave-faced merchants, their importance evident in their gold chains and richly furred robes, up to the far end of Cheapside where a group of aldermen were inspecting the conduit heads upon which the city's water supply depended. I remember all this so acutely, for as I walked I became aware of danger, of something wrong. Perhaps the press of people who tried to attract my attention knew something for, when I turned, I got the impression of someone just slipping out of sight.

I suppose you expect danger when you trail the streets of the city at night but not on a bright morning when all of London is alive and busy around you. I decided to stop and take some refreshment and walked into a tavern, the Holy Lamb near St Paul's cathedral, for a jug of ale. The place was brisk with people from every walk of life, the knifeman, the courtier, the upstart, the cleric, a captain home from the French wars, the usurer, the bankrupt and the scholar. I looked round at each face, trying to shake off the feeling of disquiet, of danger, of being watched or pursued. I saw a young man swoon before a farmer who bent down to care for him, while the young gentleman's accomplice sidled up and cut the fellow's purse before slipping away into the crowd. Then some mountebank asked for our attention, claiming he possessed the very chair in which Julius Caesar had been stabbed and that he could sell the stones Satan brought to Christ when tempting Him to turn them into bread. The last claim brought gales of laughter, and empty tankards and scraps of food were hurled at him so I decided it was time to go. I left the tavern and turned down a narrow alleyway leading to St Paul's where gossips and scriveners of the city took up residence. I knew some of them for they kept me informed of any news about the Lollards or the whereabouts of Oldcastle or his accomplices.

My stay in the tavern had restored my good humour and I was surprised to find a figure loom out of the darkness and block my path. 'Stand aside!' I shouted good-humouredly but the man lunged towards me. I thought he was drunk but then the light caught the glint of steel in his hand and I realised the danger. Heart pounding, throat dry, I quickly rolled my cloak into a shield around my arm and drew my long stabbing-knife. Now, I know, I am a coward, but I always believed the difference between a coward and a brave man lies in the eyes of other people, not himself. That day I fought bravely, albeit from sheer terror. It was none of your courtly duels or prettified tourney. Once we were close, we grappled and clashed. I think the man would have killed me, he was agile with muscles like whipped steel yet, as I fought, I realised he was no city ruffian sent to dispatch me. As it was, the fellow nearly did. He had me down, my face against the hard cobbled stones, one hand against my throat as he scrabbled to bring his other up for the killing blow. Suddenly I heard shouts, the man got up and I watched him run, black against the light at the far end of the alleyway. I heard a scrape of cord, something hissed over my head and my assailant flung his arms out as if greeting some lost friend and fell hard against the earth. I got up, turned and saw that my rescuers were two soldiers, both dressed in the livery of Beaufort's household. I recognised one as the captain in the Bishop's retinue, a thin, sallow-faced man with hard, brown skin and close cropped hair.

'You are fortunate, Master Jankyn,' he rasped. 'We almost lost you in the tavern!'

'Who sent you?' I snapped ungratefully. 'Have you been following me?'

The fellow shrugged. 'For a soldier back from France, a veteran of Agincourt,' he jibed, 'you seem to display little military knowledge, Master Jankyn. We have been following you for days. Ever since you left the Bishop's household.'

'To protect me?' I asked.

'Yes,' the man answered unconvincingly. 'To protect you.'

I knew he was lying and the Bishop still did not trust me. 'Well,' I sighed. 'It seems you killed my assailant. It may be interesting to find out who he was.'

I left the body to them and trudged back to my lodgings grateful at being saved though angry at Beaufort's lack of trust in me. I suppose it is a characteristic of the professional liar. We do expect some measure of trust. Otherwise how can we betray it? I knew that my attacker had not been some London ruffian from Southwark or the Smithfield area, such creatures hunt in either pairs or packs and rarely launch such a clever attack. I was proved correct. The corpse was examined by the coroner of St

Paul's, who actually described the man as a murderer who received his just deserts. His chattels were declared forfeit to the crown. They did not amount to much, the most notable thing being a purse which held a few coins and a list of horses stabled at the manor of Almery in Herefordshire. This document was brought to me at my lodgings by a messenger from Beaufort with a covering letter pointing out that Almery was Oldcastle's principal manor house. Beaufort added the surprising thought that Oldcastle might well have returned there in the hope that officers of the King might never dream that a rebel would return so brazenly to his own home. The following morning I packed my possessions on a sumpter pony and rode through the city gate and took the road west.

The weather was cold but with promise of an early spring and this made travelling easy. The roads had not yet dissolved into muddy morasses and I made fair distance, staying by night at lonely farms or in sheltered hamlets, buying a space on the floor, a dish of hot, greasy food and a cup of ale for a few pennies. I had very little idea of where Almery was except that it was in the shire of Hereford but, by asking directions of tavern-keepers, peasants and traders, after eight days' travelling, I found myself on the brow of a hill which overlooks the village of Almery.

Looking down I could see a cluster of cottages, farms and a small village with a square-towered church and a large manor house nearby. This was on one side of a small river, on the other were meadows where the village flocks and herds were pastured during the lean time of winter. Between the meadows and the woodlands on the far horizon were three open fields, divided into strips by narrow grass paths or baulks as the country people call them. It looked a homely scene, a prosperous village preparing for spring and the hard task of sowing for a good harvest. Plumes of black-blue smoke rose against the winter sky, there seemed no hint of menace and I decided

that the best approach was an honest one. I urged my horse
down the hill, along the dirt-beaten track and into the
village. The place was relatively deserted, a few dirty children playing, and I remembered it was Sunday and most of
the villagers would be in the local church. There was a
derelict house with an ale-stake above it so I tethered the
horse outside, slipping a coin into the calloused hand of
some yokel with sharp words for him to guard it until I
returned.

Inside, the tavern was slovenly and dark, an earthen floor
covered with dirty rushes, a few ramshackle tables with
upturned barrels for seats and, in the far corner, a row of
tuns with dripping spouts. A slattern asked my business, so I
ordered a mug of ale and some bread. I sipped the ale and,
pretending to be some honest traveller, asked who was the
lord of the manor. The slattern mumbled something and so
I asked if it was Sir John Oldcastle. She threw me a slightly
mischievous look and after that refused to speak any
further. The place began to fill, the morning Mass was over.
In the main they were simple peasants, clumsy ham-fisted
men with raw faces, peeled by the sun and wind. They gazed
at me curiously but never approached. I heard the slattern
whisper 'Oldcastle' and they glanced strangely at me but
nothing else until a large, portly, rather well dressed man
came over. He introduced himself as Thomas Lavenham,
Constable of the parish. I am always wary of such fellows.
Dangerous men who wield as much power in their own
communities as Beaufort did throughout the realm, with
their right to duck the village scolds or throw charlatans,
thieves and brawlers into the stocks. Their power is absolute, supervising the lives of the villagers, seeing that flesh
was not eaten on fast days and that everyone went to church
on Sundays. Petty tyrants. This one was no different with
his fleshy face and slack wet lips. In a loud voice he began to
question me as if I were a child. 'Who was I? Where had I
come from? What business did I have in Almery? Had I
been to church?'

I sat and watched him act his play in front of an audience of open-mouthed villagers. I let him rant on and rose, dug into my wallet and brought out Bishop Beaufort's warrants. 'I am,' I proclaimed for all to hear, 'here on the orders of Bishop Beaufort, Bishop of Winchester and Chancellor of England, to question you, sir, and any others who have information on the whereabouts of Sir John Oldcastle, wanted by the King for treason, rebellion and divers other felonies against the crown!' The villagers almost cheered to hear such authority whilst the Constable simply deflated like some pricked pig's bladder.

The man spluttered, lips moving furiously as he tried to recover his pride and hide his fear. 'I am sorry,' he muttered, 'I did not know who you were. Forgive me. Sir John Oldcastle is no longer in the manor. It has been empty and in the King's hands for over five years now. It is managed by Sir Griffith Vaughan of Welshpool in the shire of Montgomery. One of his sons resides there as Steward until the King decides what to do with the manor and its appurtenances.'

I nodded gravely and brought my hand down with a smack on the fat man's shoulder. 'Come, Sir Constable,' I said, 'if you would be so kind as to take me across the manor and then return to stable my horse, I promise you that I will remember your services when I return to London.'

The fat fellow positively beamed with satisfaction and I followed him as he waddled out of the inn, oblivious of the hum of conversation which broke out behind us.

We crossed the village street and went up the beaten causeway to the manor-house. It was a two-storied affair, moated and walled, though the drawbridge had been removed and replaced with a wooden footbridge. We crossed this, the Constable banged on a small postern gate, a stable-boy creaked it open and we entered a deserted quadrangle. I suppose it had once been busy, now it was deserted; stables and outhouses along the walls were derelict. A few scraggy chickens pecked in the dust and the place was littered with rubbish and weeds. The house itself was a heavy-walled building of timber, brick and flint with narrow apertures and the occasional window. The constable imperiously waved the scruffy stable-boy away and walked up the main path fringed by sprays of hedgerows. We were greeted at the main door by a young, thin-faced man with watery blue eyes and thin mouth who introduced himself as Geoffrey Vaughan, son of Sir Griffith Vaughan of Welshpool. He led us into a deserted oak-panelled main hall; I whispered to the constable that he could go whilst Vaughan went into the buttery for a flagon of wine which was as bitter as the young man who served it. He informed me that Almery had been in the King's hands for a number of years and his father had been entrusted to look after it. He, in turn, had given it to one of his sons who was evidently not pleased with the task.

'I don't like it,' Geoffrey mumbled in a sing-song accent.

'Why not?'

The fellow glanced sideways and gulped from his cup. 'Sir John was a strange man,' he replied, 'not liked by many of his tenants. He involved himself in things no manor lord should.'

'Such as?'

'Lollardy, heresy. Rumours of witchcraft.'

'And the Whyte Harte?' I interposed.

Vaughan grimaced as if he had smelt something nasty. 'That nonsense,' he replied. 'I tell you, Master ...'

'Jankyn,' I reminded him.

'Yes, Master Jankyn,' he retorted. 'You see, we on the Welsh march have had enough of civil war and the fate of kings. First Glendower, then Percy's rebellion against Henry IV. Each time the royal troops come down upon us like flies on a summer dung-heap. They plunder. They pillage. They requisition stores and after them come the royal purveyors, taking goods in the King's name and

offering us worthless tallies in return.' Vaughan sighed
and chewed on his lower lip. 'Of course,' he said, 'there are
always young men looking for excitement. Some fight for
the King and are killed or injured. Others choose the
losing side and end up wolf's heads or swinging by the
neck on some crossroads scaffold.'

'And Sir John Oldcastle,' I reminded him. 'He was never
caught?'

'No. Like summer mist or some will-o'-the-wisp, he
comes, causes trouble and then disappears.'

'So, he never returned?' I asked.

'Why do you ask?'

I told Vaughan about the attack in London, how I had
almost been murdered by one of Oldcastle's retainers.
Vaughan shook his head and informed me that the
assassin would not have come from the manor but
probably was one of the young hotheads who had marched
with Oldcastle years ago. 'I tell you,' he continued,
'Oldcastle was never liked here and, if he returns, my
father has issued instructions for him to be taken dead or
alive. He has been considered Utlegatum, outside the law –
to be taken or killed on sight!'

I looked around the deserted hall. 'And Sir John's
property?' I asked. 'His possessions, his movables? What
has happened to them?'

The fellow grinned maliciously. 'It costs money to run
an estate,' he said. 'The King will not repay my father, so
my father does what he can. But there are certain things
you never touch. Come.' He took me up a stone staircase
and pushed open a metal-studded, heavy-timbered door.
If the hall had been deserted and meagre then this was
positively sumptuous. The floor was inlaid with chequered
tiles, lead windows with horn glass, an oaken cupboard
stood in one corner and in the other, a richly carved chest
with intricate bands and locks of wrought steel. A huge
four-poster bed dominated the chamber with the curtains
pulled around it so that it seemed some sort of tent or

pavilion. On these were embroidered in red and gold silk, a gentle white hart sitting on a golden field beneath silver rose trees.

'Sir John lived well,' I commented enviously, 'for a man involved in spiritual affairs. You have not sold these yet?'

'Oh, no, the royal exchequer has this room inventoried,' Vaughan replied grimly. 'But, come, look at this.' We crossed the room, Vaughan pressed a wooden wainscotting and opened a door concealed there. The chamber beyond was small, bare and gaunt. The floor was paved stone, the walls whitewashed with meagre light from two arrow-slit windows.

I have been in many places but never experienced the terror and sadness I felt in that room. It was like standing in a house of death or meeting with the evil which stalks at mid-day. I always pride myself on my total lack of conscience for my finer feelings were never allowed to develop. But in that room I sensed an abomination, something cold and malevolent.

'What is it?' I whispered to Vaughan.

The man sighed and hugged his arms to his chest as if he was cold. 'I do not know,' he replied. 'We found the remains of a child beneath the flagstones here and this ...' He moved into the shadows and brought back a small box of white and blue velvet. He opened it and inside encased in tawny sarsenet was a small phial filled with a red, sluggish liquid.

'What is it?' I asked hoarsely.

Vaughan snapped the box-lid shut and returned into the shadows. 'I do not know. We found this room and the box only weeks ago. My father believes it is something to do with Oldcastle's dabbling in the black arts.'

I left that chamber and the deserted house as quickly as I could though Vaughan promised that he would inform me if Oldcastle ever appeared in the area. I thanked him profusely and was gone, instructing him to send messages not to me, but direct to the Chancellor.

14

I spent the succeeding months travelling from town to town and shire to shire. Now and again I returned to London to deliver messages or see if any instructions awaited me from the Chancellor. Travel is never easy for me but, in those months, I became an expert horseman, someone who knew the quickest routes from city to shire and back to the capital. Oldcastle, however, always eluded me. He was in Northampton, then in Norfolk, on the Welsh march, or in the taverns and stews of Southwark. He had his friends, for I knew his glib tongue could persuade anyone to give him shelter. Oldcastle knew he was being pursued and twice I was attacked. Once by a secret but clumsy assassin. Another time, outside Newark, a well aimed crossbow bolt flew within inches of my head. I never really cared. I was obsessed with finding and killing him. Sometimes he was almost within my grasp. I knew from covert glances and secretive expressions that Oldcastle had been in a place sometimes only hours before I arrived.

In the late summer of 1418 I fell ill with a fever and had to return to London. I recovered and was preparing to leave when I received the incredible news that Oldcastle had been captured. I was disappointed that I had not been in at the kill but took solace from the fact that perhaps my relentless pursuit had worn him down. Oldcastle had been seen in the neighbourhood of St Albans in the house of one of the abbot's serfs but a raid on this place revealed nothing. Next he was seen in Byfleet in Northampton where two husbandmen and their wives comforted and sheltered him. For this all four were hanged. Then Oldcastle reached Almery where he tried to coerce some of his former tenants into providing him with food and shelter but Sir Griffith Vaughan sent a party of men to arrest him. I laughed to the point of hysteria when I learnt the details. For Oldcastle, the redoubtable street-fighter, was finally brought down by a woman cracking him on the shin with a stool. So serious were the injuries that the rebel knight had to be taken back to Westminster in a horse-drawn litter. The King was in France but his ministers were ecstatic with Oldcastle's capture and I received letters of congratulation from Beaufort. Oldcastle was committed to Newgate. I asked permission to see him but this was refused. Beaufort told me that no one was to see the prisoner until after his trial, although I was invited to attend that.

Of course I had to fight my way through the crowded throng at Westminster Hall to get a good view of the great red baize table, the symbol of King's Bench, the tribunal before which Oldcastle was brought. The hall was packed with lawyers in their scarlet clothes and striped, silken hoods. The clerks appeared with bundles of parchment, stacks of pens and trays of inkpots. These would advise the five judges who sat before the great bench in their crimson miniver, their close-fitting white hats or coifs clasped round their heads and fastened under their chins.

There was a trumpet-blast and from a side chamber came a troop of serjeants wearing the King's insignia and between them, chained, stumbled Oldcastle. He was dressed in a sober brown tunic lashed at the waist by a piece of rope, his feet thrust into a pair of simple, open sandals. He seemed a little older, greyer and shorter than I remembered him but there was still the old arrogance, the supercilious smile, the cold, sharp eyes. He turned to survey the packed hall and dismissed us all with a flicker of his eyes before turning to present himself at the wooden bar and glare at the judges. He had chosen to defend himself, denying the charges of heresy while, at the same time, attacking King Henry's right to try him, proclaiming in his loud, rich voice that Henry was no true king whilst Richard was still alive in Scotland. The judges did not care to or could not answer this, even though Oldcastle's assertion brought loud sighs, even cheering from the crowded hall. Of course, the verdict was a foregone conclusion. Oldcastle was adjudged a traitor, a heretic and a felon and sentenced to die by burning at Smithfield the following morning. I was in the far corner almost parallel to where Oldcastle stood at the great wooden bar of the court and, though I hated him, I admired his cool courage as he received the sentence passed on him with a shrug of his shoulders and a supercilious smile. Then he disappeared in a swirl of soldiery. I was content for, just as the trial had begun, Beaufort had sent a warrant allowing me entry into Newgate to see Oldcastle.

I went there that afternoon, concealing my dread on returning to that terrible place and not at all eager at renewing my acquaintance with the chief gaoler, Bothelmans. He was as fawning, devious and sinister as ever. Bowing and scraping with a knowing look in his eyes, he shoved away Beaufort's warrant as if we were old friends who had no need to stand on such formalities and led me across to the heavy oaken door in one of the small towers.

'Sir John has been placed here,' he muttered, almost apologetic as if expecting me to be angry that Oldcastle had not suffered the same humiliation as I had in one of the underground dungeons. 'Do you wish a guard?' he asked.

I shook my head. 'Is the prisoner chained?'

Bothelmans nodded.

'Then,' I said, unsheathing my dagger, 'I will be safe.' I wanted to sound brave, though I had secret fears about Oldcastle, chained or not. I knew the man and would only rest assured when he was dead.

I entered the bare, stone-vaulted chamber. Bothelmans

was correct. It was a more palatial residence than my underground cell. I suppose even when it comes to treason there is always a distinction between the high-born and the rest. Oldcastle sat, half resting on a truckle bed, his arms and legs secured in iron gyves by chains to the wall. He peered through the gloom and the shadows caused by the cell's sole flickering flame. 'Oh, it's you, Jankyn,' he greeted me, almost as if we met every day and I was making a routine visit. I glanced at the balding dome of his head, his now gaunt face, steeling myself not to be caught by those entrancing eyes or listen too carefully to that honeyed voice.

'I would have preferred to have captured you myself,' I commented. 'I would have liked to kill you myself. You owe me that, Oldcastle. You owe me your life. For what you did to Sturmey, Mathilda and all the other poor bastards you enticed to their deaths!'

'It was all for a cause, Jankyn,' Oldcastle replied, almost sadly, like some monk listening to a sinner's confession.

'For what cause?' I tartly observed, wishing to smash his arrogant face against the cold, stone wall. 'For Lollardy? You forget, Oldcastle, I have been to Almery. I have seen the secret chamber beyond your bedroom and heard the stories. You don't believe in any god or any church. Or any of the forces of powers we poor sods do.'

Oldcastle shrugged, almost boyishly now he had been caught out. 'For the Whyte Harte, Jankyn,' he said. 'For Richard's cause.'

'Why?' I begged. 'Why Richard? What does it matter who sits on the throne? They are all the same and Richard was no different. He extorted, bribed, crushed and manipulated as much as Henry of Lancaster or his son have done. What did he promise you? An earldom? A bishopric?'

'Is that why you are here?' Oldcastle replied truculently, 'poor old Jankyn still stumbling around in the dark. You don't understand, do you, Jankyn, what it means to serve a lord and see that lord betrayed? You just don't understand. Our good King Henry does. He is frightened of the Whyte Harte.'

'Is the King alive in Scotland?' I asked.

'No,' Oldcastle mockingly replied. 'The King is in France.'

'You know what I mean. Is Richard II still alive in Scotland?'

'Richard is still alive,' replied Oldcastle carefully, 'though it depends on what you mean by alive, but the truth is more terrible than that. Just think, Master Jankyn, our present Lord King is killing Frenchmen in their hundreds, drenching the fields of Normandy with blood, but it will not clear this mystery away.' Oldcastle leaned forward until the chains creaked in protest. 'Listen, Jankyn,' he whispered, 'and listen carefully. Our King is obsessed with Richard. He knows the secret. He knows what was done. He knows the truth but cannot live with it. I would hazard a guess that he almost wishes Richard were alive in Scotland and that, Master Jankyn, is all I am going to tell you.' He stared at me for a few seconds before throwing his head back and bellowing with raucous laughter. I walked a little closer and watched him lying there, shaking with mirth.

'The same Oldcastle,' I muttered, 'all mouth and words and no answers.'

Oldcastle stopped laughing and stared coldly at me. 'And the same stupid Jankyn, all questions and no answers. For God's sake go!'

I left Newgate feeling bitter at the encounter, sorry that even on the verge of a horrible death, Oldcastle could still outwit me, taunting me with mysteries, puzzles and riddles. I spent the rest of that night getting drunk in a Holborn tavern and fighting with some wench in a dirty, flea-infested corner. By dawn, however, I had sobered up, I suppose I am a vindictive man, I wanted to see Oldcastle die and I was there when they brought him out of

Newgate. They had dressed him in full knightly regalia, a doublet of purple and black with parti-coloured hose of red and gold and costly leather boots clipped with an ornate pair of spurs. He stood before the entrance of the gaol while lords and ladies fought to get a good view, sipping from goblets of hippocras, malvoisie or muscadet. All London seemed to have turned out. The rich burghers in their tawny gowns of fur with black doublets and liveries of red and white silk, hats of velvet and fur, and shiny leather boots. There were goldsmiths in their gowns of scarlet cloth, adorned with silver bars and dotted with golden trefoils. Young gallants of the court in doublets with their fiercely padded shoulders and suave tight waists. These young men stood wanting to be seen as much as to see; hands on hips to display their sleeves, wild concoctions of velvet damask and satins, and belts of jewelled leather, while all the time they chattered to their ladies who were equally adorned with fancy head-dresses in the shape of horses, butterflies or crescents; their eyebrows and forelocks severely plucked, their soft bodies covered in a profusion of crimsons, gold and black velvets, silks, fur, miniver and ermine.

This ring of riotous colour stood in the great forecourt of the prison while Oldcastle was taken to a specially erected scaffold draped in black. Here, on a rough post, hung his shield bearing the Oldcastle arms though they were now upside down and smeared with black pitch. Two serjeants-at-arms brought Oldcastle beneath this, while twelve surpliced priests took up position and began to sing in a low monotone the Vigil of the Dead. As each psalm ended, after the Gloria, the priests paused and a third serjeant stripped one piece of clothing after another from Oldcastle's body, beginning with his hat. Eventually he was naked, apart from a loincloth. The reversed shield was taken down and broken into three pieces and a pitcher of dirty water poured over his head to the open derision of the onlookers. Once it was finished, Oldcastle was strapped to a litter hurdle which was dragged across the ground to a nearby chapel, accompanied by a friar who began to intone the office of the day. Oldcastle bore himself courageously enough, though I could see him twist his face and curse the friar who followed him. The crowd began to break up, satisfied at what they had seen, though for Oldcastle the real agony had only just begun. The hurdle was dragged back down the steps of the church and fastened with ropes to a horse. Then, preceded by bagpipes and kettle drum, the macabre procession began its long route from Newgate up to the execution ground of Smithfield.

The lords and ladies, of course, did not follow but I did, determined to be there to the bitter end. The soldiers kept the crowd and commoners away as the horse pulled its burden through the mud and offal of the city streets. The track was rutted, the hurdle little protection for Oldcastle's bare back. The crowd on either side pelted him with dirt, rocks and mud, even carrion picked up from the streets. By the time we reached Cock Lane at the beginning of Holborn, Oldcastle was smothered in dirt and blood. I followed, watching his face, and for a second remembering my own grim march after the terrible defeat outside St Giles.

Smithfield itself was packed by the time the procession reached there. It was early in the morning but many Londoners had turned out to see the famous heretic and rebel die. Torches flickered in great iron-black sconces driven into the ground in the centre of Smithfield. These torches were arranged in a circle around a great pyre of faggots and straw from which a stark wooden pillar rose. Strapped to this was an oaken barrel. Oldcastle was taken from the hurdle, dragged by the soldiers up the pyre and hoisted into the barrel, his hands and legs being chained to the post. The end was very quick. The priests began to intone the Miserere and the crowd fell silent. A soldier thrust a lighted torch into the faggots. I saw a fine wisp of smoke and a yellow tongue of flame which gradually scaled the pyre until everything was covered in a curtain of flame. I saw Oldcastle move twice from side to side. I thought I heard him call out but then everything was smothered by a haze of flame and smoke. I turned and walked free of the crowd. Oldcastle was dead, my grudge with him settled but I knew that the search for the truth, the hunt of the Whyte Harte had only just begun.

PART TWO
The Hunte of the Whyte Harte

15

In the winter of 1418, the date of Oldcastle's death, Henry V had been king for five years and was still slaughtering the French with furious abandon as he pursued his claims to the French throne. Beaufort summoned me to see him, closeted in his red-and-white-tiled chamber near the great hammer-beam hall of Westminster. He always loved his luxury did Beaufort, with his polished oak desk, sweet-smelling braziers, beeswax candles, his rich carpeted floors and walls adorned with arras and tapestries, a wild profusion of colours. He offered me a cup of hippocras, blood-red wine spiced with ginger, cinnamon, sugar and sunflower seeds and sat and looked searchingly at me as if I was some penitent sinner returning to the fold.

'Master Jankyn,' he began, 'so far, you have served me well. In France and in bringing Oldcastle to justice, but there is still the cause of the Whyte Harte. His Grace, the King, wants the matter fully investigated.'

'My Lord,' I interjected, 'the present king's father had Richard's body brought from Pontefract Castle and buried at Kings Langley. Then our present Lord, King Henry V, had it exhumed and brought in gorgeous splendour to lie in Westminster Abbey. So the King knows the truth. Why does he need to bother with legends and rumours of a king who never dies?'

'You don't understand, Master Jankyn,' Beaufort snapped back. 'There is a problem here. I have told you many times before, our King feels guilty about Richard's

death. King Henry is haunted by nightmares and wants
the truth to be known.'

'Did Oldcastle reveal anything?' I asked.

Beaufort shook his head. 'No,' he replied, 'he told us
nothing, perhaps because he knew nothing.'

I knew that Beaufort was lying. There was something
concealed, hidden, which Oldcastle had refused to tell me.
Beaufort looked at me sideways, cradling the silver-chased
cup in his hands. 'The King has asked me,' he said, 'to set
up a commission. A secret committee of the chancery with
orders to investigate the conspiracy of the Whyte Harte.
To seek its origins, find the truth and extinguish all the
rumours. You, Master Jankyn, because of your tenacity,
your logic, not to mention your cunning and ability to
survive, will be a member of that commission. It meets
tomorrow in the White Tower. I expect you to be there
shortly after Nones. About 11 o'clock.'

I admit I groaned. I had found security in Beaufort's
household. A pardon for past crimes, an easy path. I had
the reputation of being a veteran of Agincourt, a scholarly
man, a trusted yeoman. A stout sort of fellow by common
report. Admired by men, pursued by the ladies. I had a
sweet-faced, soft, white-skinned mistress. The daughter of
a mercer in St Marks Lane. She thought I was the
reincarnation of King Arthur and would do anything for
me, in bed or out of bed. A comfortable life. The life of the
professional liar or rogue and I did not want it threatened.

Nonetheless, the following morning, I left my lodgings
cursing as I splashed my way through the muddy runnels
of London. I pushed aside leather-aproned bakers and
butchers, who clawed at me with their greasy hands
offering 'Fresh bread!' 'Hot ribs of beef!' and made my
way down to the riverside. I hired a barge or wherry and
soon a gap-toothed, wizened-faced bargeman was pulling
at its oars as we made our way through the cold morning
mist. The Tower of London is built on a small rise, a huge
fortress dominated by its white keep which is surrounded

by concentric and crenellated rings of walls and towers. A bleak place, it was still a royal residence, the king's private wardrobe containing arms, saddles and weapons of every kind. It also housed the many records and was a safe place for men with secret plots and stratagems to meet. My boatman dropped me on the quay and I made my way through the enormous yawning gate. The Constable, wearing the royal tabard, greeted me and, after questioning me closely, led me up the cobbled pathways through more gateways into the large open area which surrounds the White Tower. I reflected on the irony of meeting Beaufort's secret committee in such a place. Little did he know (perhaps he did) that I had been instrumental in freeing Sir John Oldcastle from this very prison only a few years before. I could not help laughing at the idea, the Constable looked at me strangely and I am sure he wondered if I still had my wits about me.

We entered the White Tower up a winding, bleak staircase, across St John's chapel and into a small adjoining room which probably served as a vestry. A luxurious place, with its black-and-white tiled floor and its crimson and white tapestries adorned with the heads of griffons, dogs, leopards and lions depicted in a rich dazzle of colour. Outside it was cold and dark but, there, a fireplace heaped high with logs, the flames already greedily spluttering round them, kept back the cold while around the walls there were braziers, cresset torches flickering in their sconces and a row of wrought-iron candelbra. I always remember the impression was one of heat and light and I thought it strange that such a room should be the meeting place for secret devious business. A huge oaken table dominated the room, its polished top gleaming and winking in the light. There were chairs on either side and Beaufort, dressed in a black ermine-trimmed gown, sat at is head. He rose as I entered and gracefully gestured for me to sit. I was late and too embarrassed to look at the others who sat there. A servant brought me a cup of spiced

wine and a sugared wafer. I nibbled and sipped while
Beaufort named my companions. Sitting next to me was a
small, innocuous man whom Beaufort introduced as John
Prophett, clerk of the Chancery. I dismissed him as a
nonentity with his drab brown robes, furtive eyes and buck
teeth. He looked and acted like a frightened rabbit. On the
other side sat Sir Thomas Erpingham, resplendent in a
green silk doublet and piripipe. He was middle-aged with a
red, honest face and a circle of white hair. He looked a
pleasant country squire but I knew his sort. A shrewd
soldier of redoubtable fire, a close confidant and friend of
Henry V. I was not tricked or traduced by his cheery face
and bluff manner for he had the hard, cold eyes of a
venomous snake with the reputation to match. Sitting next
to him was Matthew Glanville, thin, ascetic-looking, with the
sharp eyes and cruel face of a hunting falcon. He looked
what he was, a skilled lawyer who constantly regarded the
world with cynical disbelief. He sat huddled there in his
grey and white cloak trimmed with miniver. He had the
manner of a man who did not care but his eyes and ears
greedily drank in every experience for his shrewd mind as
grist like a mill does wheat. I knew as soon as Beaufort had
finished the introductions that this was no petty committee
but one with a purpose. I already decided that my three
colleagues were Henry's men while I was Beaufort's nominee. I realised that then, I only wish I had remembered it.

Matters began smoothly enough. Beaufort finished the
introductions, ensured we were comfortable, dismissed the
servants and launched into a well prepared sermon. 'You
now know each other. You four, Sir Thomas Erpingham,
knight banneret of the King's household; Matthew Glanville, lawyer in the King's Bench; John Prophett, chief clerk
in the King's Chancery; and Matthew Jankyn, trusted
yeoman from my household, have all been appointed by His
Grace and me to investigate a most serious matter, the
problem of the Whyte Harte and the mystery surrounding
Richard II's death.'

'Surely,' Glanville interposed in dry, sardonic tones, 'the problem is quite simple? King Richard II was deposed in 1399 by Henry of Lancaster and placed in Pontefract Castle where he died in the winter of 1400. His body was later taken to Kings Langley from where our present king exhumed it for burial in Westminster.' Glanville paused to look swiftly at Beaufort. 'That, my Lord,' he continued, 'is half the problem. The other side is a tissue of lies about a Pretender who now lives at Stirling Castle in Scotland claiming to be Richard II. This latter is a fool, a mammet, a tool of the Scottish court who may want to use him against our King.'

'True! True!' Beaufort replied smoothly. 'But the problem is not as simple as that, nor are the solutions. First, our Lord the King considers there is a problem, so,' Beaufort beamed round the table, 'one exists. Secondly, this mammet, as you call him, is and has been the centre and focus for conspiracies and rebellions against the English crown. It is important to find out who he is. Perhaps,' Beaufort paused and pursed his lips, 'even kill him.'

I could see Glanville was not pleased with this reply, his sallow face flushed as he leaned on the table to stare down at Beaufort. 'Is it, my Lord,' he continued, 'that our King's father seized the crown so the King feels guilty at wearing it? After all the King is laying claim to the throne of France and the French have not been slow in pointing out that he has little claim to the crown of England, never mind that of France!'

'You utter treason!' Sir Thomas Erpingham stirred in his chair, he spoke softly but menacingly, his hard eyes and rat-trap mouth betraying his anger. 'Richard of Bordeaux,' he continued, not even bothering to give the deposed king his true titles, 'was a despot and, through God's grace, he was deposed and the crown given to the House of Lancaster. A divine act, Master Glanville, just as the crown of Israel was taken from Saul and given to David.'

'Our King therefore,' Glanville replied coolly, 'is a true
Solomon. I do not deny that nor do I speak treason. I
simply stated the opinion of the French. I never said it was
mine.'

Erpingham simply snorted and slouched back in his
chair as Beaufort gently rapped on the table. 'Gentleman,'
he exclaimed, 'you are to act in concord. This is an
important matter. I do not doubt that you are both correct,
but so is the King. So am I. Richard II's personal emblem
was a Whyte Harte. It was, and still is, the cause and agent
of both treason and rebellion. The King wishes us to
discover the truth behind this matter.'

I had to smile at Beaufort's words. Oh, he was a skilled
liar. A teller of tales. No wonder he had such power over
the King or got a cardinal's hat from the Pope. I bet he lied
himself into Heaven and is now a rival to St Peter himself.
Beaufort was Lucifer in all his glory. He certainly was that
cold morning in the Tower as he went on to insinuate that
our King had been Richard II's favourite and, for want of
a son, his possible heir as well. Only God and Beaufort
know the truth of that. Beaufort concluded by emphasising how important our task was and swore each of us to
secrecy on a leather-bound, gold-clasped copy of the
scriptures. Once this was done, he crossed the room and
unlocked a great oaken, iron-bound chest and drew out
four red-rimmed, leather chancery pouches and gave us
each one.

'In there,' he said, 'you will have a full and complete
memorandum on the deposition of Richard II, his
imprisonment, death and burial. You will also find the
different plots and conspiracies hatched and devised by
followers of the Whyte Harte over the last eighteen years.
The memorandum has been drawn up by our clerk, John
Prophett, who has used his considerable skill in searching
the records of the Chancery, Exchequer and King's
Bench.' We all looked at the smiling, rabbit-faced clerk
who almost squirmed with pleasure at such eloquent

praise. Beaufort then instructed us to study the memorandum and meet him again at a banquet at the Bishop of Ely's Inn near Holborn. We were then dismissed though he caught my arm, as the others filed out, and asked me to stay.

Once the chamber was cleared, the Bishop called a servant and ordered food and wine to be brought up from the Tower kitchens, giving detailed instructions on how the meat was to be cooked and which cheeses and wines were to be served. While we waited, he discussed household matters, scandals of the court, the King's war in France and the possibility of the French suing for peace. The meal was served. Beaufort ate sparingly, plucking at the crisp, white flesh of a capon, or picking at the doucette pastries of flowers of violet – a concoction of almond milk, rice, flour and sugar. Nevertheless, he urged me to eat heartily, refilling my cup with thick red Muscadet wine while he questioned me.

'What do you think of your fellow commissioners?' he began.

I shrugged. 'Prophett,' I replied, 'is an administrator, a trained chancery clerk who would serve the crown if it were worn by an ape from the menagerie. Erpingham is from the royal household and therefore the King's nominee.' I smiled at Beaufort. 'Jankyn is definitely your man which leaves Glanville who, I suspect, is a compromise between you and the King.'

'Shrewd, sly Jankyn,' Beaufort gazed at me speculatively while toasting me with his cup.

I ignored the flattery. 'Glanville is a lawyer?'

'From King's Bench,' Beaufort replied.

'He has a lawyer's brain,' I continued, 'and, despite Erpingham's nasty aside, his question still stands. King Henry V is busy conquering France, England is peaceful, Scotland involved in its own affairs. Richard II and the cause of the Whyte Harte are merely an irritation. So why all this fuss? The secrecy?'

Beaufort swilled the lees of the wine round his cup. 'You have told me,' he answered, 'how your life and your dreams are dominated by a Whyte Harte. Our King is no different.'

'But there is something else?' I asked bluntly. 'Some dark secret?'

Beaufort stared at me. 'Yes,' he replied, 'there is, but I only suspect it. You must find the truth. You may find it in the memorandum drawn up by Prophett. Study it well.'

16

Beaufort diverted the conversation into other matters before dismissing me. I gathered my cloak, dagger and the leather chancery pouch and made to leave. The day was almost drawing to a close. I left the White Tower and walked through the fortified gateways which led from the inner to the outer bailey and down to the wharf beside the Tower. A thick, heavy sea-mist was rolling up the Thames and I did not relish the journey back along the dark, choppy water. Nonetheless, I hired a boat and steeled myself for the trip. The river mist was thick, almost like a blanket, the boatman was quiet and I sat thinking about the commission, Beaufort and the cause of the Whyte Harte. Beneath it all was some terrible mystery and the secrets of the mighty are best kept concealed from little men. I shivered and pulled the cloak firmly about me, conscious that the thick river mist was nothing compared to the frightening task in front of me. I stared, peering through the haze, wanted to keep contact with the river-bank. The heads of hanged river pirates bobbed quietly on the water as the river began to cover their rotting bodies. Bonfires and huge iron-sconce torches glowed along the quayside. A boat carrying dung and refuse collected by the gong farmers from the cesspits and laystalls of the city punted out to dump its refuse in the water. I heard the boatman curse and promptly covered my nostrils against the rank stench.

At last we docked at the quayside, I paid the man his pennies and began my journey back up Thames Street to my lodgings. The day was done and the city was preparing for the night. Scavengers and rakers were collecting cartloads of refuse from the fronts of houses: apprentices were dismantling their stalls and putting up boards, while householders hung lantern horns to gleam dully through the dark mist. The wood and wattle houses loomed above me. I passed through street after street, a whore in bright red taffeta called out to me but I hurried on: the mist was thickening, the streets becoming deserted. A beggar on hands and knees, his stumps encased in wooden sleds, clattered out from the shadows and whined for a penny. I threw him a coin and hurried on. Two boys baited a pedlar standing in a pillory at a crossroads, a Jew in his yellow hood shuffled by and I was almost knocked to the ground by a group of knights, mailed and helmeted, who swept by on their great destriers, their colours and pennants muted in the misty twilight.

I was suddenly afraid, conscious once again of how alone I was and that something, beyond my usual cowardice, threatened me. I was almost relieved to hear the booming of church bells for Vespers and stopped to watch a quarrel between some petty city official and a harridan of a housewife about the latter's use of a cellar in her house as a piggery. I needed human company, and near St Marks Lane almost ran into the comforting warmth of a tavern. Filthy, and smelling of the refuse beneath layers of dirty rushes, it was still busy with custom, potboys and slatterns running from the huge butts at the far end of the large room with jugs and pots brimming with frothy ale. Dried

hunks of meat and vegetables hung from hooks in the
low-slung, smoke-blackened ceiling while the furniture
was rough trestle tables, three-legged stools, barrels and
benches. I went into a corner and ordered a jug of ale and
a potage of meat, leeks and onions garnished with herbs
and spices. I was not really hungry but cold, lonely and
curious. Since leaving my boat at the quayside, I had been
terrified, an uncertain vague feeling of menace. I thought
it was just the task, the intrigue and mystery surrounding
it. Yet, there had been something else, a feeling of physical
menace, of something scuttling behind me in the darkness,
I was being followed, I sat eating my food, watching
through the faint light.

At last he came in, dressed in a brown fustian cloak and
hood which he pushed back as he sat at a table looking
everywhere except at me. Small, squat with yellow, dirty
hair and the bulbous face of a baby mastiff, I sensed he
had been following me. I chewed my food, trying to ignore
the tang of rancid food beneath the savoury spices. I
watched him closely but secretively, quietly rejoicing in the
knowledge that he thought I was an unsuspecting quarry. I
finished my meal and went out. It was dark, the mist
swirled through the narrow streets. A dog howled, baying
like a demon into the darkness. I began to walk down the
centre of St Marks Lane, my ears pricked like a hunting
fox. I heard it, the slither of leather on wet cobbles and I
turned, unsuspectingly like a child turns to greet its
mother. He came closer, I saw the lantern in his left hand
but his right was concealed. 'Good friend,' called I, 'I am
drunk and have lost my way, for pity's sake help me!' I
staggered towards him and placed one hand on his
shoulder while the other pushed my dagger up into his
soft belly. I saw his bulging eyes start as the blood seeped in
drops through his lips and he crumpled slowly to his knees
with a sigh. I bent over his prostrate body and pulled back
the cloak. He was dressed in boots, hose, shirt and leather
jerkin. His right hand still grasped a long curved

evil-looking dagger. I searched his large purse, he had a cluster of silver coins which I pocketed, but nothing else except, strangely, an empty leather chancery purse similar to the one I carried.

I left the body and hurried on. I was responsible for his death but wanted no guilt attached to me because of it. I reached my lodgings, terrified and drenched with sweat, pushing past my landlord, muttering some excuse, fearful of the light and wondering if my clothing bore any bloodstains. I reached my garret, a small though comfortable chamber under the eaves of the house, furnished with a bed, table, chairs and two iron coffers. It was my home. Beaufort had restored my father's estates but that was a grandiose title for a farm in Shropshire which I had sub-let. The Bishop had granted me lodgings in his own palace with licence to draw on his central wardrobe and supplies but I wanted privacy, so I commuted his grant into money which I banked with a respectable goldsmith.

I was glad of such privacy when I returned that evening. I carefully lit a small brazier and cresset sconce bearing oil for six lamps, a dangerous task for I was always fearful of fire. I undressed, inspecting each of my garments for blood, there was some on my boots and around the sheath of my knife. I carefully washed these and poured a cup of wine to warm my belly, trying to forget that my assailant lay frozen in his own blood only a few yards from the house. I knew it was no night-time robbery, but why? Was it a Lollard still angry at my involvement in the destruction of their leader, Sir John Oldcastle? I concluded I would never know and was fearful of future attacks.

The next morning the mist had cleared. I kept to my own room, even though I was aware of the cries and shouts below as the corpse of my attacker was discovered. The ward watch was summoned, officials from the mayor's office, the coroner and many more. Later I heard that a jury was empanelled but reached the unsurprising verdict that the stranger was murdered by person or persons unknown. The death did not bother me. The man had my murder planned and what could I do? I had killed in self-defence. I dismissed him from my mind to join the many spectres which haunt my nightmares and turned to the document Beaufort had given me.

Written on white, soft parchment and tied with a red chancery tag, the document drawn up by Prophett was an impressive compilation of thorough research into the royal records. I still have my copy now. It was the evidence on which I acted and contained conclusions which resolved the mystery of the legends surrounding the Whyte Harte. It goes as follows:-   'A memorandum drawn up by John Prophett, chief clerk in the Chancery, at the behest of his Lordship, Bishop Beaufort of Winchester, and to be distributed to members of the secret commission with a copy to His Grace the King, concerning the mystery and speculation surrounding the imprisonment and death of Richard II.

'Richard Plantaganet, the only surviving son of the Black Prince, succeeded to the throne in 1377 and ruled this kingdom for twenty-two years. He was married to Anne of Bohemia but, after her death in 1396, wed a child bride, Isabella, daughter of the French King. Richard Plantaganet, Richard of Bordeaux, or King Richard II as he is known, began his rule as a young man endowed with all the physical and spiritual attributes one would expect of a king. During his twenty-two-year reign, however, he proved himself a tyrant, forming his own bodyguard of two thousand Cheshire archers called Valets of the Crown, who wore his livery of the Whyte Harte, Richard's mother's personal insignia had been a Whyte Hind.

'The King used these archers and other means to abrogate the laws of Parliament and force his will upon the people. No man was safe, judge, justice, bishop, lord, merchant or commoner. Richard was opposed by his premier earl, Henry of Lancaster, who resisted Richard's attempt to exact heavy fines known as "Les Plesaunces", but the earl was eventually driven into exile, whereupon Richard unjustly seized his estates and decreed that Lancaster was not to return to England on pain of death. Richard continued his high-handed actions even though he was warned by a hermit "to mend his ways or he could shortly hear such news as would make his ears tingle". Richard replied that the hermit should prove he was a prophet by walking on water and, when the man refused, cast him into prison.

'In 1399, Richard decided on the conquest of Ireland. He held a great feast at Windsor, where he took an affectionate farewell of his child queen and, a few days later, at the end of May 1399, crossed from Milford Haven to Waterford in Ireland. Meanwhile, Henry of Lancaster, with the support of the Pope, and aided by others, landed at Ravenspur in Yorkshire. The people greeted him as a saviour. The Duke of York, Richard's regent in England, immediately surrendered and took his troops over to Henry of Lancaster. When King Richard heard the news he swore a terrible oath that the Duke would die a death which would make a noise as far as Turkey and immediately returned to north Wales. Although aided by the earls of Worcester and Salisbury, Richard found himself unable to raise any troops prepared to fight for him and, tearfully bewailing his hard fortune, he wandered restlessly from castle to castle until he decided to hide in Conway. When Lancaster heard of this he sent the Earl of Northumberland and Archbishop Arundel to Conway to speak to Richard. Whereupon the King, realising he had lost the goodwill of all his estates and community, agreed to surrender.

'After this, Richard was taken to Flint, where Lancaster met him on the 19th August. The earl greeted his royal cousin with outward respect and it is untrue that the King travelled on to Chester on a sorry hack worth only a couple of pounds. On the 21st August 1399 the journey began to

London. At Lichfield, a favourite spot of Richard's in happier times, the captive King escaped through a window by night but was retaken, whilst between Lichfield and Cambridge, Earl Henry's army was attacked by bands of Welshmen and Cheshire archers still loyal to the captive King.

'On the 1st September 1399 Henry's armies reached London where the mayor and citizens came out to congratulate Henry and greet him as their saviour. Richard was taken to Westminster before being lodged in the Tower, pending a meeting of a Parliament summoned for 30th September. In the meantime a committee, learned in the law, met to report that there were sufficient grounds for Richard's deposition but recommended that, before he was deposed, Richard should be informed of this matter. On the 21st September this committee met Richard in the Tower and, a week later, a second committee of the Lords visited the imprisoned King to receive his abdication which Richard insisted on reading himself. With a cheerful expression, he renounced the crown for which he declared himself unworthy and expressed a wish that God's will be followed and Henry of Lancaster should be his successor. Indeed, Richard took Lancaster's hand and placed on his finger a royal signet ring.

'The next day the Lords of Parliament assembled around the vacant throne in Westminster Hall to accept Richard's abdication and express their determination that, by right of conquest, Henry of Lancaster should occupy the vacant throne. These same peers consulted as to what means, short of death, must be taken to render Richard powerless, advised that he should be confined to some secure and secret place. Accordingly, Richard was taken, disguised as a forester, to Archbishop Arundel's castle of Leeds in Kent and then to Pickering, Knaresborough, and finally Pontefract in Yorkshire, where he was placed in the custody of Sir Robert Waterton and Sir Thomas Swynnerford.

'But this was only the beginning of trouble: on Twelfth

Night 1400, Richard's birthday, certain lords who were
friends of the deposed King conspired to murder Henry
and openly proclaimed that Richard had escaped from
Pontefract and was residing at Radcot Bridge. King
Henry, saved by a few hours, escaped with his son to the
city of London. Here, the King assembled troops and the
traitors, losing heart, retreated west to Cirencester in
Gloucestershire. Henry IV followed in hot pursuit vowing
that if Richard was still alive and they should meet, one of
them would surely die. At Cirencester the rebel army, led
by the Earls of Kent and Salisbury, attempted to make a
stand but made the mistake of dividing themselves from
their forces. They lodged at the chief inn of the city while
the bulk of their troops were quartered in the surrounding
countryside. At dawn, the day after they arrived, the town
was surrounded by an armed mob and the two earls were
forced to surrender. One of the Earl of Kent's chaplains
tried to set fire to the town in order to divert the citizens to
the protection of their homes. It failed, and the loyal
citizens, so incensed by such actions, bustled the Earls of
Kent and Salisbury into the market place where they were
beheaded. Other leading rebels met similar just deserts:
the Lord de Spencer was lynched at Bristol, the Earl of
Huntingdon torn to death by revengeful men of Essex; at
Oxford twenty-six knights and squires were executed in
the city ditch, their bodies quartered after the manner of
beasts and, partly in sacks and partly slung on poles
between men's shoulders, these were carried to London
where they were salted and exposed to public view. Others,
including Richard Maudelyn, one of the deposed King's
favourite chaplains, who was, in almost every respect, a
double of his master, met with a grisly death by hanging at
Tyburn. The traitors were brought to nothing by God's
grace but their malice was evident for all to see for they
even visited King Richard's young widow at Sonning in the
hope of enlisting her support in the rebellion. By the 8th
January 1400, the conspiracy and rebellion were crushed.

On the 31st January, King Charles VI of France issued a proclamation that Richard was dead and the great French fleet assembled in the channels ports to invade England was disbanded, while two days previously, King Henry IV and the French signed a truce bringing the hostilities to an end.

'On the 14th February 1400 Richard of England, who had not escaped from Pontefract Castle, but had hoped that the actions of his traitor friends would be successful, died from enforced starvation. On the 17th February money was issued by the Exchequer to carry Richard's body from Pontefract by easy stages to London. The face of the corpse was exposed to the people so that all men might know that Richard was dead, not by violent means or through weapons or poison but that he had pined away. At every chief town on the way south, a halt was made to display the corpse until the procession finally reached Cheapside where the body lay exposed outside St Paul's Cathedral, being viewed by vast multitudes of the city. I, John Prophett, the writer of this memorandum, saw the body in the lead casket. The head lay on a black cushion, the face exposed from the lower part of the forehead, with the rest of the body being concealed. The corpse was buried in the Dominican Priory of Kings Langley in Hertfordshire and only transferred to Westminster Abbey in January 1414 with the gracious permission of the Lord King.

'In 1400, the Scots reneging on their promise and the will of God, waged a terrible war against our King in the northern counties but, due to God's intervention, the Scots were defeated at Homildon Hill where Prince Murdoch, the Earl of Douglas, Scottish knights and thirty French knights sent there by King Charles VI were captured.

'In May 1402, a proclamation was issued in the northern counties condemning those who claimed that Richard of Bordeaux was still alive. In the June of that same year, another proclamation was issued condemning rumours and stories that King Richard had not died at Pontefract but had escaped to Scotland and was still alive. Much mischief was caused by such legends and stories and many Franciscan convents in particular were rife with rumours that Richard was still alive. So serious did these rumours become in all the shires, particularly Norfolk and Kent, that the royal justices had to question many Franciscans who were openly declaring themselves exceedingly glad that King Richard was still alive. Eventually, two friars, Roger and Richard Frisby of the Leicester convent, who had cherished and spread these rumours, were brought before the King himself at Westminster to answer the charges levelled against them. Information was given to the court how the friars had assembled five hundred men who would march to find and join the forces of Richard II. King Henry IV immediately issued a proclamation prohibiting all friars, on pain of life imprisonment, to utter any word either about the dead King Richard or himself. He also questioned Roger Frisby and I give this conversation verbatim from the records of the court:

The King: "Did you say that King Richard is alive?"

Frisby: "I do say that if he is still alive, he is the true king of England."

The King: "Richard abdicated."

Frisby: "He did so but under compulsion and that is not valid."

The King: "He was deposed."

Frisby: "You usurped the crown."

The King: "I did not usurp the crown but was duly elected."

Frisby: "An election is null and void while the legitimate possessor is alive and, if he is dead, you killed him, and if you are the cause of his death, you forfeit all title and any right which you have to the kingdom. It was not, as our enemies say, our intention to kill you or your sons but to restore you to the dukedom of Lancaster which is what you ought to hold. I repeat, you forfeit all titles and rights."

The King: "By this head of mine, you shall lose all your rights."

'The said Frisby was later adjudged a traitor and sentenced to death but still the conspiracies continued:- 'Item

– in 1403 the Duke of Northumberland and his son, Henry Percy, popularly known as Hotspur, rose in rebellion against the King, issuing proclamations that Richard was still alive and in Chester Castle for all to come and see him. The said rebels were, by divine grace, defeated at Shrewsbury by loyal forces in the summer of that year.

'Item – in the winter of 1403/1404, Princess Isabella, widow of Richard of England, tried to land in England but was prevented by storms and ill winds. In 1404 William Searle, Richard II's secretary, who had fled to Scotland, was captured and brought south to London to meet a deserved traitor's death. A proclamation was also issued against Thomas Ward of Trumpington, near Cambridge, a former student of the university there, who bore a striking resemblance to the late king and actually claimed to be Richard II, giving out that he escaped from Pontefract Castle and fled to Scotland.

'Item – in 1405 Sir Robert Waterton, gaoler of the dead King, was captured by Northumberland, though later released.

'Item – in the June of that year, the Earl of Northumberland, still a rebel against the King, sent a message to the Duke of Orleans in France saying that "if King Richard is still alive, then he should be restored to the throne."

'Item – in 1414 Sir John Oldcastle and other Lollards, proclaiming that Richard was still alive, attempted to seize our King but their plot was brought to nothing.

'Item – in 1415 Sir Richard Grey and the Earl of Cambridge also plotted against King Henry's V's life, claiming that both King Henry and his father had usurped the throne, that the House of Lancaster should be extinguished and Richard was alive in Scotland and should be restored to his rightful status.

'This memorandum shows the truth about Richard's death and the vexatious rumours which have disturbed, and still persist in disturbing, the King's peace with legends

about the cause of the Whyte Harte and King Richard's
supposed survival.

'Signed and sealed by John Prophett. Chief Clerk to the
Chancery.'

Some of these items and pieces of information I knew
already but I could scarcely believe what Prophett had
written. Richard might well have died at Pontefract, been
buried at Kings Langley and reinterred at Westminster,
but why was it that so many people over such a long period
of time, not just Oldcastle and other crack-brained traitors,
but priests, lords, powerful nobles and barons had been
prepared to rise in rebellion? They really believed Richard
had escaped and was alive and well in Scotland. Other
questions and problems surfaced like bubbles of air in a
pool. I could list and analyse them, but provide no
solutions. These could only be given by men like Beaufort,
even King Henry V himself. I studied Prophett's
document most carefully, going over it time and again like
an actor learning his lines or a student preparing to
discourse upon his thesis. I had always believed that the
cause of the Whyte Harte was something shadowy,
insubstantial, a ghost which haunted my mind and that of
others. The Prophett memorandum clearly depicted a
matter of grave cause. Richard, his memory and the
emblem of the Whyte Harte had consistently caused
plotting, treason, rebellion and death over the last twenty
years. It was not just that the deposed king might still be
alive but almost a spiritual quest, something which drew
men on just as surely as the Holy Grail fascinated Arthur
and his knights. Yet this was no spiritual search, it was
death. The Whyte Harte might trip across green fields but,
as in my dreams and nightmares, it drew men of every
degree and profession into the dark blood-wet woods of
death. For the Whyte Harte, men have died in battle, been
murdered, strung up on gibbets, hacked with axes or
consumed in flames at Smithfield. Only the truth would
clear such phantasms of the night.

17

On the day appointed I made my way up Newgate towards the Bishop of Ely's Inn in Holborn. I gathered from members of Beaufort's retinue that the banquet was in honour of the Portuguese envoys who had come to London to reinforce their treaty with England and ask for Henry's help against the northern kingdoms of Aragon and Castile. The occasion was used to conceal a meeting of the secret commission and, at the same time, reward its members with the good things of life. Beaufort had commandeered this private inn for his own use and huge beacons and braziers had been placed along Leverhulme Lane to light the pathway to the residence.

I arrived early and entered the great hall which had been cleaned and prepared for the feast; hundreds of wax candles glittered and flickered in their iron holders whilst torches, carefully placed along the walls, glowed and brought alive the splendid scene. A huge table at the far end on the dais with trestles down each side of the hall; the walls were covered with thick costly drapes of black, purple and white; and fresh crushed violets had been scattered on the floor to give a perfumed smell. The four bay windows had been shuttered and covered with tapestries; one bore an amazing conglomeration of peacocks, vines, wheels and platters, another festooned with red and white roses and the heads of graceful greyhounds. The tables had been covered with white lawn cloths bearing the golden leopards of England or the silver lion of Portugal. There was a richness of golden vessels, cups and plates, all chased with silver rims and festooned with sparkling rubies and diamonds.

The banquet began late in the evening, Beaufort, dressed in scarlet robes trimmed with the purest white fur, welcoming his dark swarthy guests, the perfect diplomat, ushering them to seats while I and others had to take care of ourselves. I looked around and noticed courtiers, some wearing the colours of the King's livery, others in paltocks of silk with hose of two colours, their girdles bound with silver cords, their shoes curled more than ten fingers high and fastened to the knee with chains of gold. No wives had been invited but high-class courtesans and ladies of the town dressed in kirtles of Indian Sendal lace, small, pretty and trim or decked in mantles of green, blue and gold velvet, embroidered in gold and fringed with costly grey fur. Their faces were painted white, eyes ringed in black kohl, long hair hanging like sun-shot silk, garlanded with gay coronas of gems and other costly stones. Beautiful women, adept in court fashion, they each took their place alongside the invited guests. Beaufort's cooks proved that the Bishop laid one of the most sumptuous tables in Europe. Wine from Bordeaux, the Rhineland and Italy flowed like water. The food was served on huge silver platters, venison cut into strips and put into a sauce of wheat boiled in milk to which yolks of eggs, sugar and salt were added. There were soups of beef and fish mixed with ground almonds and sweet wine: chopped roast pork, fried onions, followed by other meats doused with strong wine, blended with powdered cinnamon and fortified with soft pine cones, white sugar and cloves. Course after course was served whilst a group of minstrels kept up quiet soothing tunes on trumpet, tabar, rebec and small pipes. I did not eat much, determined to keep my mind clear, and I was more than pleased when the assembly broke up and one of the Bishop's household told me to go into a small chamber off the great hall.

Other members of the secret commission were already there, Erpingham slightly drunk, Glanville flushed and bright-eyed, still carrying a goblet of wine. The clerk,

Prophett, eager and inquisitive, ready to begin upon the business of the night. Beaufort, sipping iced sherbet, seemed cool and collected. Torches and candles were lit, two or three of the small braziers had been wheeled into the room to give it warmth. The door was closed and Beaufort rapped on the table to call us to order.

'We have,' he began, 'had an opportunity to study the excellent memorandum of our clerk, Master Prophett, and all of us must have reflected on what we have read and learnt. I have assembled you on this festive occasion to rejoice and relax in the pleasanter forms of politics and diplomacy and, at the same time, give me your considered thoughts on what you have read.'

In the ensuing silence no one spoke until Glanville cleared his throat and came abruptly to the point. 'My Lord, it is apparent that there is enough evidence to cast doubts on the accepted story of Richard II's deposition and death. It would seem that many powerful men really believed Richard II escaped from Pontefract to become the focal point of conspiracy and rebellion over the last nineteen years.' He coughed and cleared his throat. 'Of course, men will say that the King's father, Henry IV, displayed the corpse in public and had it buried with full public ceremony but the rumours continue.'

'I agree,' Prophett squeaked. 'Many kings who died violent deaths are alleged to have survived, Harold the Saxon, King John who signed the Magna Carta, Edward II, great-grandfather of Richard II, and more instances can be found abroad from other times and other places.' Prophett paused and looked round as if to give importance to his words. 'Nevertheless,' he continued, 'such rumours always die within a short while of the King's death. In this case they have persisted for almost twenty years. There are a number of questions we must address. First, is Richard II alive in Scotland? If he is, why did he flee there and not to Wales with Glendower's armies or to France? The Welsh were always supporters of Richard whilst the French regarded him as an ally. Secondly, if he did die at Pontefract, why have so many English lords believed he is alive? Men such as Oldcastle, Sir Thomas Grey and the Earl of Cambridge. More importantly, his own wife, Isabella of France, refused to marry again on the grounds that her husband was still alive.'

'Look,' I interrupted. 'The accepted story is that Richard died at Pontefract and, my Lord,' I turned to Beaufort, 'is there any evidence to suggest that Richard escaped?'

Beaufort shook his head. 'None,' he replied. 'Richard's gaolers, Sir Thomas Swynnerford and Sir Robert Waterton, were Henry IV's men. They have both maintained that Richard was in their custody all the time.'

'Well,' I concluded, 'our first task is to seek out who this person in Scotland really is. He claims to be Richard II. We must, somehow, determine if his claims are true.' There was a silence as everyone looked at me and Beaufort smiled.

'Then, Jankyn,' he said sweetly, 'you must be off to Scotland!'

'My Lord,' I replied glibly, 'that is easier said than done! Scotland under its Regent, the Duke of Albany, is not friendly with England. There are border disputes. How on earth can I travel through half-hostile country to Stirling, where this Pretender resides?'

'If you go, Jankyn,' Erpingham commented, 'you should, like any good English spy, go in disguise.'

'Go as what?' I jibed.

'Oh, quite simple. Go as a leper. Nobody would dare approach you,' Erpingham slyly retorted.

'True! True!' Beaufort agreed. 'The Prior at Tynemouth near the Scottish border is a friend of mine. You can carry letters to him and he will arrange what we need.'

My heart sank and I glared around at their smug, self-satisfied faces, I knew, despite any protests, Beaufort would have me in Scotland.

I left London two days later at the beginning of
February 1419 around the feast of Candlemas. I had a
horse, a good sturdy dappled grey., I remember it well for
it later saved my life. My baggage was tied on a
wicked-looking sumpter pony. Both beasts were from
Beaufort's stable, together with high-cantled saddle,
sweat-cloth, breast-straps and other harness. I intended to
be as comfortable as possible. The weather was freezing
and I prayed there would be no snow. I was well armed for
the weather was not the only problem I would encounter.
Death stalks the lonely highways and roads of England, in
the shape of the outlaw, the sturdy beggar and above all,
the assassin. I had not forgotten that attack in London and
I knew it could happen again.

I left the city and made my way out on to the old Roman
road which runs north. I decided to stay with convoys of
other travellers though they were scarce, long wooden
carts from farms and manors; the two-wheeled wicker
work carts of the more prosperous peasant pulled by two
or three gaunt horses; the solitary messenger or sturdy
pilgrims bent on reaching their hearts' desire. There was
the occasional mounted convoy bringing royal purveyance
south to the Channel ports but, in the main, the roads were
deserted. I rode along under armour-grey skies, the fields
and woods on either side gaunt, brown and covered, even
at mid-day, by a white hoar frost. The villages, hamlets and
manor houses slept in frozen solitude, only long black
plumes of smoke showed there was life. The peasants had
to survive the winter. Some hardy souls tried to break the
frozen earth in earnest expectation of spring and I saw
sights which would have offended Christ, a man and a
woman pulling a plough as if they were animals and, in the
corner of the field, on a leather sheet, a small infant,
bundled against the cold, mewed like a kitten against the
intensity of winter. Christ in His goodness knows why such
people live like that. I am now a wealthy baron but I look
after my peasants, no one starves. No pillories, no gallows,

but I am still a hard man, I seduce their daughters. Yet I saw great cruelty that winter which must only have stirred the anger of God and His sweet Mother. Families froze in ditches, corpses hanging like icicles from white-frosted gallows. The peasant is condemned, so say the scriptures –

'Of the earth you shall, with sweat and swynk
Gain all you shall to eat and drink.'

But with such cruelty?

I helped where I could but I cursed to hide my compassion. I bought their stale green cheeses, paid too highly for a dish of curds and oatcakes but, Christ, I saw such poverty. Sometimes the peasants turn and rise in anger as they did some thirty years before when Wat Tyler and his merry band took and burnt London. On one occasion, outside Lincoln, I was stopped by a group of men in brown woollen tunics girt with leather girdles studded with metal-rimmed strap-holes. They were disguised by large, brown felt hats and rags across their faces. They carried rusty swords and were mounted on plough horses with hogged manes and hooves spiked for sowing. They were no real threat, their horses were only fit to sit on. I turned my own and easily outdistanced them, escaping across a field scattering the peasants who were spreading lime and marl to make the soil fertile.

Sixteen days after leaving London, I entered Tynemouth. I was wearied from the journey, tired of the taverns, the hostels, the guest-houses and, more commonly, the dirt-packed floor of some hovel with a bush above the door to serve as an ale-house. I also knew I had entered the battle-land, the wild empty march or border which separates Scotland from England. Time and again, each nation launches raids across into the other's territories and I saw the result, devastated fields, bodies rotting in ditches, burnt out houses and ravaged villages. The usual plunder were women or cattle. I cannot speak for the women but the cattle must have become dizzy crossing and re-crossing that ill-fated border.

Tynemouth with its castle and gaunt priory situated near the seashore was a haven of peace behind its grey-granite, crenellated walls. I made my way up its narrow streets, past old cottages where thatched roofs swept down so close to the street, their little windows, half hidden by heavy eaves, seemed to peer up like the eyes of a frightened animal. The streets were as crowded and stinking as London though more drab. I crossed the cobbled market-place with its heavy, planked stalls. Huge wooden forks were dug into the ground festooned with goods: dried meats, leaden vessels, iron bins, racks for fodder, basins, pepper-horns, seed-baskets, oil-flasks, drapes of clothing. All raised high to catch the eye while the people talked in a quick, clipped dialect I could not hope to understand.

I thought of stopping at a tavern but reconsidered and pushed on through a dark, narrow wynd which led up to the priory. It was deserted, quiet with menace and I was almost caught unawares as the attackers came swirling out of the darkness. Hooded and secretive they seemed to rise out of the murky shadows, prancing like dancers towards me, the weak sunlight glinting on their swords. Oh, thank God, for my cowardice! Many a man, some heroic idiot fed on the legends of Roncesvalles, would have stayed to fight and perish. Not me! I was through them, moving and screaming like the wind. I kicked my horse and broke into a gallop, the evil-eyed sumpter pony needed no urging, it clattered behind me, striking out with its iron-shod hooves doing more damage than I could ever hope to achieve. Due to my cowardice and his evil nature, we escaped with no pursuit, the cries and shouts behind me ample testimony to the wicked blows of my baggage animal.

I arrived breathless and shaking at the priory gate and tugged on the bell like a soul clamouring to get into heaven. An astonished lay brother ushered me in and led me across a dirty courtyard, gabbling in an accent I would not have understood if I had stood there till Christ's second coming. I was led up a beaten stone staircase and into a large white-washed chamber where Prior Lovell greeted me. His broad, humorous face and mop of red hair a soothing sight after the murderous assault in the alleyway. He directed me to a heavy, oaken chair and brought me a cup of wine. I did not mention the assault. What was the use? He could not help and would just dismiss it as a 'sign of our lawless times'. The attack would be assumed to be the work of ruffians but I knew better, it was planned, these assassins had been waiting for me to arrive.

Prior Lovell eagerly read Beaufort's letter which I had hidden in the stitching of my belt. He glanced through it again and looked curiously at me.

'So, Master Jankyn,' the voice was soft with a pleasant Yorkshire burr. 'I am to put you across the border on the King's secret business.' He laughed. 'It will not be the first time and certainly not the last, though the manner of your crossing will be unique.'

I shrugged and muttered something about Beaufort's schemes but the prior smiled and showed me to a small, windowless cell, telling me to rest. I did, sleeping on the truckle bed, my mind still turning and twisting over the attack and the persons behind it.

18

I stayed at Tynemouth three days, and on the fourth the prior announced there would be a ceremony in church which I would have to attend. I did, concealed behind the heavy, ornate chancel screen while the prior, dressed in a white alb and purple-gold cope, conducted a macabre

service down near the church porch. He was blessing
lepers, dismissing them from society to wander the land till
their dreadful disease consumed them. There were four,
three men and a woman. The latter was far gone, even
from where I stood I could see her white, skeletal face, the
glaring eyes and the hole where her nose had been, it
looked as if one great hideous mouth dominated her face.

I must admit I admired that prior. He stood alone
sprinkling the unfortunates with holy water while saying
'Be thou dead to the world but alive again unto God.' Then
he intoned the terrible words. 'I forbid you to enter
churches, or go into markets, a mill, or bakehouse or into
any assembly of people. I forbid you ever to wash your
hands or any of your belongings in spring or stream water
of any kind. If you are thirsty you must drink water from
your cup or from some other vessel. I also forbid you ever
to go without your leper's dress or travel abroad unshod. I
forbid you, wherever you may be, to touch anything you
wish to buy other than with a rod or staff to indicate what
you want. I forbid you to enter taverns, or to answer any
questions till you have left the road.' So it went on as these
poor persons were cut adrift on God's earth to God's
mercy. That same evening the prior, a skilled herbalist,
rubbed white chalk into my face and hair, daubing my face
and hands with red ink-paste so I too became a leper. I had
heard his instructions, how lepers move, and must be
prepared to act likewise. Also, the commissioning
ceremony would explain my presence on the road. Just
another unfortunate, no real menace to Scot or
Englishman. Who cares about the nationality of a leper?
He has none for he is accursed by all.

I left my belongings and horses at the priory and the
next morning was led out of the town on to a track running
north. I had a collection of clothes, a brown cloak, boots, a
black, broad-brimmed hat and a suitable disguise over the
hose, shirt, jerkin and dagger beneath. My fardel or
bundle contained sheets, a cup, a knife and plate and, of

course, I had a staff and a set of wooden clappers to warn all God's creatures that a loathsome disease was about.

Nevetheless, I was warm, protected and safe. None would approach me. The only danger was someone whose nostrils I might offend deciding to kill me without compunction as a farmer destroys a pest. Not that I met anyone, the land of rolling moors, gorse and clumps of dark trees were deserted. It was winter, no one travelled, not even soldiers for this was not campaigning weather. Sometimes, I thought I was in a dream, turning sharply around as if people were following me. There was nothing except the wild expanse of moor and the lonely whining wind. Perhaps the dead walked with me: my father, Sturmey, the hundreds who died for Richard and the cause of the Whyte Harte. Once, I am sure I saw it, against the darkness of the forest, a slender, snow-white hart dancing daintily across my sight, a golden crown round its elegantly curved neck but, when I looked again, it was gone. I tried to forget my fears, realising that I was going to face the possible cause of all the legends, Richard, or the man pretending to be he. I wanted this for the truth would bring me riches and exorcise the ghosts from my own soul.

I saw the decaying walls built by the magicians of Rome: huge forts and castles which now crumbled under the wind and rain. One night I sheltered in one of the ruins, ghosts all around me, I huddled over a meagre fire and heard a vixen bark under the ice-bright stars. I was lonely and tired, and I would have given ten years of my life to listen and speak to another being but there was no one. I continued my journey, avoiding villages or hamlets. The rare traveller, mounted or on foot, heard the sound of my clapper and immediately avoided me, sometimes silent, sometimes shouting, cursing or throwing stones or refuse at me.

I splashed across the Tweed, the freezing water of the ford swirling around my leather boots and I was in Scotland, a vast expanse of swamp, bog, forest and marsh.

The roads were beaten tracks which crossed and turned through low-lying hills past squalid villages, groups of hovels with turf roofs and only ox-hide curtains for doors. The womenfolk and children, however, were sturdy enough and it was pleasing to see how Scottish women were absolute mistresses of their homes, even of their husbands, in all things concerning the adminstration of their property. I say this for them, they were kind, many did shun me but not a few brought oatcakes and watered ale for me as I tried to go round their village. Is it not strange how they who have so little give so much? I felt guilty, crouching beneath some hedgerow eating the scraps these women gave me while their menfolk furrowed with wooden plough and heavy oxen the barren hillside fields which swept down to waterlogged valleys. Yes, I felt guilty at my deception but dared not reveal my true identity.

It was a lonely, cold, bleak journey. At night I felt I was in one of the frozen circles of Dante's hell: dark, yawning blackness on every side, no moon nor stars, I began to feel they had fallen from heaven. Nothing save the moaning, biting wind and the long sinister howl of a wolf. Except on one occasion when I was sheltering in the ruins of a cottage, a weak fire spluttering in the corner over which I was toasting some dry pieces of meat. I heard a sound, a footfall and whirled to meet the menace, dagger drawn, mouth snarling. I must have looked like an enraged wolf.

'Who are you?' I rasped. 'Come out of the shadow, but be warned, I am a leper!'

'Then we are well met,' came the cool reply. The figure pulled back its hood and I stared into a gaunt face with brilliant eyes, framed by straggling grey locks.

'Who are you?' I repeated.

The man undid his cloak and on the quilted jacket below was the yellow star of the house of David. 'You do not mind?' he asked.

'I do not mind,' I muttered and gestured him to join me.

I offered him some meat, he refused but produced a wineskin from the saddle pouches he carried and filled my cup to brimming. God knows, the wine was good, but the company was even better. He was a great talker. A strange man with sunburnt skin and dark glittering eyes. He had travelled to Cathay, along the roads of the Ottoman Turk, and talked eloquently of cities and peoples I had not heard of. Just before daybreak as we prepared to leave, he described Genghis Khan, the great Mogul warrior whom he claimed he had met, and his powerful army, the Golden Horde, whose dark purple banners had even threatened the West.

'Come!' I jibed. 'You could not have. The great Genghis is dead and has been for centuries!'

He continued to pack his bags and swung them over his shoulder. 'I saw him,' he replied firmly. 'My name is Joseph but once I was called Cartaphilus.' Then he trudged off into the swirling mist as I tried to remember where I had heard such names, but I could not. Only later in the day did it come to me and I gasped with surprise. Cartaphilus or Joseph were names given to the Wandering Jew of popular legend. He had not been born a Jew but a Roman who became converted and was present, so the story goes, at Christ's trial before Herod. As Jesus was led out, Cartaphilus struck Him in the back and urged, 'Go, hurry on!' Whereupon Christ turned and quietly replied, 'I will not hurry, nor will you, Cartaphilus, you shall stay on earth until I return to judge the earth with fire!' So Cartaphilus was condemned to live for ever, wandering the earth, his age fixed at the time he struck the Christ.

I often thought he was a dream, a phantasm or demon of my mind brought about by fear and loneliness, for my pilgrimage was beginning to affect me. Sometimes, I saw my father, or Mathilda, or even Oldcastle standing on a hill or river-bank beckoning me to come. Of course, the Whyte Harte was always there, slender and beautiful, tripping like a palfrey in front of me. I thought Cartaphilus was

such a vision until, strangely, years later while fleeing a
hostile mob through the heat and dirt of Rome, I saw him
again, staring wickedly at me. Strange that I should first
meet him on a lonely Scottish moor whilst hunting the
Whyte Harte.

19

It took me four days to reach Stirling. I saw its tall black
tower against the sky, the burgh, or town scattered round
it. I sounded the wooden clappers as I crossed the city
ditch and began to make my way up the narrow winding
paths just as the sturdy burgh piper began his jaunty tune
in the market streets, signalling the beginning of the day. I
passed the townspeople talking volubly in their strange
clipped accent. Up past the kirk, the Tolbooth, gaol and
courthouse to the large clear space dominated by the
market cross. Here, criminals sat in the stocks, placards
round their necks, a beggar was nailed by his ears to a
wooden post while the dismembered limbs of greater
offenders were hoist up on stakes and poles.

Stirling was a royal burgh and castle, overlooking the
Forth and the gateway to the Highlands. If Richard, or the
pretender, was here then he was well guarded for the town
was full of soldiers, fierce-looking men; from the mid-leg
to the foot they went uncovered but they were armed with
bows and arrows, a broadsword and a small halberd. I
noticed they always carried in their belt a stout dagger,
single-edged but razor-sharp, and some wore coats of mail
made of thick heavy rings. I kept a wary eye on these as I
wandered through the town, past the middens populated
with vermin, wandering dogs and swine. Beneath the

castle walls, near the shambles and the bloody work of the fleshers' knives was a laundry well and I kept this under sharp observation. One night, the second after my arrival in Stirling, I drew water from it and with soap and ointment, washed the clay from my face and hair and changed my clothes, dressed simply in brown jerkin, leggings and boots. The next morning I was free of my disguise and desirous of getting unobserved into the castle. I thought it would be difficult but it was not. The Scots expected no attack, the castle was open, no check being made on who entered or left. I strolled up the rock and across the broad, cracked wooden drawbridge. The deep gateway was guarded by town militia clad only in a linen garment sewed together in patchwork, well daubed with wax or pitch and an overtunic of dressed deerskin. I wandered in, my pack slung across my shoulder like the pedlar I professed to be, who had travelled north to shelter from the winter. I felt elated, excited but frightened. Would I meet Richard? Or an impostor? I did not care. The cause of the Whyte Harte had drawn its strength from a man, claiming to be Richard II, who had shut himself up in Stirling Castle. Now I was to see him.

Inside the castle, I crossed the bailey, a hollow, square courtyard formed by the battlemented and gated walls. It was full of horses, doves, fowl and dirty bales of hay and straw. There was confusion and bustle. No one really noticed a pedlar and I slipped into the great hall, brushing aside the wolfhounds who lounged near the door. It was a long raftered room, clouded with smoke from its turf fires though I could see the stone walls were warmed by coloured drapes. Flemish linen was spread across the board of the long table on the dais at the end of the room which was dominated by a great silver-chased salt-cellar. It was mid-morning and people sat at the table eating, men and women, with heads covered as is the Scottish custom, for only servants are hatless. The air was thick with dust and sour with the stench of discarded food. Spluttering sconce torches flickered in reflection on pewter and the occasional dish of gold probably looted from some English Church. The wooden clogs or slats of the servants grated on the floor and waiting hounds yawned, scratched and kept a wary eye on such scraps of food as were thrown at them.

Small boys brought metal finger-basins to the guests at the high table, I sat on one of the benches running along the wall, drew a penny from my purse and beckoned one of these boys over. He looked curiously at me because of my accent but listened politely to my questions. 'Oh, yes,' he replied in a piping voice, 'the people on the dais are the governor, his lady, family and the King of England.'

'Oh,' I said, my heart beating with excitement. 'Which is he, but do not point. I am curious yet do not wish to give offence for I have heard of this Prince.'

The little fool ignored my words and threw out his hand. 'He is there, the King of England is to the right of my Lord!' His clear voice carried like a bell, silencing the hum of conversation at the end of the hall. A thick-set, red-haired man dressed in a blue, quilted jacket, rose hurriedly to his feet, glared down the hall and beckoned me to approach. I was terrified. If I obeyed his command I would be discovered, if I attempted to escape I would not leave the castle alive. I put a brave face on, hiding the agitation in my belly which threatened to turn my bowels to water. I picked up my pack, strode up the hall and went on one knee before the table. I bowed my head and looked up into the thin white face the young page had pointed out. I was so surprised I could hardly talk, the blond hair, the beard, and the deep-set blue eyes and prim lips. I had seen a painting in Westminster Abbey and knew I must be looking at the true likeness of Richard of England. Of course, he was older, the skin sagged round his neck, the face, especially the eyes, were lined with age and worry but he was a regal figure. Dressed in a blood-red doublet, cambric shirt peeping out underneath, a gold necklace slung round his neck, his long white fingers studded with precious gems.

'Sire,' I began desperately trying to collect my thoughts. 'I come with messages from your loyal subjects in England.' I lied in my terror. 'They could not be trusted in writing. In case I was taken! They are verbal messages!' I explained as a white hand was raised, the fingers snapping.

'What if you were taken?' The voice was hard and brutal.

'I would not be here and you, Sire, would not receive the messages.'

'In Scotland?' the thick-set man almost bellowed and I surmised he must be the Governor. I looked into his piggy eyes and brazenly lied. It is always the best way.

'In Scotland,' I replied, 'there are those sent and paid by Henry of Lancaster.'

'And the messages?'

'Only for his Majesty,' I bowed.

'His Majesty,' the Governor retorted, 'will only meet you in my presence.'

I felt the figure in red stiffen with annoyance but the moment passed.

'Your name?' the Governor asked.

'Matthew Jankyn,' I replied, 'of Shropshire. My father died for King Richard as did my friends and leader, Sir John Oldcastle. I took part in the rising of 1413 and was a close friend of Swinderby, the Norwich tailor, who visited his Grace here some years ago.'

I must admit I was proud of my speech, a clever farrago of truth and lies. I saw the King (or so he claimed) smile, the Governor pursed his lips and there was a sudden lessening of tension. The Governor ordered a chair to be brought and I was invited to dine, eating from the dishes of carp, venison, sturgeon and bream which littered the table while my cup was constantly filled with a cool white Rhenish wine. Of course, they questioned me. How had I travelled? How long had it taken? Was I in any danger? I sipped the wine carefully and dealt with their questions,

constantly turning the conversation to give as much
information as I could of my Lollard past and links with
the cause of the Whyte Harte.

All the time I watched that figure in scarlet as he daintily
plucked at his food, lapsing into certain French phrases
and wiping his lips with a small patch of lace-trimmed silk
which he would push back under the cuff of his sleeve.
According to what I knew, he looked like Richard, had his
size and colouring, talked French and displayed the
famous handkerchief which the King is supposed to have
introduced from France. But was he Richard? Was he the
Whyte Harte, whose emblem was stitched on the right of
his doublet? He had a regal manner and I began to
question my own secret mission. Of course, I kept such
doubts to myself as the governor (I think his name was Sir
Archibald Douglas or something of that ilk) introduced me
to his wife, his two daughters, whose faces were as empty
and vacuous as the governor's. One girl did catch my eye,
her glossy, black hair gathered up under her veil, a serene,
olive face with dark, wide eyes and full red mouth. She
smiled sideways at me and eventually leaned across to
introduce herself as Amasia Deyncourt, the daughter of a
French knight who had settled in Scotland, marrying into a
local Scottish family and inheriting estates just south of
Stirling. She told me this with a candid frankness and I had
to remember that in Scotland, women did not accept a
subservient place and Amasia took full advantage of this
custom. She was vivacious, her eyes bright and alert. She
chattered merrily, asking questions about my life,
innocent, innocuous ones, or apparently so, but I soon
realised she was the most dangerous person at that table as
her questions were simple, her manner frank and
welcoming. I knew I could easily trap myself with answers
which contradicted each other.

I was more than relieved when the governor rapped on
the table and a venerable old monk stood to mumble 'the
Benedicamus.' We all rose, I bowed to Amasia, hiding my

fears though aware of the sweat which soaked my body. It was almost a relief to be away from her and following Douglas and the King up winding, wind-chilled stone stairs into a spacious chamber at the top of the keep. I gathered it was Richard's, large spacious and luxurious. The wooden floor was a polished sheen covered in thick, multi-coloured woollen rugs while the grey granite was cleverly disguised with ornate tapestries; one in green, red and gold depicting the fall of Jerusalem, another the victories of David, while between the great bay windows hung a huge purple-gold banner bearing a glorious Whyte Harte in all its pure splendour. Chests and casks littered the room, their lids pushed open by the silk, damask and velvet clothes which spilled out on to the floor. Boxes of jewellery and pouches of gold were heaped in one corner, a suit of plate armour made of fine Milanese steel chased with gold hung on a prop in another. The room was dominated by a great four-poster bed, its curtains of deep purple fringed with silver tassels, the bed-cover, a cloth of gold, decorated with the dainty white head of a hart.

This was majesty and, amidst such splendour, I lied for my life. I spun a story which Chaucer would have envied. How I had been sent by certain lords in England (who for the time would remain nameless) with messages of support from them as well as powerful London merchants eager to end the war with France and return to pouring their gold into commerce, not the yawning pit of constant battle. Oh what a tale and what a teller! They took it like hungry carp seize the bright-coloured bait. I was accepted for what I claimed to be and not questioned on what I could be. Nevertheless, Douglas said he would send messengers to the Regent of Scotland, the Duke of Albany, and I knew I could stay, at least for a while. I was given a small, smelly chamber in the keep, a chest, a truckle bed and the right to draw on provisions in the castle. I settled down, confident that the weather would hinder messengers and give me sufficient time to ferret out the truth.

I concentrated on talking to Richard, observing him sharply, setting small traps to catch him out. He seemed to be what he claimed. He was majestic, cold and distant with a deep loathing for the House of Lancaster and a fierce determination to be revenged but, from the beginning, I felt there was something wrong, lacking or missing. Oh, I searched for proof but he always hid it; his signature was Richard's, he bore his own secret and chancery seals to mark documents. Yet, I still felt uneasy. On one occasion I discussed philosophy with him, criticising the writings of Thomas Aquinas and praising those of Marsilius of Padua and the Nominalist Occam. He joined in with spirit, showing his knowledge, commenting with an acid wit and, as he did, something stirred in my memory but it was only a shadow and I could not grasp it.

Of course, I acted the role of the faithful retainer, the ardent partisan and crafty spy. I convinced Douglas, though I kept a wary eye on Amasia, who seemed to take a liking to me. God knows why. She delayed her departure and sought me out. I think she both cared for and was intrigued by me. A flattering situation which I exploited for my own use. I wooed her with subtle compliments and courtly courtesy and she responded, still I suspect she saw me for what I was, a rogue, a charlatan, a liar. God save me from intelligent women. They can always see the truth. I think Amasia did and quietly mocked me for what I was.

As the days passed, we became friends and then lovers. She came to me one evening, knocking on my door, slipping into that dingy chamber to mock and tease me. We kissed and she disrobed, stark naked, save for a white silk ribbon round her neck, and we made love, turning and twisting on the bed. She, moaning with pleasure, as I kissed her small, round breasts and lay between her legs, seeking comfort in her soft silken warmth. In moments of passion she would cry out in French and I would answer her in that tongue. We accepted that as our language, talking in English whenever anyone was present but lapsing into French when we were on our own. She was fluent and would tease me on my atrocious accent for, though I had mastered the tongue in my studies and my stay in France, my ability was only in the written form. She often said I spoke her language like a Spanish cow and made me laugh at her savage caricatures of my accent. Not that I had much time to improve. Most of my days were spent with Richard, listening to his ravings against the House of Lancaster and his schemes of vengeance whilst I supplied information on what I knew about the English court, gamely lying as I tried to work out the truth.

I seized every opportunity to question Richard on how he secured the royal signet as well as other jewels, furs, velvets and riches belonging to the crown. He claimed these had been hidden on his return from Ireland and despatched north by friends and retainers. He also explained how he escaped from Pontefract. A squire in Sir Robert Waterton's household had smuggled in women's clothes and then started a fire. In the confusion he had managed to escape and reach the Lancashire coast. From there he had taken ship to the Orkneys where he had been recognised and brought to Stirling.

'But the body?' I exclaimed. 'The corpse buried at Langley and reinterred at Westminster?'

Richard smiled. 'An impostor,' he replied. 'Probably my chaplain, poor Richard Maudelyn. After execution, his body was sent back in a solemn black farce.'

I nodded understandingly, it was not too nonsensical though I still felt there was something amiss.

I stayed at Stirling for it became impossible to leave. Two days after I arrived, the snow fell, carpeting the surrounding countryside and freezing on the turrets, walls and parapet walls. It blocked all paths, buried hamlets and outlying villages. Nothing moved in that death-white world; villagers tried to shelter in the castle but were turned savagely away. The castle rations were reduced to bread and rancid meat which stank despite the heavy

garnish of spices. I spent most of the time either talking to
Richard, spinning a web of lies about a mythical conspiracy
in England or trying to find out if his story was true.
Sometimes I nearly grasped what was amiss, as when I
walked into his chamber, thinking it was empty to find him
lolling on the great bed, humming a tune which he
stopped as soon as he saw me. I thought the tune familiar
but could not place it. Of course, there was Amasia whose
passion and energy did not abate. My only worry was her
continuous presence or wild, abandoned cries when we
made love, which would create suspicions even in the dim,
dull minds of the governor and his family. We spent our
nights, naked under the blankets of my truckle bed,
wrapped round each other for warmth and passion,
listening to the chilling howl of wolves, long, dark,
dangerous shapes who slunk out of the woods to bay
beneath the castle walls.

Gradually, a thaw set in, the snow disappeared,
unfurling like a tapestry to reveal the destruction and
death beneath. The frozen corpses of villagers, men,
women and children, together with their beasts, killed by
the murderous, cruel winter. Perhaps we are like the
seasons. Whatever we claim to be, eventually the truth will
out. It happened so at Stirling, quickly, almost without
effort. I was in Richard's chamber listening to his array of
questions, when Amasia joined us. She wanted to tease me
and did so in French, fast and voluble before I laughingly
drove her away.

'What is wrong with Amasia?' Richard asked, half
distracted as he examined a torn fingernail. There was a
momentary silence.

'Oh,' I replied slowly, 'she wants me to take her out of
the castle and escort her on a ride. I refused.'

Richard smiled, nodded, and I knew he was a liar.
Perhaps I should have just gone, said nothing, ignored the
beating of my heart and the pounding of blood in my
head, but Amasia returned to pick up a small phial she had

forgotten. She was about to leave when Richard suddenly called out.

'You should not ask to be taken for a ride, Amasia. It is still unsafe!'

Amasia turned and pouted at me. 'I asked for nothing of the sort!' and flounced out, crashing the door behind her. I stared silently at the figure before me, my hand stealing under my cloak as I watched the pretender, the impostor, the mammet of Scotland, slouch on the bed, his hand beneath one of the large, red silk bolsters. He had a clever, knowing smile on lips and I knew I would find it easy to kill him.

'Oh,' he began softly, 'that was clever, Master Jankyn.'

'Yes,' I retorted, my hand firmly clutching the bone handle of my dagger, 'it was clever. Richard of Bordeaux was fluent in French and would not need to ask for a translation. You, however, can only mutter a few phrases, spice your conversation with specially chosen words to give the impression you understand the tongue. But there was more. Richard hated the study of philosophy, yet you are well versed with Aquinas' works. Richard liked music but not the student ditty I caught you humming. Strange, the last time I heard that was at Oxford, but you learnt it at Cambridge, where you were better known as Thomas Warde of Trumpington!'

'But the jewels, the robes?' came the cool reply. 'The signet ring?'

'Not sent to Scotland,' I heatedly replied, 'but brought here by William Searle in 1400, a few months before he heard of you. An impostor, a pretender, an actor who liked to play roles.'

The creature laughed. 'Oh! Good! Good!' he replied delightedly. 'You are clever, Jankyn. I enjoy the life of a prince and the rare possibility of gaining a crown. Why should I object?'

'Does the Governor know?'

'No, but Albany does.'

'That is why he does not produce you in public?' I asked.
'Perhaps!'

'Did Oldcastle know?'

'I think he did.'

'So, Richard did not escape from Pontefract?'

'Ah,' the creature smiled knowingly. 'I did not say that. The truth, perhaps, is even stranger.'

He looked at me, the smile dying around his thin lips. 'But, Jankyn, you do not mind? It changes nothing!' I suddenly realised that, though I knew him, he did not know about me.

'Oh, no, Master Warde of Trumpington. It changes nothing. It does nothing. It causes nothing. It does not bring my father back to life or my friends, or restore the wits of the one woman I loved. Oh, no, it does nothing for the scaffold, for the rope, the axe, the burning thorns, for you are nothing!'

He must have seen the murder in my eyes for he scrabbled for the knife beneath the bolster but my dagger was out and streaking for his heart. He moved sideways and it caught him in the muscles beneath the shoulder. He screamed as the blood spurted out, gushing on to my knife, then he slumped unconscious on to the floor.

Perhaps I should have killed him, but I fled the chamber and hurried up the icy, slippery stairs to my own garret. I packed my bundle and quietly stole down the stairs, crossing the inner and outer baileys, pretending I was going into the town and hoping no one would think it strange I carried a pack. Luckily, it was cold, already half dark and no one cared enough to stop me. I was soon through the postern gate under the muttered curses of a frozen sentry and slipping down into the town. My heart pounded, my chest heaved in rapid gasps for air. I was waiting for the hue and cry, the shouts of 'Harrow! Harrow!' as the pursuit began, pounding footsteps, shouts, the angry whirr of a cross-bow. But there was nothing. Only silence, as I slipped across the snow through the quiet, soaking town and into the surrounding countryside.

20

The thaw had come but the paths were still soggy with snow-drenched icy mud and deep drifts still lay hidden, traps for the unwary. God knows how I travelled, sometimes ploughing chest-high through drifts like a swimmer in icy water, splashing across freezing, swollen rivers, sometimes missing my footing on the slippery ford bottom. I intended to journey back disguised but there was no time. Once or twice I saw horsemen, dark cloaks flapping as they pounded along the edge of a hill so I hid amongst the hard, frozen bracken. I stole, begged and wheedled for food, drink and fire and only Christ knows how I survived. One night, shivering with the fever, I dreamt I was surrounded by scores of Whyte Hartes, all staring at me, their black mouths open, but when I awoke they were only patches of snow.

I pressed on but realised I could not cover the vast open countryside which rolled down to the Tweed and the English border. Desperate, I turned due east, making for the sea and the small fishing villages sprawled along the coast. I found one. A God-forsaken, damp place reeking of rotten fish but with a small, dirty hovel above the sand dunes with an ale-stake pushed into its eaves. There I drank hot bowls of fish soup and a flagon of thick ale till I thought I would be sick. I threw a coin at the small, dishevelled landlord and slept on his dirt-beaten floor, one hand tightly clenched around my pack, the other on my dagger.

I must have arrived late in the morning for it was night

when I awoke, bleary-eyed, my body aching and my mouth thick with the taste of the soup. I ate again, this time questioning the owner who stared greedy-eyed at the coins I laid before him. He extended a claw-like hand, moaning with greed, but I drew my dagger and he adopted his usual servile stance. He understood what I wanted and scuttled through the leather curtains which served as a door. He must have been gone some time and I was beginning to doze when he returned with two others, fishermen of the town, red-faced, bluff fellows who looked askance at both me and the landlord. Nevertheless, I trusted them. Thank God for a lying heart and a treacherous mind: the landlord was a weasel, I recognised the type but these were dull yet honest, brave men. They understood English, the coastline and Tynemouth and agreed to take me there for two gold coins.

We left on the morning tide in a small, one-sail herring boat which did little to diminish my fear of the sea. I once said my journey to France with the army of Henry V was the worst voyage of my life. As usual, I was lying. The journey to Tynemouth was a descent into Hell. The boat, dirty and battered, with water seeping through the pitch and tar, nosed its way out and into the misty, choppy sea. I just crouched in the stern amidst greasy nets, hooks and rotten fish and prayed to every saint I knew. The voyage took two or three days. I did not keep count but the two fellows bundled me ashore and I parted with more than two gold coins. I huddled for a while against the sea-wall before wearily dragging my way up the streets to the priory. At one time I collapsed and only moved when a mongrel dog, urged on by a gang of young ruffians, came up, sniffed at me, and was about to cock its leg against my shoulder. I cursed, rose to my feet and struggled on to the priory.

The prior welcomed me, exclaiming in astonishment when a lay brother almost dragged me into his clean, whitewashed chamber. I heard him speak, issue orders with a clapping of hands and whispered instructions before I collapsed in a faint. I spent a week at the priory, staying in their infirmary while an austere, black-habited physician looked after me. He was the best of his kind: he did not bleed me, cast horoscopes or fasten slimy leeches to my limbs, but made me eat and sleep while I dreamed about traitors, armies on the march and the mystery surrounding the Whyte Harte. I had unmasked the pretender at Stirling but felt that it proved nothing but the obvious. To quote a proverb, so far I had only spooned the cream off the milk.

Of course, I would have immediately travelled south to London but the prior, a friend of Beaufort, insisted otherwise, saying I was not strong enough for such a journey and he would arrange for a ship to take me back to London. I cried out in alarm, cursing him, but eventually I conceded. I was bundled aboard a small, squat cog carrying coal and iron and within a week was back in Westminster, with no further mishap than a hatred for the sea and a weak, retching stomach.

I stayed two or three days in my garret before sending a messenger to Beaufort. A day later one of his household came and took me down to Westminster through the milling crowds and busy courts to a small painted chamber where Beaufort and the Secret Commission were waiting for me. They sat there, like a tableau, and I felt angry at their smug security. What did they know of men armed with daggers secretly trying to kill me? Hungry wolves, freezing snow and other secret terrors? Then I remembered Amasia, her long, sweet throat, her head thrown back moaning with delight as I kissed her breasts, as well as the pleasure of plunging my dagger into the impostor's body, and I felt better.

I sat staring down at Beaufort's angelic face and told them all I could, omitting only those details I wanted to. They listened and then came the questions. 'So,' Glanville summarised, 'Richard of Scotland was a mammet, an impostor and stands unmasked as one. At least,' he looked sideways at Beaufort, 'to us.'

'But not to the world,' the Bishop replied. 'Let us realise that we suspected the man in Scotland was an impostor and not the Whyte Harte. So what is there left?'

'For the love of God,' Erpingham broke in, 'Richard is dead, he starved himself to death at Pontefract. Why all this foolery?'

'Ask the King!' I retorted angrily. 'After all, he nominated you to do this commission. There is,' I added slowly for effect, 'the admission of the impostor in Scotland that things might not be as described in Prophett's memorandum, excellent though it was.'

Erpingham was about to question me further when the clerk intervened.

'My Lord,' Prophett almost squeaked, 'there is one further path we may go down.'

We all looked at this small, insignificant man who positively blushed with embarrassment at the attention he drew.

'Oh, Scribbler!' Glanville commented drily. 'What is it?'

'Oh, Lawyer!' I jibed. 'More than you can ever offer.'

Glanville glared across the table and I saw the murderous hatred in his eyes.

'Master Jankyn,' he replied, 'I find it hard to sit with a thief, a rogue, a heretic and a traitor. Know your place before someone succeeds in showing you it.'

I could have smashed my fist into his dry, sardonic face but Beaufort, who seemed to enjoy the conflict, intervened, demanded silence and, turning to Prophett, told him to continue.

'It is Queen Isabella,' Prophett excitedly announced. 'In 1400, when the rebels tried to assassinate the King's father, they went to her at Sonning. In 1402, after her return to France, she issued a proclamation saying that Richard was still alive and twice tried to land in England. She always refused to accept that Richard was dead, unwilling to marry again until ordered to do so by her father.' Prophett turned to Beaufort. 'As your Lordship knows, she eventually married the Duke of Orleans' son and died in 1408 whilst in childbirth.'

'Yes, yes,' Glanville testily interrupted. 'But what is the point?'

'The point,' Prophett replied, 'is that her husband succeeded his father as Duke of Orleans and fought at Agincourt where ...'

'Where,' Beaufort triumphantly broke in, 'he was captured and brought here to be imprisoned in the Tower until his ransom was paid!'

'Exactly, your Lordship,' Prophett concluded, 'and I am sure you have reached the same conclusion as myself. Isabella must have talked with Orleans, told him something about Richard's death or the mystery of the Whyte Harte. Why, even when he was imprisoned in England, Orleans is said to have become involved with people who talked of restoring Richard. So much so, that his Grace the King moved Orleans to Pontefract as a grim reminder of what can happen even to princes. I understand,' Prophett continued, 'that Orleans has now learnt his lesson and been restored to his apartments in the Tower. I believe he should be questioned.'

I watched the pleasure in Beaufort's eyes and knew Prophett was right. I envied his tidy mind, his ability to ferret out facts, connect events, and looked at him with new respect. Despite his rabbit-frightened looks, Prophett might be a dangerous man.

'Jankyn!' Beaufort caught my attention. 'You will go to the Tower and question the Duke.'

'My Lord,' I answered wearily, 'cannot someone else go? I have travelled ...'

Beaufort stopped me short by slamming his hand on the table. 'This commission,' he announced angrily, 'serves the King and will complete its task without rancour or quarrelling. Jankyn, you will go!'

I nodded meekly. Beaufort picked up a small silver bell and rang it until a clerk scurried in with a writing-tray slung round his neck. At Beaufort's command he hastily wrote out a warrant permitting me to visit Orleans in the Tower. Beaufort read the document, clicking his tongue at the clerk's mistakes, before ordering the wax to be heated and a small pool of it poured on the parchment which Beaufort promptly sealed and handed to me. I rose, bowed and dejectedly made my way down to the quayside.

The Tower was as bleak and lonely as ever; huge ravens with cruel, yellow beaks and hard, black eyes jabbed at the muddy soil in front of the main quayside gate, scattering with raucous cawing at my approach. There were the usual interminable questions and checks from the guards as I entered the darkness of each gateway which controlled the entrances through the concentric ring of towers. Inside one of these I was stopped and made to wait until a royal sergeant brought the constable, a fat, dapper little man with sandy hair, florid face, and eyes no kinder than two piss-holes in the snow. He introduced himself as Sir Aubrey Fordin, constable and governor. He looked me up and down, smiled as if he recognised me for what I really was, scrutinised Beaufort's letter and beckoned me to follow him up the steps of the large donjon-like tower. Half-way up were guards lounging outside a heavily padlocked, iron-studded door. Sir Aubrey muttered an order, a guard fumbled with the keys, unlocked the door, and we entered a spacious room. It was luxurious, with clean rushes on the floor, a huge bed ringed with half-drawn purple-and-gold curtains which revealed a beautiful blue canopy decorated with silver fleur-de-lis and pearl-white bolsters. The walls had heavy blood-red drapes, there were chairs and tables, stools and a row of wooden chests spilling out clothes, belts, hose and other belongings. The windows were made of horn, there were sconce stones and iron cresset-holders for light.

At the far end of the chamber was a half-open door

which, Sir Aubrey explained, led on to a parapet walk
along the battlements. He coughed and slammed the door
behind us to indicate that we were present. There was the
patter of footsteps and a figure entered the room from the
parapet walk. He was slender, of medium height with
white skin and rather long, fiery-red hair, blown and wet
from his walk above the river.

'My Lord,' Sir Aubrey said. 'May I introduce Matthew
Jankyn, a member of Bishop Beaufort's household. He has
come to ask you certain questions.'

The duke approached. He looked as arrogant as a
peacock: a beak of a nose rose above thin lips, his eyes were
heavily lidded and I was surprised to see they were of
different colours, one a bright blue, the other dark brown.
He saw my confusion and smiled thinly, sardonically
welcoming me in fluent English while he dismissed Sir
Aubrey with a flick of his fingers as if shaking off dirty
water.

Once the constable was gone, Orleans relaxed and led
me over to the two chairs placed before a small
iron-capped brazier. He opened this, stirred the coals with
a rod until they spluttered and glowed, threw a handful of
aromatic herbs in and lowered the cap. He poured two
goblets of wine and, giving one to me, sat opposite,
carefully sipping from the cup. I knew he had used these
ordinary tasks to give himself time to think, recollect and
quietly study me. He had been held in prison for four
years, whilst his relatives in France collected the huge
ransom demanded by King Henry. He talked of this,
recalling the battle where he had been captured and we sat
like two old veterans discussing tactics and condemning
the mistakes of our leaders. He was proud but, beneath
this courtly hauteur he was just another prisoner in a
foreign land.

'Well Monsieur?' he eventually said. 'Bishop Beaufort
did not send you here to enquire after my health or to
discuss the strategy of the Agincourt campaign. So why?'

'Richard II,' I abruptly replied and watched the hooded, guarded reaction in his strange eyes.

'What is that to me?'

'Enough to start plotting for his supposed return, even here when you were sheltering after your capture at Agincourt.'

Orleans threw his head back and laughed softly. 'Oh, that,' he ruefully admitted. 'Nonsense. Play-acting. Revenge on King Henry. Nothing more. I have now learnt my lesson.'

He looked at me. 'King Henry, you know, moved me from the Tower to Pontefract. I was placed in the same room as your ill-fated Richard. I questioned many who served in the castle. They all claimed Richard was always there. Never once was he hidden away and his refusal to eat was well witnessed. Nor,' Orleans drily concluded, 'was there any attempt to hide his corpse. It was dressed for burial by local physicians and exposed in the great hall of the castle for all to see.' Orleans paused. 'Yet still it is strange.'

'Why, my Lord?' I asked.

Orleans smiled secretively. 'Why should I tell you, Master Jankyn?'

'You were married to Richard's widow, Isabella,' I replied.

'Ah!' Orleans exclaimed. 'La petite belle Isabella! But my question, Master Jankyn. Why should I tell you the secret conversations between a lord and lady?'

I thought hard and quickly. 'Bishop Beaufort could arrange more comfortable quarters.'

Orleans laughed and airily waved his hand round the chamber. 'This is enough for any prisoner. Besides, I would miss baiting that stupid oaf, Sir Aubrey.'

'His Lordship,' I began slowly, 'Might arrange a reduction in the ransom demanded for you in France.'

Orleans straightened in his chair. 'Oh!' he said softly, 'that is worth any conversation. And,' he added, 'is there anything else?'

'No,' I replied truthfully, a rare occasion for me. 'Nothing, except my father, my friends, the woman I loved, all suffered because of Richard and his Whyte Harte.'

Orleans pursed his lips and turned to gaze into the glowing coals. 'I have never told anyone this,' he began. 'Isabella always believed Richard was still alive. She wanted that for she adored him. She never accepted his death.' Orleans paused to pluck at a loose thread in his dark-blue hose. 'She claimed that Richard wrote to her.'

'A forgery,' I interrupted. 'I have seen similar.'

'Oh, no. No forgery,' Orleans replied. 'The letter bore a secret code known only to the two of them.'

'Henry of Lancaster,' I said, 'may have allowed Richard to write from gaol.'

'But,' Orleans teased, 'in this letter, dated December 1399, Richard claimed he was free, though in hiding, waiting to stage his own restoration.'

'What?'

'Yes,' Orleans continued remorselessly. 'There is more. Isabella claimed to have seen her husband alive and well after his supposed imprisonment at Pontefract.'

'Where? When?'

Orleans squinted at the far wall while he tried to remember. 'The Queen,' he murmured, 'was at Sonning in Burk ...'

'Berkshire!' I corrected.

'Yes, Berkshire, just after the New Year, the one after his deposition by Duke Henry.'

I sat speechless. According to Orleans, King Richard was free, writing and visiting his wife when, state records claimed, he was in prison at Pontefract.

'Isabella must have been wrong,' I answered. 'She did not see Richard, but Maudelyn, her husband's chaplain. He was the King's twin, so alike was he to Richard.'

'That may be true,' Orleans replied, 'but Isabella claimed Maudelyn was also there!'

'So, who was in Pontefract? There cannot be two men identical to Richard!' I insisted. 'Surely Isabella was mistaken, overcome with grief. She may have imagined what she saw.'

'I could believe that,' Orleans replied, 'if she had been the only one, but there was another, Jean Creton, a French squire and Richard's personal body-servant. He was with Isabella, saw Richard and received letters from the King the same time as the Queen did.'

'Are these letters still extant? Did you see them?'

Orleans shook his head. 'No. I think they were kept hidden, perhaps destroyed when Isabella died.'

'And Creton?'

'Oh, he is still alive. A clever clerk. I believe he works in the Louvre Palace in Paris.' Orleans paused and stared at me. 'If his Lordship, Bishop Beaufort, sent me a tun of good Bordeaux wine, I would even write letters of introduction and safe conduct for you.'

I smiled and nodded. Orleans knew that what he told me was a revelation and, as Isabella was now dead, it would be crucial to meet Creton. This French lord's story was radically different from Prophett's memorandum and, for the first time, I began to wonder if that little chancery clerk was not deliberately misleading us.

It was already dusk by the time I returned to Westminster: cresset torches had been placed in the great hall now emptying for the night. A long line of felons, bound by halter ropes around their necks, were being led away by city bailiffs and pursuivants. Judges in their fur-trimmed caps strode purposefully from the courts pursued by a gaggle of weary clerks, their arms clutching rolls of parchment. A baker with a tray of hot pies and buns was being forcibly ejected from the hall amidst catcalls and jeers. A dog pissed amongst the rushes and then barked at a huge white-bellied cat, which slunk by, a young rat in its jaws. I tried to ignore this confusion and eventually caught the eye of one of the ushers. He looked suspicous when I asked to be taken to Bishop Beaufort but quickly co-operated after I slipped a coin into his hand.

Beaufort was in the same chamber where the Secret Commission had met earlier that day. He was wrapped in a thick, woollen cape, a beaver hat on his head, booted and spurred, looking more like a prosperous merchant than a bishop.

'Ah, Jankyn,' he greeted me. 'So you have returned.' He waved a gloved hand round the empty room, the red ruby on his forefinger winking and sparkling in the candle-light. 'See, your colleagues have gone before you.'

'Not for the first time, my Lord,' I observed bitterly, 'and I think it will certainly not be the last.'

Beaufort walked over and grasped me by the arm. 'Matthew,' he said softly, 'I trust you. You know the city. You can survive. Can you imagine the others? Erpingham perhaps, but he is the King's man and,' Beaufort broke off and shrugged. I had the impression he was going to say more but he let the matter drop and asked me to report on my meeting with Orleans.

When I had finished Beaufort's lips were pursed, his eyes bright with excitement. 'Orleans may have his tun of Bordeaux and you, Master Jankyn, are off to France!'

'But the others?' I protested. 'They do nothing. France is a battleground. The sea voyage. I cannot go!'

'You will go!' Beaufort snapped. 'I have need of you there. You will be well rewarded. Have no fear of that.'

'What is the use of rewards if one is dead?'

'What do you mean?'

I told him about the attacks on me. He did not look surprised but nodded sagely like some doctor listening to some childish list of ailments. I didn't think he even cared. I should have known better. Beaufort, the clever bastard, cared about everything. He told me to be wary and on my guard, I sardonically thanked him for the advice but he just patted me on the shoulder.

'Matthew,' he said firmly, 'you are for France. You must

be prudent, realising we are approaching the heart of this mystery.'

Oh, Beaufort should have been called the Chrysogonous or the golden-mouthed with his clever ways and artful suggestions. I wonder, now, scores of years later, why I followed his orders. Perhaps the money. Perhaps the hope of a solution. Perhaps I had nothing better to do. No family. No friends. No religion. God had never talked to me and I had stopped talking to Him ever since I lost Mathilda.

I left Westminster and its dark pools of intrigue and returned to my lodgings to pack my saddlebags and put my affairs in order. I drew up a will leaving my lands and chattels to Mathilda, witless as she was, I lived on in hope that one day she would recover. I sat once more reading through Prophett's memorandum and something stirred in my soul. A faint shadowy idea but it evaporated as my tired brain tried to grasp it.

Two days later I returned to see Beaufort. He was gone but his chief notary had already drawn up letters for my passage to France and had obtained similar letters from Orleans. There was some money and permission to take horses and sumpter ponies from Beaufort's stable.

'Oh,' the clerk concluded, 'His Lordship said your colleagues would be busy during your absence. They are to question Sir Thomas Swynnerford and Sir Robert Waterton.'

I was pleased. Beaufort also realised that the heart of the mystery was Richard II's alleged imprisonment in Pontefract. I left London the same day and joined a military convoy on the road south to Dover.

The port was a hive of activity, the castle fortified with mangonels and other machines of war; the garrison at full strength, workmen reinforcing the walls, while along the cliff-top wine-barrels had been stacked on top of each other to form a series of beacons. The harbour was full of ships whilst out on the sea roads, huge merchant cogs with all their armaments patrolled the coastline. A soldier informed me that news had arrived that Castile, France's ally, had put its fleet to sea and an attack on Dover had not been ruled out.

21

I groaned at the prospect of being drawn back into King Henry's horrific war and cursed even louder when I was unable to find a bed in the crowded port, having to sleep in a draughty warehouse on the quay alongside the troops all waiting to embark for France. I remember that time, March, I think, March 1419. A cruel month with blustery gales and driving icy winds. I spent days on the chilling quayside trying to obtain passage. It was difficult, the ships were full to capacity, each waiting for a break in the weather and assurances that the sea was free of the Castilian armada.

Eventually I was lucky and paid for a place on the *Saint Nicholas*, a converted merchantman packed with men and supplies bound for the English-held port of Calais. I secured passage for my horses and equipment though it cost me, or rather Beaufort, dear, and soon afterwards put to sea, for messages had arrived that the Castilian armada was not in sight. The *Saint Nicholas* looked capable of defending herself. She had a bluff hull or cut, in sailors' parlance, raised at the stern to form fighting-castles protected by gaily painted palisades, and one monstrous mast with a lookout point posted just beneath the red and white pennant. I felt safe enough as we turned for the open sea with the ship's jagged, black bowsprit jutting out in front and the royal banner of England trailing from the

stern. As we left the port, the master began to issue a spate
of orders to loosen the sail, followed by shouts and the
stamp of bare feet as sailors climbed the rigging or
loosened the cords from their clasps. A young boy, nimble
as any squirrel, climbed up to the yard and with a bellow of
words about 'hauling the bowline' and 'veering the sheet',
the great square sail was lowered, fastened and bellied
forward in a strong wind.

It was a pleasant enough crossing though the *Saint
Nicholas* was packed with archers, men-at-arms, scullions,
pit boys, friars, monks, clerks and all the other professions
which keep a great army on the move. Under a grey sky,
the ship seemed to skim the waves as a strong north wind
caught and filled the sail. On board we had to find shelter
where we could in nooks and crannies under the rails and
mast, only to be soaked or pushed and shoved with curses
by the sailors who openly rejoiced in our discomfort.

I knew enough of sailing to avoid both the wettest part
of the ship as well as the stench and noise of the pumps. I
sat near the forecastle and wondered how my meeting with
Creton might solve the mystery of the Whyte Harte. I
knew that Orleans' confession was important and revealing
enough to excite Beaufort. But what lay behind it? I
remember crouching in that cold ship and itemising for
the hundredth time the implications of Orleans' words.
First, if Isabella was correct, how did Richard escape from
Pontefract and yet maintain the pretence of being there?
Did Maudelyn take his place? If so, he must have had the
full connivance and co-operation of his gaolers, Sir
Thomas Swynnerford and Sir Robert Waterton. Yet, these
were men trusted by Henry of Lancaster, Swynnerford
was his own brother-in-law and, after Richard's death, so
Beaufort had informed me, had been greatly favoured by
Henry. Secondly, Maudelyn could have been the one in
prison at Pontefract all the time, but this was ridiculous.
King Richard was captured and interviewed by those who
knew him well. They would not be fooled. Moreover,

Isabella said she saw Maudelyn with Richard in January 1400 and it would be the most remarkable of coincidences that there would be two men identical to Richard. True, there had been the mammet of Scotland, but he kept himself from public view, especially from anyone who really knew Richard II. Those who did see the impostor had probably never seen the deposed king, while any changes noted by them would be dismissed as the result of years of enforced exile. Even so, the mammet had certainly not convinced me and confirmed my suspicions with little or no effort. I concluded that neither Richard nor his chaplain, Maudelyn, could be in two places at the one time. So many questions and problems, so few answers or solutions, I was still trying to resolve the matter when the *Saint Nicholas* entered Calais.

Nevertheless, the mystery kept my mind off the voyage and I disembarked safe and well on the busy port quayside. Calais, itself, was a busy war-camp. The castle, walls, houses and fortifications were thronged by English troops. The inns, taverns and bawdy houses were busy with trade which never ceased. Calais was the great war-base for Henry V and through it poured men and supplies for his campaign in Normandy. The city was packed with soldiery; archers in their brown leather jackets, foot soldiers in leather sallets, flat, iron caps and boiled leather leggings. Some nondescript, others wearing the livery of the different lords. Great war-horses, caparisoned and harnessed for battle, plunged and reared in the narrow streets and fought to clamber on to the plump haunches of some mare or snapped viciously at the sumpter ponies. Carts filled with supplies: bread, cheeses, cooked meats, tuns of wine and hogsheads of beer. Behind them the arms-wagons, the instruments of war peeping out from their leather coverings; bows of yew, arrows in their thousands all capped with shiny, Sheffield steel; halberds, axes, daggers, clubs and swords. Supervising them all and trying to make sense out of the chaos were the

lords and knights in half-armour, their squires beside
them holding banners and pennants with the flaming
tinctures of heraldry; deep azure, blood-red gules the
black sable of night, greens, purples and golds. I could
distinguish the English, who forbade the same colours in
the one coat of arms, but those of Henry's European allies
blinded me with their glorious colours and emblems, some
recognisable, others flaunting dragons, griffins, gorgons
and strange salamanders.

Oh, it was a glorious sight. Men in all their glory, terrible
as an array of bloody banners, as they prepared to go out
and slaughter their own kind for the highest possible
motives. I kept clear of their fiery natures and warlike
stances, leading my horse and sumpter pony through the
icy, choked, stinking streets, patiently waiting my turn,
eyes down, unwilling to be drawn into any of the sudden
squabbles and vicious quarrels which flared up like banked
fires. I finally reached the fringes of the town where I
spent the night in the retching stench of a warehouse
before joining an English Military convoy making its way
south, following the Seine down to Rouen, Normandy's
capital.

I was aware of the situation in France. King Henry, bluff
Hal, the ideal king and perfect warrior, had continued to
cut his way through living bodies as he tried to grasp Paris
and the crown of France. Agincourt had only been the
beginning of Henry's systematic conquest of Normandy,
reducing the fortified towns and castles with his inimitable
ferocity. Charles VI, sick and senile, could do little to
oppose him, his wife Isabella of Bavaria too interested in
her cohort of lovers and troupe of monkeys. Wits said it
was difficult to tell the difference between the two. Henry
could have been stopped by either the powerful Duke of
Burgundy or the Armagnacs who had retreated south
under the Dauphin. Yet they hated each other more than
the English, so our King moved between the two and
advanced on Paris.

Strange! Good, strong Hal trying to take poor Charles'
crown while secretly trying to justify his own. I often
wondered if Richard's death and deposition were the real
cause for the untold misery in France, the rapes, the
murders, the plunder and burning. Was Henry like some
nervous boy who hides his own anxieties by a blustering
attack on others? Christ knows the French paid for this.
Two months earlier in January 1419, the great city of
Rouen had eventually fallen to Henry. He had ringed it
with fire and steel the previous July and set his face like
stone against the defenders. The latter had attempted to
send out what soldiers call 'useless mouths', those French
unable to take part in the defence of the city, the women,
the young and the old. The defenders of Rouen hoped
Henry would let them through his lines. They should have
known better. Henry refused and the poor bastards died
in their thousands in the city ditch. Oh, the cause was
Henry but behind him was the Whyte Harte with its sad,
reproachful look, the dead hand of Richard clawing from
the grave, prodding Henry with a thin, skeletal finger to
prove he really was a King.

Now Henry aimed for his greatest prize, the French
crown and the white, satin-soft body of Katharine,
daughter of Charles VI and younger sister of Isabella,
Richard II's former queen. Here, too, I wondered, was
Henry trying to prove he was Richard's equal as well as his
rightful successor? I learnt about Henry's war in France
from the soldiers guarding the convoy as it wound its way
south to Rouen. It was led by a knight banneret, a captain
from Henry's own forces, Stephen Brabazoun, a fair-
haired, boyish-faced knight from Dorset. A young man
already marked by war with his lined, furrowed face and
diamond-hard eyes. The convoy he led was a string of
carts, guarded by mounted men-at-arms and archers. The
countryside we passed through had already been scorched
by war; black gibbets at crossroads, bodies gently swinging
from the long branches of a line of elm trees, burnt-out

villages, polluted streams and wells. Death riding a Whyte
Harte had passed through the flat countryside and dealt
out savage retribution.

In theory, Henry was conqueror and possessor of this
ravaged, depopulated land though the Armagnacs or
Burgundians could launch a surprise attack. The French
still had to learn from their defeats in battle for our convoy
was attacked in the same manner as at Agincourt. Our
scouts first brought in news that groups of cavalry were
massing to the south-east. The information kept flowing
in; the cavalry was hostile, bearing the blue and gold
colours of Armagnacs, the personal colours of the
Dauphin; the horsemen had made contact with our
outriders and were now approaching. Brabazoun ordered
the carts to be formed in a square, the men-at-arms were
placed in the centre, mounted, while the archers, on foot,
took up position behind the carts. I stood in the middle,
confident that I would be protected by the milling mass of
bodies.

I felt the same as I always do when fighting men prepare
for the kill. I trembled, quaking with fear, trying to hide
the terror in my heart and the quickening grip of fear in
my bowels. Oh, I hid it well, as I always do, in a show of
false courage and bravado, issuing orders, shouting
encouragement and waving my arms. I shut up when I saw
the French, they swept down in an arc of coloured steel,
snapping banners and thundering hooves. They were
brave but foolish: Brabazoun snapped out an order 'Aim!
Steady!' Rows of bows, a mass of wooden death lifted their
vicious steel points to the sky. 'Loose!' A black cloud of
arrows sped towards the French, followed by others, to fall
amongst the charging riders. I saw the lines of horsemen
waver, come on, tremble and sink into chaos. Horses,
caparisoned in gorgeous hues, crashed to the ground, they
and their riders pierced by clusters of arrows. Brabazoun
kept rapping out his simple orders till a ring of bloody
colour, screaming and shouting, lay around the carts. One

of these was pulled aside and the mounted men-at-arms streamed out, followed by the archers. They took no prisoners, cutting the throats of the wounded and then stripping and plundering the dead. Brabazoun's serjeants, aided by a trumpeter, eventually restored order. Scouts were sent out, they reported that the survivors of that furious charge had fled. The wagons were reformed and the convoy continued its way south, Brabazoun and his companions wearing the expression of men content with a good day's work.

Three days after this we reached Rouen in the middle of a drenching rainstorm. God knows I have seen forsaken places, but Rouen, that wet, miserable afternoon, was something out of Dante's vision of the bowels of Hell. The dead, women and children, still lay in piles; gibbets, five or six-branched, stood heavy with swollen bodies; the city ditch was rich with the stink of rotting corpses. The walls were still broken, dented and stained with boiling oil.

I had seen enough. I thanked Brabazoun and skirted the city. I was now moving into the area round Paris untouched by war and protected by the fragile truce recently negotiated between Henry and Charles. As I followed the Seine south, the land became softer. I passed through small villages of scattered cottages; each wood and daub building enclosed in its little patch of land by an old thorn hedge and a shallow ditch bridged by a plank. I often stayed in one of these cottages with their three rooms for family, fodder and animals. The peasants, because of their close proximity to Paris, were protected from the devastation of war and lived in relative comfort. To them, I was just another highly paid, overfed official with a strange accent. Nothing too strange to arouse their suspicions. For a price, which calmed their surliness, I could share their fire of peat and logs and dip into the blackened kettle which always hung from a pot-hook over the fire. Taverns and inns were rare and I felt too afraid to sleep in the open countryside. During the day, I joined

other travellers, courtiers, carters, pilgrims and even
groups of soldiers. The latter were usually mercenaries.
Undoubtedly, they would have robbed me but I showed
Orleans' warrants to their captains and it drew the respect
I really did not deserve.

For all my world-weary knowledge and travels, I was
excited by the prospect of Paris. It had outgrown the walls
built by Philip Augustus but the English invasion had
meant new fortifications; heavy chains across the road,
barricades and constant cavalry patrols. I understood from
a merchant it was not only the English the city feared but
the Jacquerie or peasants, landless, desperate men armed
with scythes and billhooks. Crushed by the French lords
and ravaged by the English, they had recently risen in
rebellion against Paris and devastated it, slicing the heads
off any who opposed them. Charles VI of France believed
it might well happen again and the Provost Marshal, based
at the Chatelet, the city prison, governed Paris with a
ruthless militia who patrolled the borders and eleven
crossroads of the capital. As I entered, I saw proof of their
dedication at the gibbet of Montfaucon. A huge, stark,
four-branched scaffold each bearing its load of rotting
human fruit. Beside this, on a broad raised platform, was a
huge wheel with a criminal strapped to it. At every turn of
the wheel, a gigantic, red-hooded executioner brought his
iron hammer down on the unfortunate's arm and leg, till
the sweating, blackened body danced and jerked with pain.
I hurried on, fully aware a similar fate awaited me if I was
arrested as an English spy.

I did not immediately search out Creton. My curiosity
quelled my terrors and I decided to gain some
acquaintance with the city. First, because I wanted to, and
secondly, like every good rat, I wanted to find the
bolt-holes. Paris is built on the Ile de la Cité in the middle
of the Seine and contains the lofty towers and vaulting
pillars, buttresses and stonework of Notre Dame, the
Louvre Palace and the Hotel Dieu or public hospital. The

Palace, where I hoped to meet Creton, was a collection of stone and wood buildings connected by covered passageways and ringed by a defensive wall. I noticed that all the gates were heavily guarded and I wondered how I might safely contact Creton.

I crossed to the left bank of the Seine and wandered through the students' quarter, no different really from Oxford except for the abundant display of books chained in displays in the countless bookstalls. I passed on, noting the many fountains which were fed by aqueducts bringing water from the hills north-east of Paris while I was astonished to see windmills so close to the city.

I forget the actual date of my arrival in Paris, but it was a spring morning and a warm sun had brought the crowds down to the riverside to await the barges bringing produce in to the city. The prospect of war seemed to recede as I pushed through the colourful crowds in their crimson and gold apparel. Unlike London, the main streets were paved and were broad enough to permit two carts abreast and these were packed with soldiers, mules, tradesmen and pedlars, many of the latter confined to the city by the war. Shopkeepers were not allowed to show their wares so huge, crude signs carrying an enormous tooth, glove, hat or pestle proclaimed the particular trades. Despite the sunshine and usual routine, however, the gaiety was forced, the townspeople fearful of the savage bands of peasants marauding in the hills above Paris or the great armies of England, Burgundy and Armagnac, which manoeuvered and turned like swordsmen, each viewing Paris as the prize.

I found a tavern and sat in the shade drinking wine and eating a stew of bread, meat and vegetables as I considered the best approach to Creton. In the late afternoon, with a plan half formed, I wandered out into the streets. Beggars, many of them wounded veterans of the wars, sat by the church doors asking for alms, Franciscans and Dominicans begged for food and sustenance for the prisons; jugglers

performed in the squares, while minstrels narrated tales of
fabulous journeys to the end of the earth where yellow kings
ruled vast, opulent lands from palaces of shimmering ivory.

Evening drew in. At the crossroads bonfires were lit and a
huge, flaming, tallow candle placed in a niche holding a
statue of the saint of the quarter. I knew the Angelus bell
would signal the curfew, proclaiming the danger of staying
on the street when bands of Tuechiens literally kill-dogs,
sturdy vagabonds, roamed seeking their prey. I secured a
room in a hostel on the right bank of the Seine and stayed
there till the following morning when I hired a boy to take a
letter across to the royal palace. It was addressed to Creton
and I could only hope he was still there. The boy returned,
said he had delivered the letter to an usher but, though I sat
for a whole day, no one came.

The same happened the following day and I was
beginning to despair when late in the evening, a soberly
dressed man in a dark-green doublet and hose, swathed in a
common brown robe, entered the inn and crossed to a table
where he ordered wine and food. He ate and drank sparingly, never stared round but acted as if he was a regular
visitor to the tavern. Once he had finished, he pushed his
hood back and stared across at me.

'Monsieur Jankyn?' he asked softly, I nodded and he got
up and joined me. A long, bony hand, which I hastily shook,
was thrust across the table. 'I am Jean Creton,' he said in
French. 'I received your message. Only someone close to
Richard would know that I, too, served him well.' He
pushed a parchment across to me. 'Here. This is the Duke of
Orleans' letter you sent to me. He vouches for you. So,' he
shrugged, 'what is good for him is good for me!'

I gazed at his long, mournful face, dark-ringed, sad eyes
and felt I could trust him. Creton ran a hand through his
shoulder-length, blond hair and stared around the deserted
tavern. 'I think we can speak in English,' he said in a
half-whisper. 'What do you wish to know?'

'It was in my letter to you,' I replied. 'Richard II was

imprisoned in Pontefract in 1400 but Orleans claims you saw him free and received letters from him during the rebellion in England in January 1400.'

'Yes,' Creton replied. 'I did see him in January 1400 and I did receive letters from him. I continued to disbelieve the stories that he was dead and, when I heard that he was in Scotland, I travelled there in 1405 to see for myself.'

'The man in Scotland,' I harshly interrupted, 'is a liar and a scoundrel!'

'I know, I know,' Creton said sadly. 'But I lived in hope. When I returned to France I informed the French court that Richard was truly dead.'

'So, the French, too, believed Richard was alive for a while and not in Pontefract?'

'Of course. I sent Richard's letters to France. That is why in December 1399, just before the earl's rebellion, King Charles VI massed his fleet in the Channel. He intended to launch an invasion to help Richard but when the rebellion collapsed and Richard was taken back to Pontefract to die, the French King cancelled the venture.'

'So you believe Richard escaped from Pontefract?'

'Of course!'

'But his gaolers swear that he was there all the time!'

'Then they are lying, Monsieur.'

'It could,' I continued, 'be that they held someone who looked like Richard.'

'Impossible!' Creton almost hissed. 'The only man who resembled the King was Maudelyn but he was with Richard.'

'Look, Monsieur,' I said wearily, 'please tell me about the conspiracy and what you saw.'

Creton picked some crumbs off the table and crushed them to a fine powder. 'Richard II was deposed in the autumn of 1399,' he began. 'His army was disbanded and many of his generals made their peace with Henry of Lancaster. The young queen, Isabella, was treated most courteously and placed in the royal manor of Sonning in

Berkshire. I had followed Richard from Ireland and been with him right up to his surrender at Flint. The English would not let me stay with him, so I sought refuge in Queen Isabella's household.'

'What was Richard like, I mean, just before his forced abdication?'

'Defiant,' Creton answered. 'Fully determined to fight against Henry of Lancaster.'

'Yet there are those who say he co-operated fully, was dejected, sad and subject to fits of depression which made him starve himself to death.'

'I know nothing of that,' Creton replied bluntly. 'When Richard was captured he only co-operated in the hope of gaining time. Anyhow,' he continued wearily, 'after his capture, I joined Isabella at Sonning. We thought the King's cause was lost, finished, then we heard rumours. At first vague, but then both Queen Isabella and I received letters from Richard. We could hardly believe it yet we knew they were from him, sealed with a secret cipher known only to the two of us.'

'Where are these letters? What did they say?'

'For the moment, Monsieur, for the moment, leave that. Suffice it say we were overjoyed and drawn into the plot to kill Henry and restore Richard. You probably know the details. Those earls loyal to Richard rose in rebellion and seized Windsor, only to find their quarry had escaped so they marched up the Thames to Sonning. The first we knew about it was when their outriders entered the manor forecourt. The earl's army then arrived, they tore down the standard of Henry of Lancaster and ripped off the collar insignias of Henry's retainers.'

'Was Richard there?'

'I did not see him at first. I saw his double, Richard Maudelyn, then the King appeared in the Queen's chambers where I had taken shelter. He looked thinner, more gaunt, but it was the King. I fell to my knees and kissed his fingers. He patted my head and said God had delivered him and would do so again. He asked me to withdraw and I did, so he could talk to the Queen. When I returned he had gone but I saw Maudelyn later as he left the manor. I went in to the Queen, Isabella was ectastic with happiness, promising me that the old days would return.' Creton's voice trailed off. 'You know the rest. The earl's army was defeated. Richard was recaptured and despatched to Pontefract to die. Maudelyn was captured and sent to London to suffer the unjust and disgraceful death of a traitor.'

'You are sure it was Richard?' I asked.

'I am certain.'

'And Maudelyn was there?'

'I swear, I saw him!'

I stared through the open shutters at the gathering darkness. It made no sense. 'The letters, Monsieur Creton? You mentioned letters.'

'Not here, Sir,' Creton replied. 'Tomorrow, King Charles VI rides through Paris to meet the English envoys. They will dine at the royal palace. I have only one letter. The rest are gone. I will let you read it there.' He looked round the now darkened room where only tallow candles spluttered faintly. 'I have said enough. Good night, Monsieur. Present yourself at the Palace gate. Au revoir,' and he slipped away into the darkness. I sat for a while thinking about what I had learnt. A faint glimmer of light had appeared but I dismissed it as nonsensical. I was tired and made my way out of the inn into the deserted streets. Luckily, my own lodgings were near, and I almost ran, breathless with hidden fear, grateful to reach them safely.

22

I was up early the next morning and joined the throng of people near one of the bridges which crossed from the right bank of the Seine to the Ile de la Cité. The crowd was tense and expectant: the King was returning from one of his outlying manors to begin formal negotiations with the English envoys and I wondered who these were, hoping they would provide some shelter in this alien city. The morning wore on, the crowd grew restive, pedlars, tinkers, sellers of wine, food, and sweetmeats moved in anxious to make a profit. A pickpocket was discovered and hounded out like a rabbit trapped by the beaters. Just before noon the huge bells of Notre Dame began to boom out, their clamour drowning the growing noise. A row of soldiers, all wearing the blue and silver livery of the royal household took up position, clearing the crowd and guarding the approaches to the bridge. After a short while, the royal cortege appeared, led by the marshal of the royal household and his guard, resplendent in blue and gold wearing two swords and plumed, ruffled hats. These were followed by a squad of the King's heralds, flourishing bright pennants from their silver trumpets, which shrilly brayed the approach of the King. Next came lords and a long parade of prelates, nobles, judges, councillors and officers of the royal household, each group uniformly dressed according to function. Chamberlains wore parti-coloured velvet in two shades of crimson, stewards in sky-blue velvet and lawn, valets de chambre in striped black and white. After these followed a group of mounted knights in shining, silver half-armour, lances raised, their blue and scarlet pennants snapping in the breeze. They were grouped round a number of people, one in crimson, and a subdued growl arose. Someone hoarsely whispered '*Les Anglais*' and I looked closer, peering through the forest of lances and almost fainted in surprise when I saw Beaufort, dressed in blood-red, trimmed with white fur, mounted on a silk-black destrier, his face a mask of peace and resignation.

The English party swept along, the onlookers now ominously silent. I later learnt it had been decreed that anyone who raised a hand or voice against the English envoys would hang at Montfaucon. Finally, ringed by a royal bodyguard, came the scrawny, long-necked Charles VI, slumped on a white palfrey and wearing a scarlet mantle, his thin, vacuous face peeping out from beneath an ancient-looking beaded hat. His passing raised a faint cheer before he was gone and, as the soldiers lining the way grouped into a phalanx behind him, I followed them across the bridge.

On the Ile de la Cité, no expense had been spared. Silken drapes had been fastened high across the streets which were lined with children dressed as angels sweetly singing. Fountains at the crossroads splashed red and white wines. There were pageants and dramas on makeshift stages, with glorious coloured tableaux from the bible or the third crusade. One scene in particular caught my attention and I felt a shiver of fear claw at my spine. On one corner, just as we entered the palace, I saw a bright orange tent but open wide at the front to display twelve maidens dressed in cloth of gold, armed with naked swords defending a large, beautifully sculptured white hart from a predatory lion and a huge, cruel eagle. It was like something from one of my nightmares. I am sure Beaufort saw it too, a quiet, malicious reminder of Richard II's deposition by Henry V's father.

The royal cavalcade disappeared into the wide-flung gates of the royal palace, the entrance being guarded by a phalanx of royal spearmen. I approached warily, wondering how I would meet Creton. There was no difficulty, dressed in blue and red livery, he was standing by the gate-pillar away from the guard. He beckoned me over, his long, sorrowful face anxious and tense.

'Come, Monsieur,' he muttered and, with a few mumbled phrases to the captain of the guard, led me through the lines of soldiers into a large paved courtyard or bailey, with a fountain splashing coloured water. It was crowded with grooms looking after horses, while ushers in white and fawn tried to organise the riders to follow them into the palace.

Creton forced his way through, taking us up wide, sweeping stairs, down a corridor into the great hall. It was gorgeous with colour and thick with cloth of gold, ermine, velvets, silks, crowns, jewels and all the baubles which bedeck the mighty. Fresh rushes sprinkled with rose water were strewn on the stone floor, and silken banners depicting the arms of France and England hung along the walls or from the thick lofty beams. Sunlight poured through the horn-glazed windows and hundreds of pure beeswax candles burned sweetly in great multi-bracketed candelabra. Through the haze and dust, I saw Beaufort to the left of the King, on the great dais which overlooked the rows of trestle tables covered in white damask that ran down the full length of the hall. There was confusion, shoving and pushing, as people fought and squeezed for tables. Servants hurried around with huge bowls of perfumed water, napkins stacked along their arms, for guests to wash their fingers. A page dropped a flagon of wine and was beaten whilst the dogs barked excitedly, cocked their legs against the wall and urinated. Eventually, trumpets shrilled and the banquet began. Creton and I seized places near the door at the far end of the hall. I watched the high table but could see very little. The King was slumped in his chair while Beaufort sat, sipping fastidiously from a jewelled, chased cup.

I turned to Creton. 'I did not realise Beaufort would be here,' I said. He looked frozen-eyed at me and I realised I had spoken in English. I coughed and spluttered to cover my confusion and repeated the remark in French.

'Yes, Beaufort is here,' Creton sardonically observed. 'Probably because he is trying to please his master.' He caught my quizzical look and shrugged his shoulders. 'You must know,' he added, 'Pope Martin has bestowed a cardinal's hat on him, but King Henry V has opposed the idea. Or so the rumours go, men say Beaufort flies too high and King Henry wishes to clip his wings.'

I nodded as if I understood (of course I didn't) and gazed at that silent, devious figure at the far end of the hall. So Beaufort, I thought, is in trouble with his King. But why? Was it linked to the Secret Commission? The cause of the Whyte Harte? Or was it more? I remembered that Beaufort's family were the illegitimate issue of John of Gaunt, Henry V's grandfather. Was Beaufort aiming higher? It is hard for me now, an old man, to remember everything from my youth, blessed, even as I am, with an excellent memory, but I do remember as if it were yesterday, the fear I felt in that banqueting hall. A fear I knew well for it sprang from my own sensitive desire for self-preservation. If Beaufort fell like Lucifer, then he would drag me down through the stars of heaven.

I tried to concentrate on the sumptuous food: roast capons, civets of hare, meat and fish aspics, lark pastries, plover garnished with white leeks, fruit wafers, iced pear and thick, mulled wine. All served in dishes and cups of heavy silver, jewel-encrusted, though none too clean. I played with my food, unwilling to be drawn into conversation with Creton lest my accent attract too much attention. Then, just as the last courses were to be served, a servant plucked my shoulder and bent over to whisper in my ear. I could not understand the message so I asked him to repeat it. He did so while Creton listened, before departing as silently as he came.

'The Bishop,' Creton observed, nodding towards the high table, 'wishes to see you here, tomorrow, at noon. I will not be here so it is best if I showed you what you came for.' He looked at me curiously. 'You are,' he muttered, 'a man with strange masters. You have the personal recommendation of the Duke of Orleans yet you are also known to Bishop Beaufort of England. You should remember the scriptures, Monsieur Jankyn, a man cannot serve two masters!'

I smiled to hide my confusion. I was surprised that Beaufort had even noticed me, but I should have known better. I was also wary of Creton. I did not wish to alienate him. However, he asked no further questions, but took me into an alcove in the passageway outside the hall, dug into his wallet and pulled out a fine, thin roll of parchment. It had been sealed once in shiny red wax now chipped, dry and broken. I carefully unrolled it. The vellum had turned a shiny brown, but the ink was still a bright mauve. It began with the usual phraseology. '*Richard, Roi d'Angleterre ... á notre cher esquier Jean Creton.*' I glanced immediately at the bottom of the page and noted that the scrawled 'Richardus Rex' looked geniune enough.

'This is the only letter extant,' commented Creton. 'You may read it now but you cannot take it with you. It's my last contact with the King.' His voice trailed off. I nodded and quickly read the letter. It said very little but I noted the important points: it was dated December 1399 when Richard was supposed to be in Pontefract; the King was joyful that he had escaped the clutches of his enemies, his friends were working for his restoration but, for the time being, he was sheltering in a place which Henry of Lancaster would, in the near future, find difficult to control. I handed it back to Creton.

'Did you know where the King was hiding?'

He shook his head. 'No, there were rumours it was Wales. But where?' He shrugged. I thought he was correct. Scotland would have been too dangerous and, in the autumn of 1399, Wales was seething with discontent. It was also near Ireland and only a short distance from Cheshire, the county most loyal to him.

'Did the King say anything when he came to Sonning? How was he dressed?' I asked.

'Very soberly in a long, miniver robe.'

'Were he and Maudelyn so alike?'

'Yes, in almost everything except height. Maudelyn was slightly taller,' Creton replied.

'Is there anything else you can tell me?'

'No, Monsieur, there is nothing else.'

I felt a tension between Creton and myself. There would be nothing else. I extended my hand and he clasped it. 'Thank you,' I said. 'Whatever you may think, Monsieur Creton, I do wish to find a solution to this mystery.'

'If that is so, I wish you good luck. Adieu,' Creton replied and, swinging on his heel sauntered back into the hall. I did not follow but left the palace and returned to my lodgings.

I spent the rest of the day reflecting on what Creton had said and the letter he had shown me. He believed (and I had no reason to doubt him) that Richard did escape from Pontefract, hid probably in Wales, sent him that letter and joined the earls' rebellion against Henry IV. But how did he escape? Who was it in Pontefract Castle? What happened to the King after the revolt failed? The questions whirled and turned in my brain. It was no clearer the next day when I prepared to return to the palace to meet Beaufort. I could only comfort myself with the thought that the Bishop might provide some answers.

I walked back through the now empty streets, the tatters and remnants of the previous day's pageants still clinging to pillars or lying along the rutted track. I crossed the bridge and went down a winding street alongside the cathedral. It must have been Sunday, the bells were clanging, their peals rolling like thunder above me. I remember the street narrowing, as it approached the square before the palace. I saw the sunlight on the square and, just in time, the shadow of the assassin as he struck out of the darkness.

I am, I admit, a fearful man, full of terrors. People will talk of the horrors of the battlefields, the ambuscade, or the siege, but nothing equals the silent assassin who strikes at mid-day. My legs turned to water, my belly and heart jerked in terror. The assassin was simply there, quiet, dark and threatening, the cruel sword and dagger glinting in the light. He was squat, black-haired with the pitted skin of a boar and the face of a monkey. He shuffled towards me, I drew my own dagger and adopted what I thought must be a fighting-stance. I have, over the years, been involved in many street and tavern brawls. Never, of course, of my own making, but I will say they are all the same. No romance, no heroic duel, no clash of arms in golden lists. The attack in Paris was no different. We closed, hugging and panting like lovers. He was thick-set, over-confident and allowed me inside his guard so he could not use his sword, which he dropped as he tried to twist his dagger for the killing thrust. I saw his eyes, smelt his body and felt the usual twinge of regret as his sweaty wrist slipped off mine and I dug my dagger deep up into his belly. He jerked, eyes staring, almost curious, and collapsed to his knees choking on his own blood. A few seconds later, he coughed, sighed and slid on to his stomach. I stood gulping air before tilting him over, trying to ignore the open sightless eyes staring up at me. He was well dressed, his purse was full, so I took it, together with a small roll of parchment from his wallet. I unrolled and read it, and rage replaced my fear. The man was Stephen Ludgall. He was English, a member of Beaufort's retinue. I pissed over his body and strode down towards the palace.

The guards slouched around the main gate, eyed my dirty, bloody clothes suspiciously and the captain in charge agreed most reluctantly to take my message in. He returned, snapped his fingers at me to follow and took me across the now empty bailey and in through a small tower door. Beaufort occupied the main hall or solar, a huge room hastily decorated to cover the bleak, stone walls and floor. He was seated at the top of a long polished table, surrounded by a pile of documents with two clerks at either side, their writing-trays before them. Beaufort rose, smiling, as I entered the room, he dismissed the clerks and held out a soft, beringed hand for me to kiss. I ignored it, throwing the parchment I had taken from the assassin on to the table. Beaufort stared at me curiously before picking it up to read.

'So,' he said, letting it drop from his fingers. 'This is a safe conduct issued by me to a member of my retinue. Why do you have it? And why should it make you so surly?'

'I took it from the assassin who just tried to kill me!' I snapped.

'So?'

'He was from your retinue!'

'Are you saying that I sent him?'

'I repeat, he was from your retinue!'

'But not from my household. Look!' Beaufort spread his hands, 'My retinue includes many people I do not know, so, tell me what happened!'

I did, sparing no details. When I had finished he shook his head. 'I swear, Matthew,' he said softly, 'I knew nothing of this and accept that someone in England wishes you dead. A person who knows not only that you are here but why.'

'A member of the Secret Commission?' I asked.

'Perhaps. There could be others. The cause of the Whyte Harte and the memory of Richard have not yet faded. You have seen the devastation in France. Richard still haunts our own King, even the French know that. You saw the tableau the day we arrived in Paris. The maidens defending the trapped Whyte Harte?'

I nodded while Beaufort stared dully at the table before rousing himself. 'Well,' he said, 'your journey to France.

Has it been profitable?'

I told him about my conversation with Creton, the letter
and the conclusions I had drawn. He agreed with them but
his eyes were guarded as if he knew more. 'So you will
search in Wales?'

'Perhaps,' I lied. I did not tell him that Prophett's
memorandum had indicated the place I should visit. I did
not trust Beaufort. Cunning, devious. I think he saw me as
a pawn in his own complex game of chess. Moreover, the
fewer who knew where I was, the safer I would be. I also
felt angry at the attack on my life and Beaufort's smooth
explanation and half-truths. I could not leave without
showing him that he did not fully control the game.

'My Lord,' I began, 'I am sorry to hear of your
difficulties with the King.'

Beaufort's eyes narrowed and I felt the tension which
gripped him. 'What difficulties?' he muttered.

'Oh,' I answered vaguely, 'the rumours that His Grace
has not accepted too kindly the Holy Father's enhance-
ment of your position. It is ...'

'A pity,' Beaufort interrupted sharply, his mouth now a
thin steel trap. 'A great pity, Master Jankyn, but,' he waved
a hand airily, 'these setbacks occur. However, I thank you
for your concern.' He smiled. 'I am also concerned for you,
Matthew. You are not safe here. You will leave for
England. Members of my household, with an escort of
French knights, leave tomorrow for Rouen and then the
coast. You will go with them. You will be safe.' He gave me
further details and then extended his hand for me to kiss
as a sign the interview was over. This time I knelt and
Beaufort lightly touched my shoulder. 'I think you are
near the truth, Master Jankyn, and feel you cannot trust
anyone. But trust me and all will be well.'

I left the palace, cheered by his words but fully
determined that of all the people I should trust, His
Eminence Bishop Henry Beaufort of Winchester, was
certainly not one of them.

I followed Beaufort's instructions and returned to the palace the following day. I had packed all my belongings and had to wait in the crowded bailey while the escort prepared to leave. Beaufort's retainers, clerks, messengers and officials were ready to travel light. They sat muffled in their cloaks though I could see many were well armed, distrustful of the country and, perhaps, their hosts. The French escort, a group of knight bannerets dressed in half-armour, were surly and sullen. They hardly bothered to talk to us, except in terse, sharp sentences but they were professionals, they formed a ring about us and led us safely through the narrow streets of Paris.

We came to no harm except for odd curses or pieces of filth thrown at us and soon we were through the city gates where the cavalcade broke into a quick canter, travelling fast through the countryside. We stopped one night at a small fortified manor house. Our escort kept to itself while we, too tired to talk, ate our scanty rations and gratefully curled up on the dirty hall floor. By the following evening we were approaching Rouen. English scouts and patrols stopped us and carefully examined our warrants and passes before letting us proceed. This proved too much for the French who objected loudly amongst themselves at being stopped and searched in their own country. At a ford across one of the many tributaries of the Seine, their leader waved in front of us, shouting 'Rouen! Rouen!' then he rasped orders to his companions. They obeyed immediately, turning their horses and thundering off in a cloud of dust along the road they had come. We resigned ourselves to their departure, slightly relieved they had gone, and continued on our way to Calais.

It was a dangerous journey. Although nominally controlled by the English, the countryside was plagued by free-booters, mercenaries and outlaws, as well as members of the Jacquerie and Tuechiens. The latter were fearsome and I heard rumours from my companions that they not only killed but also ate their victims. The countryside we

passed through was ideal for ambush, undulating fields
dotted and broken up by clumps of wood and forest. The
villages, or villettes, were deserted, burnt-out settlements,
few moved along the road while ditches were polluted with
the rotting corpses of animals. Once we were attacked by a
band of outlaws but they were not mounted and we
managed to break through. On another occasion we came
across the hanging bodies of what must have been two
English archers. They swung from the low-lying bough of
an oak tree. Beneath each of them were the remains of a
fire. The unfortunates, probably messengers, had been
hanged and left to die above slow, burning fires. We
pressed on, riding fast, until we entered the protecting
English pale round Calais. The port was as busy as ever but
we welcomed the bustle and frenzied activity after the
sinister silence of the countryside. We stayed one night
there and easily secured passage on an empty merchant
ship returning to Dover. So relieved was I to be out of
war-torn France I even forgot to be seasick.

23

I landed at Dover at the beginning of Holy Week. The
church bells were quiet, the townspeople involved in the
sacred three-day ceremonies; it was customary for the
government in London to be suspended while men turned
from temporal things to meditate, at least for a while, upon
the mysteries of Christ. Although I still prayed to the
Virgin, I felt little attraction in observing the sacred feasts
and decided to take advantage of the lull to ride to Oxford.
I stopped for a while in London to rest my horses and
check upon my belongings in my garret and the goldsmith

who banked my money and valuables. I studiously avoided visiting Westminster or any of the usual haunts where Beaufort's retainers might see me.

Two days later, as the bells of Oxford rang to announce Easter Sunday, I returned to the university town where my involvement in the cause of Richard II and the Whyte Harte had begun. It is strange that when you return to a place from your past, everything always seems narrower, smaller, not as massive as you once thought. The halls of residence were there, great timbered houses with their black beams and white facings, the narrow cobbled streets, the wide expanse of Broad Street and the parchment sellers and taverns of Catte Street. Here, almost ten years before, I had fled from a vengeful crowd and sought shelter in Sturmey's house, only to watch Oldcastle destroy him and Mathilda. She was still looked after by an aged nurse, sitting marooned in time, believing her father would soon return from business. There was little change, except her black hair was streaked with thin strands of grey, her white face drawn and lined, her eyes blank though, once or twice, I caught glimpses of intelligence, flickers of recognition, but they spluttered and died like coals in a dampened fire. The old nurse was kind enough and I made sure that all Mathilda's affairs were in order. I was about to leave, kissing her gently on the brow and turning to go, when suddenly she rose and called out my name, 'Matthew'. I turned, expectant, but she stood, eyes staring, mouth half open, and I realised she had forgotten what she was about to say.

I made my farewells and by the end of Easter week was back in London, going direct to Beaufort's chambers in Westminster Hall where I received a message to meet John Prophett, the silent, ubiquitous clerk to the chancery. I found him in his chamber at the back of the hall, a small, lime-washed room bare of any ornaments, smelling of wax, tallow and parchment. There were rolls of vellum piled high on shelves around the room, trunks, caskets and chests packed to the top with memoranda, letters, indentures and all the other paraphernalia of good government. Prophett seemed genuinely pleased to see me. He looked expectantly at me but I told him I could not yet report on my mission to France. 'Oh,' he replied disappointedly, wiping ink-stained fingers on the front of a dirty, stained gown. 'I thought you would bring us some news, some more information.' He ran a bony hand through his straggly, grey hair and turned, muttering, to scrabble amongst the parchments on his desk. 'Here,' he said triumphantly. 'This is the report of the Secret Commission's discussions with Sir Thomas Swynnerford and Sir Robert Waterton, Richard II's gaolers. It is worth reading.' He cleared a stool, so I sat and read the document. It began with the usual official statements.

A report drawn up by John Prophett, chief clerk of the chancery and a member of the Secret Commission set up by Bishop Beaufort to make enquiries and obtain answers from Sir Thomas Swynnerford and Sir Robert Waterton, gaolers of Richard II at Pontefract Castle in the first year of King Henry IV's reign 1399/1400. Both knights had been summoned under the secret seal to the meeting of the Commission held at Westminster Hall in March 1419. Sir Thomas Swynnerford had to be carried to the meeting because of an ulcerous leg, whilst Sir Robert Waterton had become enfeebled by his long years in the King's service. Each man was questioned separately and yet both came up with the same account. Richard II had been captured at Flint and brought across England to the Tower where his abdication had been accepted. Under oath the two gaolers stated that they had collected King Richard from Leeds Castle in Kent and taken him to Knaresborough before transferring him to Pontefract in Yorkshire. They maintained that Richard had been quiet and co-operative; he had not uttered curses or attempted to escape but accepted heartily the arrangements made for his incarceration.

Both knights agreed that they had attempted to taunt and bait him, pointing out how his stubborn pride had brought his downfall. The deposed king, however, had reacted without malice, saying little except to curse the perfidy of his own subjects and openly avowing that Henry of Lancaster would find it harder to keep the crown than to seize it. At Pontefract Castle the King was placed in a chamber in one of the towers. He was not chained or ill-treated but provided with the necessities and even comforts, such as fire and light. Both swore with solemn oaths that during the rising in January 1400, King Richard had not escaped from Pontefract and was seen by them and many others in the castle. On further questioning on how the King died, Sir Robert Waterton believed that when the King heard that the rising had been such a failure he fell into a black melancholy, refusing food and drink, and eventually starved himself to death. Sir Thomas Swynnerford corroborated this, pointing out that they had often tried to force food and water into Richard's mouth, but he had stoutly refused to eat or drink.

Sir Thomas Erpingham, a member of the Secret Commission, asked if the King had said anything significant when the news arrived that the earls' rising had failed. Sir Thomas Swynnerford said he had heard nothing except moans of despair, though Sir Robert Waterton claimed that Richard had asked time and again what had happened to the leaders of the rebellion. Both knights assured the Commission that by the middle of February 1400 Richard was dead. A messenger had been sent posthaste to London to inform the King and preparations were implemented to bury the body. The corpse was dressed by a local physician in the presence of a number of clerks, servants and gentry holding land around Pontefract Castle. Sir Robert Waterton had insisted on this so that no future allegation could be made that they had murdered the King. Indeed, Waterton maintained, the physician had also been instructed to check for signs of poison and to look for the usual effects, such as discoloration of the skin. The physician had pronounced that no traces could be found.

The body was placed in an open coffin, the head resting on a black cushion, the face exposed from the lower forehead to the chin. It was then encased in lead and transferred south on the King's own orders, stopping at principal towns and meeting-places so people could view Richard's corpse. Both knights swore they could

*not understand how the rumours grew that Richard had escaped
from Pontefract or that he could still be alive. They saw him die,
dressed for burial and actually accompanied the body to its resting
place at Kings Langley. Both men also swore oaths that the King
had not been murdered at Pontefract or allowed to escape, even for
a few minutes, from their custody.*

I rolled the parchment up and slipped it into my wallet.
'It is not much,' I observed drily. 'Waterton's and
Swynnerford's story is the accepted one. They took great
pains to condemn as false tales about Richard's either
escaping from Pontefract or being murdered there.'

Prophett looked at me. 'Yes,' he replied slowly, biting his
lower lip with small, discoloured teeth. 'I cannot
understand what has happened. On the one hand we have
Richard safely in Pontefract Castle, and on the other he is
wandering around England stirring up revolution.' He
paused to sigh deeply before continuing. 'Of course, there
are always legends that a king never dies but this story is
believed by Franciscans, leading churchmen and some of
the principal lords of the realm. It would be pleasant to
believe that the mammet in Scotland was the cause of all
these rumours but he does not appear until 1404 and even
you,' his little black eyes flickered towards me, 'even you,
who had not known Richard, soon discovered he was an
impostor. So why the mystery?'

'Look,' I retorted, 'I know, Master Prophett, that you are
a most able clerk, proficient with documents, memoranda
and ferreting out facts and drawing up lists. Your work,' I
flattered, 'is excellent, but surely you may have missed
something? Some important item in the documents for
that year 1399 to 1400. Some clue which may help us to
resolve this problem. I cannot ask you,' I added hastily, not
wanting to offend this self-important little man, 'I merely
beg you to scrutinise once more amongst the documents
for that year, the household accounts especially, to see if
you can find that clue.'

Prophett rubbed his eyes until they were red-rimmed. 'I

will see what I can do,' he answered. 'And if there is any information, I can contact you where?'

I informed him of where my lodgings were, the street and how to reach it, he nodded, wrote the information down and I left him scurrying like a rabbit round his small hutch of a room.

I rode back up Fleet Street into Bowyers Row past Paternoster Row and entered Cheapside. The crowds were still celebrating the feast of Easter and the main thoroughfare was packed with revellers, small children carrying green boughs, and young girls and women with wreaths of spring flowers in their hair. I stepped into one of the many taverns for food and ale whilst considering what I had learnt from Prophett's memorandum. The conclusions were not much. I was inclined to accept as truth that Richard II had been imprisoned in Pontefract Castle and died there of natural causes, but it still left other problems to resolve. Why did so many people believe, especially Isabella and Creton, that they had seen Richard during the revolt of 1400 and actually received letters from him? Perhaps there was some shred of evidence we had overlooked? Somebody was lying, but I felt as if I was simply stumbling in the dark.

I was also concerned by the attack on me in Paris and felt that even here in London I was still in danger. Nothing significant or extraordinary, just a feeling of unease, like a cold draught upon your back. I wandered out of the tavern down into Poultry and there at the junction of Cornhill and Lombard Street I stood and watched a miracle play being performed on a crude stage. It was pleasant to feel the warm spring air and forget my own problems. Keeping my hand firmly on my pouch against the many pickpockets who ran like rivers through the crowds, I watched a scene from the Gospel, the beheading of John the Baptist; the actor was cunningly whisked away in exchange for a fake corpse and a false head spilling ox blood while the audience shrieked with excitement. I think it was then, watching this scene, that the seeds of an idea began to grow in my mind. The actors had transferred fakes around the stage to provide an effect, the deception was so successful because it was so quick and I wondered if this is what had happened to Richard II. People appearing where they were not supposed to be. A well organised and staged event. I also realised the weakness of Beaufort's Secret Commission. So far we had been spectators, reacting to whatever was displayed for our view, but we had made no attempt to discover if what we saw was fiction or fact. All the documents we examined were those issued by King Henry IV and the people we interviewed and questioned were, in the main, supporters of King Henry. Surely there was somebody from Richard's party still alive who could provide another perspective?

The following day I went along to the chancery records in the great store-rooms behind Westminster Hall and went through the assize documents of 1399 and 1400. These were records of the courts of the King's Justices in Eyre before whom were tried all those implicated in the conspiracy of 1400 against Henry IV. Surprisingly, there were none. Only entries that such and such a person was tried before the King and condemned to death. I took along Prophett's memorandum and went through the entire document and realised that there were no recorded transactions because the rebels were caught in arms against the King and therefore immediately (or ipso facto as the lawyers would put it) guilty of treason and sentenced to instant execution. Men such as Maudelyn, Richard II's chaplain, were simply brought in front of Henry at Oxford, condemned and taken to the Elms for the grisly spectacle of public execution. There was not a shred of evidence to indicate they were given any chance to answer the accusations put before them.

I searched amongst the records, long rolls of vellum entered by some anonymous pen cataloguing the passions, emotions and, on some occasions, deaths of people who

had fought on behalf of Richard. Most of the entries gave
few details but finally I came to one containing items of
interest. This was a report of the Justices in Eyre who had
toured Cheshire in 1400. The records were rich in their
references to treasonable conspiracies, plots, covens and
minor rebellions on Richard's behalf. I scrutinised each
entry until I found the section I wanted. A group of men,
thirty in all, mostly from the village or suburbs of
Nantwich in Cheshire. They had been arraigned before
the King's justices for attempting to free the captured
Richard II as he was moved from Wales in the late summer
of 1399 to Westminster. I had read of this in Prophett's
memorandum. In the main, they were simple peasants or
archers, and so bound over to keep the peace. One,
however, was not. John Felton, master bowman, was
imprisoned in the Fleet for one year, fined one hundred
shillings and neighbours and friends had to compound a
further two hundred shillings for his future good
behaviour. This was the man I was looking for. Somebody
with personal loyalty to the cause of the Whyte Harte and
Richard II who could give me an additional view of the
tapestry of events of 1399 to 1400.

I left London the following morning, praying that
Felton would still be living in Nantwich. The winter was
dead and the warm spring sun had dried the mud and
smoothed out the rough ruts in the road. I made good
progress, riding hard by day and taking the minimum of
shelter at night, either out in the open wrapped in my
cloak or in some small hostelry or tavern. Since the attack
in Paris, I went well armed with sword, buckler, dagger
and a huge, cruel crossbow which swung from the pommel
of my saddle. In three days I was in Cheshire, saddle-sore
and weary but safe with no sight of pursuit or treachery.
On the fourth day, late in the evening, I approached
Nantwich, a small market town, a mixture of black-and-
white-timbered merchant houses as well as the usual hovels
and cottages of the poor peasants. I reasoned that Felton,

if he was still alive, would be well known and decided not to waste time subterfuge or fraud but to confront the problem openly. I found the largest hostelry in the town, a great spacious affair bearing the sign of the Golden Eagle. I stabled my horse, secured a small chamber and walked round Nantwich.

It was a prosperous town with a number of churches and merchants grown fat on trade in wine, fish, spices, tapestries and above all, wool; smug and secure, glorying in its guilds. I walked for a while and approached the gates of the town, mapping out the routes in my mind, taking note of the tortuous alleyways and swarming narrow runnels. I observed the market, the rows of stalls with hawkers offering their fruit, chestnuts, pins and girdles; weavers' wives displayed on their arms long drapes of costly cloth woven from pure wool. There was a dispute going on in one of the churchyards over the depositing of rubbish and I followed the crowd which gathered as it stormed off to the Guildhall to lodge its protests. Here I looked for the clerk, that busy, inquisitive man who knows everything about the city's affairs and I finally found him, small, balding rosy-cheeked with the glassy eyes and long nose of the born informer. I introduced myself as a clerk from London in Nantwich to do business with John Felton, master bowman and burgess of the city. The man smirked, looked askance at my description, but nodded his head. 'Yes,' he replied, he knew Felton, where he lived and, once I had paid the obligatory bribe, he gave me directions on how to find him.

I left the Guildhall, passed the butchers and fish-mongers who polluted the lanes with reeking piles of blood, bones and entrails, down streets fouled by steaming deposits of horse and cattle, and hemmed in by the crowded tenements. After losing my way a number of times, I found the tavern nestling between a large house, its sign display-ing the crude figure of a bull with horns almost as huge as the door it fronted. Inside, dark and musty, there was the usual scattering of trestle tables and rough stools. The host approached, servile and watchful, wiping his wet hands on his greasy apron. I asked him where John Felton was, he grimaced and nodded to the far corner where a man sat slouched in a chair over a tankard of ale. I ordered two more from the landlord and went across to sit beside the fellow, who looked up blearily at my approach. In his middle fifties, Felton looked and smelt like a toper, his white, whiskered face red and sweaty with the ale he drank. 'Master Felton,' I lied, 'I would like to introduce myself as John Appleby, clerk and chronicler. I am desirous of collecting information on the reign of the late Richard II. I know, by public report and common repute, that you were a member of his royal bodyguard, the Cheshire archers, and took part in an attempt to free him after his capture at Flint in 1399.'

I suppose, looking back, it was a rather blunt introduction but I did not waste time for the man posed no threat to me. He was an old soldier and the best way to their hearts is free ale and flattering words. Felton was no different. He was deep in his cups and babbled like a brook. I will not bore you with all his ramblings, indeed, I forget most of them now, but he made two interesting allusions. First, he corroborated what Creton had said, that Richard and his chaplain, Maudelyn, were identical though Maudelyn was slightly taller than Richard. The second was much more significant. He described the attack on the convoy which brought Richard from Lichfield down to Westminster. He rambled but, in the end, gave a startling description of this would-be rescue attempt. It was organised by one of Richard's followers, the Earl of Salisbury, and the attack was launched just before Henry IV's procession entered the city of Coventry. Felton was bemused, confessing that as one of the troop commanders he had been puzzled by the instructions given to him, to attack the convoy but resist any attempt to engage in hand-to-hand combat. 'It was,' he said blearily, 'almost as if

the attack was a sham, as if we were to play a part and
nothing more. Indeed, that is how I was captured. I
thought we were there to free the imprisoned king. We
were to shower the procession with arrows and then draw
off. I ignored the order and led my small troop into the
heart of the procession where I believed Richard was
riding. Indeed, I saw him there, lashed to his horse.' Felton
blinked, screwing up his eyes in concentration. 'Of course,'
he continued, 'the attack was a failure. I was captured and
imprisoned but you know, master scribbler, even to this
day I cannot understand why the attack was launched with
so little effort to actually free Richard from his captors.'
Having said that, he stuck his nose back into his tankard as
a sign that he could and would say no more.

24

I left Felton in his dirty tavern, no wiser than when I met
him, though the vague form of an idea commenced to
grow in my soul, the beginnings of a picture of what
actually did happen rather than what is reputed to have
happened. I did not return to London but continued my
journey through Cheshire to one of its small ports and
secured passage on a fishing boat to the Isle of Anglesey,
just off the north coast of Wales. I left my horse stabled at
an outlying farm and crossed the straits safely and
securely. One of the fishermen told me that the island had
once been sacred to the Druids before the cult had been
destroyed by the great Caesar and his legions. I found it
hard to believe, the island was no more than a windswept
rocky plateau where small villages and a Franciscan
monastery huddled in dips, protected against the winds

which whipped in from the sea, though the monks had reclaimed the rocky soil, turning it into good arable and pasture-land.

They greeted me warmly, happy for any visitor, especially one with some education and knowledge of what was happening in the outside world. I recounted the scandals and gossip from the court, how the war in France was proceeding, a few stories about certain prelates and abbots and the general witticisms and items of conversation that this reclusive community eagerly lapped up. I continued my deception as Appleby, a scrivener and chronicler, from London, eager to collect information about the followers of Richard II. The prior, a small, fat, nut-brown man, was only too willing to give what scraps of knowledge he had. I knew from Prophett's memorandum that this friary had been hot in its support for the cause of the Whyte Harte and of the Welsh rebel, Owen Glendower, but this had been years past and the Franciscans involved in such affairs had either been moved or gone to their eternal reward.

I let the prior babble on about those stirring times and, when the time was ripe, posed the one question I had travelled so far to ask. 'Father,' I began gently, 'did Richard II ever visit this friary?'

'Oh, no, he did not,' the Franciscan replied in his sing-song Welsh accent.

'Then why,' I persisted in a puzzled fashion, 'did this friary so strongly espouse his cause? And, in so doing, draw every Franciscan house in Wales and England into the support of the Whyte Harte? After all,' I added, 'Richard did not support the Franciscans. His confessor was a Dominican and most of his patronage went to that order.'

The prior shrugged in ignorance. 'I do not really know,' he answered. 'Perhaps it was Maudelyn's influence.'

'You mean Richard Maudelyn?' I asked. 'The King's chaplain?'

'Yes,' the prior replied. 'I remember him. I was a novice then. He came and sheltered here, just before Richard was murdered. A strange man, Master Scrivener, they say he was the King's identical twin. I used to see him and, of course, heard the gossip about him. He was here for a short while under the protection of the prior, but disappeared shortly after Christmas in 1399 before the earls rose in rebellion against Henry IV. I know they tried to use poor Maudelyn, as the King, although common report had it that Richard was still imprisoned in Pontefract.'

'Did you see, hear or notice anything strange about Maudelyn when he was here?' I persisted, trying to hide my disappointment at what the prior had told me.

The prior paused, his eyes screwed up in concentration as he tried to remember. 'No,' he replied carefully. 'Nothing much except that he seemed to celebrate Mass in his own cell and kept to himself. Indeed, the brothers used to joke about him. They called him the hunting priest because every time they saw him he was wearing riding-boots as if he were about to join the chase.'

I questioned the man as carefully as I could but gained no further information. I accepted the bleak hospitality of another night at the friary before returning to the fishing village and buying passage back to the mainland.

Eight days after landing from Anglesey I was back in the noise and bustle of London. The news was all about the impending treaty with France and I realised why the countryside had been so empty for it had virtually been swept clean of men by the royal commission of array who were gathering a new army in the channel ports just in case the French refused to sign over their lands and their crown to King Henry of England. The news was proclaimed in Cheapside and from the cross of St Paul's. The taverns were full of chatter, gossip and hastily written ballads on one topic, the King's conquest of France. I ignored it all for it was irrelevant. The world of politics, war, battles and murders now seemed to be a dream. The Whyte Harte and the legends around it were the only reality and so, after a hasty inspection of my belongings, I walked down to Westminster to meet Prophett. I skirted Westminster Hall, searching along the offices at the back for Prophett's chamber. After a great deal of difficulty and losing my way down empty, lime-washed passageways, I found the place was barred, locked and secured. So I wandered until I met a clerk hurrying by, almost tripping over his long, ink-stained, russet gown, his arms full of sheaves and rolls of parchment.

'Prophett?' I asked, 'Master John Prophett? Is he in Westminster?'

I saw the surprise in the pale, pinched face.

'What is the matter?' I asked. 'Surely you know Master Prophett? He is the chief clerk in the chancery.'

'Master Prophett,' the man replied slowly, almost patiently, 'is dead. He was found murdered in St Marks Lane a few days ago.'

'Oh,' I replied, trying to hide my shock. 'I am sorry. I have been out of London on business. He was a friend. I did not know he had died.'

'Murdered!' came the quick reply. 'Master Prophett was murdered! His throat was slit from ear to ear.'

'For what reason?' I asked. 'He was a quiet, unassuming little man.'

'Why are men murdered?' came the sardonic reply. 'For money. Master Prophett's throat was cut and so was his purse from his belt.'

I nodded, let the man go by and returned to my own lodgings. I sat there and pieced together the facts I had gathered. I knew, vaguely, the real cause of the mystery behind the Whyte Harte and the legend about Richard II and also that Prophett had been killed not for money but because he was on his way to give me some information he had gathered.

The next morning I returned to Westminster to make

enquiries about Prophett's work in the days preceding his death. It took a lot of careful questioning, tact and diplomacy, but I eventually discovered the truth. Prophett had spent most of his time in the record or muniment-room which housed the household books of Henry IV. These are kept for every regnal year and show the income and expenditure of the royal household and provide a great deal of information about the King's business and the affairs of the court. Usually, such records are handed in at the central treasury or exchequer in Westminster for an audit to take place, after which they are kept in the record-room before being despatched to the Tower for storage. I concluded that the only way I would find out what Prophett wanted to tell me was to go through the same record-books. He had begun with the account for the year 1399 to 1400, a thick collection of folios sewn together, page after page bearing small, carefully written entries under a variety of headings: gifts, messages sent, goods bought, monies spent, monies collected, wages paid, guests entertained, the list was endless. I spent days in that small, musty room carefully reading the vexatious document which promised so much but gave so little. I ignored the protests of the clerks, their squeals and fluttering around me, angry at this intrusion into their own domain. I worked late at night but still I found nothing.

I returned white-faced and red-eyed to my lodgings and in the morning awoke with a groan as I realised that I had to return. At first I found nothing but I refused to give up and began reading again, this time paying more attention to the more boring, mundane matters of the household until I found it, a small ink-written entry under the heading 'Wages'. I stared at it in disbelief and knew then what Prophett had discovered. I found it hard to conceal my excitement. I was near to solving the mystery, I had plumbed its depths and knew more than any other of the thousands who had fought and died for Richard, the truth behind his deposition and the fascinating cause of the Whyte Harte.

Nevertheless, there was other business to attend to. It was now four weeks after Easter and I realised Beaufort must have returned to London. Common report said the King was outside Paris and I hoped that Beaufort had been dispatched home to keep an eye on domestic matters. I was not disappointed. The usual gossips reported Beaufort had returned and was residing in the royal manor of Eltham, south of the Thames.

I arrived there unannounced and demanded an immediate audience. Beaufort met me in the large, bare, wooden wainscotted hall, dressed in the full regalia of a bishop, his blood-red robes made fashionable with trimmings of white ermine and a large, gold necklace with a cluster of gems on his chest. He looked tired, his eyes guarded as if still wary of me since our confrontation in Paris. He ushered me solicitously as ever to the far end of the long table which ran down the centre of the hall, ordering wine and a tray of sweetmeats. I knew this only gave him time to study my face and reach his own conclusions.

'Master Jankyn,' he smiled. 'I have been looking for you to ask for a report. You have been most elusive.'

'Your messengers,' I replied tartly, 'did not look carefully enough. I have been in Westminster and have not moved from my lodgings in St Marks Lane.'

'True! True!' Beaufort nodded. 'Not all the men that I have are of your calibre, Matthew.'

'You mean John Prophett?' I observed. 'He was not a man of such calibre for he had his throat cut in St Marks Lane. I think it was because he wanted to see me. Common report says he was murdered by a thief but, my Lord, we both know better. He was murdered because he had information which I had asked for.' I stopped to sip from the cup of wine Beaufort had offered. 'Master Prophett,' I continued, 'was a professional chancery clerk. He had been given the task of drawing up a memorandum, which he did, but when I told him there was something missing, he went back and searched the records until he found it. I believe what he discovered cost him his life.'

Beaufort pursed his lips, nodding as if accepting as truth everything I said.

'I regret Prophett's death,' Beaufort murmured, 'and accepted it with deep sadness but have you found what he discovered? And where have you been?' he added more brusquely. 'The last time my spies provided information you were returning to London from the west country.'

'My Lord,' I replied smoothly, happy to have an advantage over him, 'I think I should leave my report until I have proceeded a little further. I have come to ask favours of you. There are other members of the Secret Commission besides myself and the dead Prophett, Master Glanville and Sir Thomas Erpingham.'

'What are these favours?' Beaufort interrupted curtly.

'I want the Commission to study two things. First, to ask the friars in the chapel of the royal manor of Kings Langley if the corpse buried there was sheathed in lead.'

'And the second favour?'

'I want the Commission to search the royal tomb at Westminster.'

'The first is simple,' Beaufort replied. 'The second may pose problems.'

'You are the Lord Chancellor and Bishop of Winchester,' I replied. 'You have the power to ask any questions you wish and seek all the answers.'

I could see that the Bishop, despite his calm demeanour, was excited and curious. 'Why not you, Master Jankyn?' he asked. 'Surely you could do this?'

'No. I would prefer to stay here safe and secure in your household. I would ask that Sir Thomas Erpingham be sent to Kings Langley and that Master Glanville carry out the inspection of the royal tomb at Westminster.'

'Then,' Beaufort said, 'can I ask the reason for this?'

'For the moment, my Lord, I would prefer you not to insist and remind you that Richard's corpse was buried twice, first at Kings Langley in 1400, and secondly in great pomp at Westminster in 1414.'

'Of course I know that,' Beaufort answered. 'Henry IV did not wish to give Richard royal honours, whilst his son later wished to atone for his father's omissions. I know all this, but why these searches, these questions? What is this to do with the cause of the Whyte Harte?'

I simply smiled, so Beaufort shrugged and let the matter drop.

I obtained and got permission from Beaufort to stay in his household, safe from any assassin hunting me in London. I passed the days pleasantly enough. I was given a small garret and moved some of my belongings in there. I obtained from the Bishop's chancery a writing-tray with inkstand, pen, pumice-stone and long rolls of polished parchment and, when I was not flirting with the servant girls, I passed the time putting down the pieces of information I had acquired, paying careful attention to poor Prophett's memorandum. I had a clear picture of what had happened to Richard II and the mystery behind the Whyte Harte, but there were other items of information I still needed.

About eleven days after I had made my request to Beaufort, I was summoned to his chamber where he was waiting for me with a rather tired-looking Erpingham. The latter ignored me whilst the Bishop sat slumped in the room's one and only chair, sipping wine from a cup. 'Sir Thomas,' Beaufort began, 'has something to report.'

'Not much,' the knight snapped. 'I travelled to Kings Langley and interviewed a number of the monks who had been involved in the burial of Richard when he was brought from Pontefract. The details are quite simple. The deposed king's corpse, sheathed in a coat of lead, was interred in a plain, wooden coffin. When Henry V exhumed the body, the wooden coffin was opened and left to rot but the corpse in its leaden sheet was placed in a new coffin and carried to Westminster. I understand from the chaplain who accompanied it that the body was not exposed to view and buried in the tomb Richard himself had provided alongside his wife in the chapel of Edward the Confessor at Westminster Abbey.'

'You are sure?' I asked excitedly, 'that the body was exhumed as you say?'

Erpingham snorted. 'I am not a liar! I spent days on the road to find such a useless item of information!'

'I do thank you,' I said smoothly.

Beaufort looked at me, eyebrows arched. 'What does all this mean, Jankyn?'

'For the moment, my Lord,' I replied, 'just another interesting piece in a complex puzzle.'

Three days later Glanville returned. When I met him in Beaufort's chamber I could see he had not liked his task. He sat and recited what he had found in a dry, legal monotone. 'Four years before he was deposed,' Glanville began, 'Richard had a splendid tomb prepared for himself and his first wife, Anne of Bohemia, in St Edward's Chapel at Westminster Abbey. A beautiful, marble sarcophagus at the back of the altar with the wooden effigies of Richard and Anne of Bohemia on top. Anne had been buried there in 1395 but, as both of you know, Richard was interred in Kings Langley before the corpse was exhumed and taken to Westminster.' Glanville turned and looked at Beaufort. 'We opened the tomb at night, removing the wooden effigies on top and the steel pins which kept the marble slab on top of the tomb. This was not easy to remove for when the Queen had been buried, it had first been sealed with a resinous cement thrust in the open joints, thus sealing the marble. When the tomb was opened and closed again after the burial of King Richard's body, this cement was not re-used but a simple mortar paste. The inside, which we examined in the light of a ring of torches, consisted of a chamber about seven feet deep, the grave itself being about two feet under the Abbey floor. At the bottom of the tomb were two coffins, both made of elm, the one on the left, the Queen's, already in a state of decay and decomposition.' Glanville coughed and cleared his throat as if trying to erase from his memory the distasteful scene. 'We saw a white skeletal leg thrust through a rotting door. The King's coffin was beginning to show signs of decay, though we had to use plumber's shears to remove the lid.' Glanville stopped speaking and breathed deeply. 'The features of the King were not apparent, the gauze sheet under the coffin-lid was rotten and the corpse itself nothing more than a skeleton, a man about six feet tall. There were no marks of violence upon the skeleton or anything worthy of note. The coffin was resealed, the slabs pulled back and cemented firm, the wooden effigies being replaced on top.'

'So,' Beaufort interjected, 'you found no signs of violence on the corpse?'

'None, my Lord.'

'No marks of strangulation, broken bones or anything to indicate the corpse was Maudelyn?'

Glanville shrugged. 'As a lawyer and a coroner, I have had to examine many corpses, even the skeletons of murdered men or women. There is always some indication of a violent death but none here.'

I scarcely bothered to question Glanville, one of the final pieces was in place and I did not want to give away the cause of my unease by any blunt questioning, so I limited myself to one. 'Master Glanville, are you sure that when the coffin-lid was removed, the King's corpse was open to view?'

Glanville flickered his narrow, hard eyes at me. 'It is as I have described,' he replied. He turned to Beaufort. 'Have you any more questions, my Lord?'

Beaufort shook his head. Glanville rose and, ignoring me, bowed to Beaufort and stalked angrily out of the chamber.

I was pleased by what he had reported and I asked Beaufort for one final favour; to order the coroners of London to search their records for a certain instruction which might have been issued by either the present King or his father. Beaufort, slightly puzzled, did not even bother to ask me the reason but agreed, promising he would dispatch the request the following morning. I already knew that the coroners would not find anything but it was a search I wanted made to satisfy my own curiosity. I controlled my excitement, carefully disguising the fact that I was now one of the few people in the kingdom who knew exactly what had happened to Richard II and the truth behind the legend of the Whyte Harte.

I think Beaufort sensed there was something wrong for, in the following days whenever we met, he stared at me carefully, slightly puzzled, as if a new element had entered the game which he could no longer control. He was right, for once, the clever bastard no longer controlled the intricate game of human chess he had set up. For myself, I was smug and content in what I knew but determined to revise everything carefully. The excitement was almost too much, I found I could not sleep at night, so I spent the time drawing up a long and detailed report which included all my findings. Once that was finished I went through it again, adding or crossing out, making other drafts until perfectly satisfied with the conclusions I had set down. Finally, Beaufort informed me that none of the city coroners had anything to report and only then did I ask him to set up a special meeting of the Secret Commission to which I could report.

25

We met a week later in a chamber in Beaufort's house. I had prepared well, happy that my Lord Bishop did not fully control the game though he still thought he did. The day before the Commission met, he handed me a letter. It was unopened but, as I broke the small, blood-red seal, I could feel the dread and hopelessness closing in. It was from Robert Arling, an Oxford lawyer charged to administer the affairs of Mathilda Sturmey of Catte Street. There were a few dry phrases which carried the heart-stopping news. Mathilda was dead, of a fever, so the letter said, though it implied that she had simply lost the will to live. I crumpled the letter in my wallet and said little and acted no differently. I suppose there are certain events and experiences which defy expression. I grieved. God knows I still do, but I hid it well. I did not want Lord Lucifer, Bishop Beaufort, to see the damage caused.

The Secret Commission met, as I have said, in Beaufort's luxurious, silk-draped, velvet-carpeted private chamber. I remember it was dark. A thunderstorm had swept in over the Thames and large, heavy drops of rain pelted the stained-glass windows of the room; wax candles winked and glittered on the silver and gold ornaments, catching and fanning the glow of a ruby, sapphire or some other precious stone. We sat round the beeswax polished table. Beaufort welcomed us, apologising for the day as if he took responsibility even for the weather. He turned to me. 'Master Jankyn, you asked for this meeting?'

'Yes, my Lord,' I interrupted briskly, 'for it may well be the last!'

I felt each of my companions stiffen. Beaufort looked surprised before his eyes narrowed to conceal his astonishment. 'What do you mean?' Erpingham broke in abruptly.

'Oh, you will see, Sir Thomas,' I answered nonchalantly. 'Be sure of that.'

'Then get on with it,' Glanville snapped.

'I will. I will,' I replied. 'But, before I begin, let me assure each of you that all I shall say has already been written down and sent, sealed, to certain people for security. They will, you may be certain, open and publish what I have written if something untoward happens to me.' I smiled expansively, savouring the moment as one does a good mouthful of wine. Beaufort stared down at the table, Glanville smiled, his half-open lips revealing broken, blackened teeth. Erpingham just gazed at me dully through heavy-lidded eyes.

'Richard II,' I began, 'was deposed by his cousin, Henry of Lancaster, in the late summer of 1399. Prophett's memorandum and the accepted, published version of events is that this King was captured in Wales, brought to London and, once the legal niceties were completed, hustled north to Pontefract Castle. The following January, certain earls sympathetic to Richard rose in rebellion. They claimed they had freed Richard from Pontefract but, of course, Henry IV proclaimed this was really Richard Maudelyn, the deposed monarch's chaplain with whom he was identical. Of course, the rebellion failed and Richard, imprisoned in Pontefract Castle, heard of the failure and starved himself to death.'

'Yes, yes!' Glanville tersely interrupted. 'But this is well known to all. So why repeat it?'

'No real reason,' I answered, 'except to dismiss it as a tissue of lies.' I held up my hand to fend off Sir Thomas Erpingham's angry exclamation. 'Let us look at the evidence,' I continued. 'Richard is supposed to have died at Pontefract, yet for years afterwards, people believed he was still alive: his second wife, Isabella; the French court; his squire Creton; the Percies, the most powerful earls in England, as well as other members of the nobility; the Franciscan order, two of whose members went to the scaffold for their beliefs. Oldcastle, the heretical Lollards, as well,' I added bitterly, 'as the hundreds of little people, men like my father, or the poor bastard Sturmey.' I saw the look of puzzlement in Erpingham's eyes. 'Oh, you would not know Sturmey, not even if you rode your horse over him!' I ignored his look of anger and continued. 'The belief of all these people, that Richard II was still alive, was the foundation-stone for the cause of the Whyte Harte. So many people believed that Richard had survived, there must be some truth in the matter.'

'So far,' Erpingham drily interrupted, 'you have spoken a lot but said very little.'

I suppose I should have acted differently but the casual arrogance of that would-be assassin stung me into a reply. 'Oh, Sir Thomas,' I said casually, 'the truth is so apparent. Richard did not need to escape from Pontefract, he was never there!' I heard the quick indrawn breaths and saw Beaufort smile in a smug self-satisfied way.

'Go on, Master Jankyn,' he almost lisped. 'Now I am sure you have our attention.'

'Richard,' I obligingly continued, 'escaped from Lichfield. Prophett says he was recaptured. He was not. Instead Maudelyn replaced him.'

Beaufort held up a slender, beringed hand to stop the flow of questions from both Glanville and Erpingham. 'But that does not make sense, Master Jankyn. If Richard escaped at Lichfield, then why did the band of Cheshire archers launch an attack in order to free him?'

'That was a sham. An attempt to convince the authorities that they still held Richard.'

'This is preposterous!' Erpingham shouted. 'King Henry IV would not be fooled!'

'Look at the facts,' I coolly replied. 'Before Lichfield, at

Conway and Flint, Richard was defiant but strangely amenable when he was brought to London and the Tower.'

'But was Maudelyn so like Richard?'

'Oh you should know that, Sir Thomas. Yes, he was, except in one respect. Maudelyn was slightly taller than Richard. A point I shall undoubtedly refer to again.'

Erpingham seemed to ignore this answer and leaned across the table, red-faced, his breath coming in short, sharp gasps. 'But King Henry would notice the physical differences.'

'Oh, I think he did,' I replied. 'Do you remember Prophett's memorandum and King Henry IV's words when he heard the rebel army had taken the field and King Richard was supposedly with them? Henry is supposed to have said that if he met Richard one of them would die. That was rather strange coming from a man who is reputed to have Richard safe under lock and key at Pontefract.'

'Are you saying,' Beaufort quietly asked, 'that Henry himself knew that Richard had escaped?'

'Yes, in view of later events I think he did. There was another entry in the council minutes for 14th February 1400. You must remember this came from Henry's closest advisers, who petitioned the King that if Richard was still alive he should be kept under close confinement. Again, rather strange that the King's own council did not know where Richard, was, yet, at the same time, they were authorising payments for him at Pontefract!'

'Jankyn,' Beaufort said silkily, his soft voice hiding the menace beneath, 'I think you owe us an explanation and the sooner we have it the better, so please continue.'

'Oh, it's a matter of perspective,' I began glibly, only too willing to annoy Beaufort even further. 'I was watching a play once in Cornhill when I suddenly realised that the reality depends upon where one stands. Actors can change scenes and make things appear, create an illusion, dreams.

Richard did that. Remember, he escaped after his capture in Flint.'

'Yes,' Erpingham interrupted brusquely. 'But he was later recaptured.'

'No, he was not,' I replied. 'He escaped. The man you recaptured was Maudelyn, or rather Richard's supporters let him be captured.'

'But that's foolish!' Glanville snapped.

'Oh, no, Maudelyn and Richard,' I continued, 'were identical, except Maudelyn was taller than the King. I suppose if we had witnesses about what the deposed king wore after his capture, certainly from Lichfield down from London and back to Pontefract, they would say he never wore boots but slippers or shoes. This enabled Maudelyn to appear shorter than he was.'

'And Richard?' Beaufort asked. 'What happened to the King?'

'He fled to Wales. The Welsh were friendly, and where better than to the Franciscan monastery in Anglesey? Near enough to Wales, close enough to Ireland, and if the situation became too dangerous he could take ship to France. Anyway, on Anglesey, he posed as Maudelyn, the priest, ensuring that he wore high riding-boots to enhance his own height. The brothers said he always celebrated Mass in his own cell, Richard, pretending to be a priest, would do that. He would never go through the blasphemy of a mock Mass in public. When the rebellion began in December 1399, Richard simply joined the rebels in their march on Sonning.'

'But, Jankyn,' Beaufort interrupted, 'you said that both squire Creton and Queen Isabella saw Richard and Maudelyn.'

'Ah!' I answered. 'They thought they did. What they saw was Richard or Maudelyn. The King in his own right or, when he wanted to, pretending to be Maudelyn the priest. He created a clever illusion which would out-fox and bewilder any spy in the Queen's household.'

'Did King Henry IV know this?' Erpingham asked.

'Oh, you know he did, Sir Thomas,' I replied. 'Of course he did! Probably at some time in London he realised the man he had captured was not Richard and that a clever trick had been staged, which is why he sent Maudelyn to Pontefract, well away from the public gaze just in case someone else noticed him. Remember the two gaolers, Waterton and Swynnerford, were selected because of their loyalty to Henry rather than their knowledge of Richard.' I paused for effect before continuing. 'I know Richard did escape. I learnt that from my meeting with Felton and the friars of Anglesey. The attack organised to free Richard after he left Lichfield was a sham. Maudelyn allowed himself to be captured while the real Richard made his way across the Welsh march.'

I stopped talking. The silence in the room was almost tangible, like a perfume or a fragrance. Erpingham's face was pale, almost sallow. Glanville was huddled in his cloak like an old woman sheltering from a biting wind.

'The tombs,' Beaufort asked. 'Why did you order the investigations into the tombs at Kings Langley and Westminster?'

'Well,' I replied briskly, thoroughly enjoying the discomfiture of my two colleagues, 'remember, Richard, or rather Maudelyn, was in Pontefract. When he heard that the rebellion had failed, like a good servant he was loyal to his cause and kept quiet. But the human heart is something that cannot be controlled and Maudelyn simply pined away. Henry must have been pleased for he used Maudelyn's corpse and had the body brought south, pretending it was Richard's, and buried it in lead in Kings Langley.' I licked my lips and took a deep breath for now I was on dangerous ground. 'Our present king,' I continued, 'probably knew something was wrong. He had the body reinterred, not just out of reverence for Richard's memory but because he needed an excuse to look at the corpse. He had probably learnt something from his father. God knows what he expected, but he had the lead sheeting removed, and the body was simply placed in a coffin in Westminster.'

'Then it is not Richard's body which lies there?' Beaufort queried.

'No,' I replied, 'that is not Richard's body. It is Maudelyn's.'

'But again I ask you, why did you ask that the tombs at Westminster be opened?' Beaufort almost snapped as if angry at losing the thread of my argument.

'Oh, at Kings Langley,' I replied, 'the body was sheathed in lead but when Master Glanville opened the tomb at Westminster, the lead covering was gone.'

'So?'

'Our present Lord King was curious, he wanted to see the remains, try and prove that they were Richard's and the nightmare which haunted him was a mere fantasy. Of course, he found little, so the body was simply reburied.'

'What is this nightmare? This fantasy?' Beaufort asked quietly.

'Soon, my Lord,' I replied softly, 'though I think it is obvious, the corpse which lies buried at Westminster will be shown to be Maudelyn's, and the coroners' reports I asked you to scrutinise show no attempt was made to discover the true whereabouts of the King's body!' I paused for effect. 'Sir Thomas Erpingham,' I continued, 'Master Glanville, aren't you interested in what happened to the real king?'

Erpingham simply glared at me, while Glanville sunk lower in his chair. 'Oh, I think you already know,' I went on. 'You see, what happened to the real Richard was that he was treated as an impostor, bound and gagged, and hanged at Tyburn like a common criminal. I think Henry IV knew that and it eventually drove him mad. He, the usurper, had a prince of the royal blood, a descendant of Edward the Confessor, the grandson of the Great Edward III, hanged like a low peasant on the scaffold! And you, Sir Thomas Erpingham, and you, Master Glanville, knew it!'

Erpingham swallowed and stuttered. Glanville interrupted, sardonic as ever, though the fear in his voice could be
detected. 'How do you know that, Jankyn?' he asked.

'Oh, I know that,' I replied, 'because that's what
Prophett found. You see, when the rebels were captured
and Maudelyn was brought south to Oxford, two men
were sent to accompany him. A young lawyer making his
way up in the royal service, named Master Glanville, and a
loyal knight banneret from the royal household, Sir
Thomas Erpingham. You took Maudelyn south! You had
him gagged throughout the journey and during his trial
because you knew he was the real Richard and you did not
want him to say anything in court.'

'You can't prove that!' Erpingham shouted. 'You can't
prove that at all!'

'Oh, no,' I said. 'I can prove very little of what I have
said, but you know the truth and,' I nodded to where the
Bishop sat passively at the head of the table, 'His Lordship
realises it is the truth. Prophett also knew the truth, that's
why both of you killed him. Just as you tried to murder me
months earlier. You gave an assassin a copy of the
chancery pouch I was supposed to carry, he was meant to
kill me and remove the information I bore, only matters
turned out differently. You also tried again in Scotland.
You knew I would enter Tynemouth and had assassins
waiting there but you failed again.'

'Are you, Master Jankyn,' Beaufort interjected, 'accusing
these men of attempted murder as well as being party to
the dishonourable death of a prince of the blood?'

'No,' I muttered, 'I am accusing them of nothing. I am
simply relating facts as I think they happened.'

Erpingham stood up. 'You cannot prove that, Jankyn,'
he said quietly. 'And you must remember that. Do you
think that our present Lord and King would want to know
that his father was party to a royal murder?'

I just stared back. Glanville rose and rearranged his
robes. 'I think we should let the matter rest,' he said. 'We

all know the truth. Let us leave it at that.' Glanville turned
to go and Erpingham, kicking the bench aside and glaring
at me, followed, but I was not finished. 'You two!' I
shouted like a schoolmaster addressing recalcitrant
children, 'do not do anything foolish! Do not send assassins
after me down the dark alleyways and streets of London.
Remember, what I have told you is not only known to His
Lordship here but lies in records in places, and with people
who would be only too pleased to use such information if I
died suddenly. It is in both your interests that I live a long
and peaceful life.'

'Long it may be,' Glanville replied. 'Peaceful, I doubt it,
Jankyn. You are a rogue and you will die like one!'

'But an honest one!' I answered quickly. 'An honest one,
Master Glanville, and that is the difference between us.
Now, sirs, good night.' Both men jerked a bow at Beaufort
and left without another word.

I turned and looked to where His Lordship, his Satanic
Majesty, sat at the head of the table smoothing a piece of
parchment between his long white fingers. 'And you, my
Lord?' I asked. 'You must have known the truth.'

Beaufort shrugged slightly, a smile on his face. 'Oh, yes,'
he said. 'I guessed the truth. Bits and pieces here and
there. Richard must have survived for such legends to
exist. His appearance at Sonning began them all. I think
our present king knows what his father did. He can hardly
live with the knowledge, that's why he hated him. I also
believe that what happened to Richard eventually drove
Henry IV to his grave.'

'Did the King really want to know what happened?' I
asked.

Beaufort smiled. 'Yes and no.'

'And did he choose Erpingham and Glanville?'

Beaufort smiled again. 'Yes and no,' he repeated. 'I
knew both men had looked after the prisoner Maudelyn
and, after their custody of him, both were rapidly
advanced in the royal service. I often wondered why.'

'So, why did you want this knowledge, my Lord?'

'Because it's knowledge,' Beaufort almost whispered. 'Don't you see, Jankyn? Even I need knowledge.'

'To use against the King?'

Beaufort looked at me. 'Why should I need that?'

'You know well, my Lord,' I replied. 'You have every office apart from a cardinal's hat, and once you obtain that, who knows, the papacy? Spiritual leader of all Christendom? Is that your aim?'

Beaufort dug beneath his cloak, drew out a thick, chinking purse and tossed it down on the table. 'My reasons are my own, Jankyn. That is for you. Here!' He took one of the costly rings off his finger and sent it spinning down the table towards me. For a brief second I thought of throwing both back in his face but then, remembering I had to live, I picked up both purse and ring and slipped them into my own pouch. Beaufort got up, walked down the table towards me and came so close I could smell the costly perfume on his skin. He took my face between his hands and for a moment I thought he was going to kiss me but then he smiled. 'Master Jankyn, we are very alike. We are both rogues and we both know it. But I believe our relationship will always be a happy and prosperous one.' Beaufort took his hand away and held it up like a juror taking an oath. 'I swear! By all that is holy I swear that you have nothing to fear from me!' He touched me lightly on the shoulder and walked out of the chamber.

I waited until the room was empty before walking over towards the window. The storm was still crashing above the palace, the raindrops smacking hard against the window. I remember standing there looking back over the past and I recalled the precious moments: my father almost pleading with me at Lilleshall to understand, my days in Sturmey's household, my love-making with Mathilda, the only person I had ever loved. Now they were all gone, lost, like tears in the rain.

Conclusion

Jankyn of course is a liar. He proclaims himself as such at the beginning of his story. However, the cause of the Whyte Harte and the fate of Richard II have been shrouded in mystery and much of the information contained in Jankyn's story is based on historical fact.

In 1399 Richard II was deposed by his cousin, Henry of Lancaster, captured at Flint and taken to Lichfield where, for a while, he did escape before his alleged recapture. After a short sojourn in the Tower of London, he was sent to Pontefract and stayed there while certain of his generals rose in rebellion against Henry IV during Christmas 1399/1400. The rebels attacked the royal palace at Sonning and tried to enlist the support of the ex-queen, Isabella.

The fate of the rebels is accurately described in Jankyn's story, as is the fate of Richard Maudelyn, who was supposedly Richard II's 'Doppelgänger'. Richard allegedly died at Pontefract and, as described in Jankyn's story, was brought south, the body being displayed for public view before being buried at Kings Langley in Hertfordshire and later reinterred at Westminster Abbey by Henry V. The deposed king's cause, however, did lead to constant rebellions for almost twenty years: the Percy uprising in 1403, the conspiracies in Wales, the support of the Franciscans, Henry IV's interrogation of the Frisby brothers, the Duke of Northumberland's constant plotting, and the fact that the Scots are supposed to have sheltered a man claiming to be Richard II at Stirling, where he later died and is buried, are all historical facts. Richard's ex-queen, Isabella, did, for a while, refuse to remarry on the grounds that she believed her husband was still alive.

The facts about the Lollard conspiracy are also accurate. The uprising in 1413, Oldcastle's constant mischievous plotting, his capture and death at Smithfield are all chronicled by the writers of the time. The same is true of Jankyn's description of the Agincourt campaign. His account is so accurate he must have taken part in the battle for he even claims to have been a friend of the one archer King Henry hanged for pillaging.

The Duke of York did die in mysterious circumstances during the battle without a trace of any wound upon his person. Jankyn is a liar but, generally, he seemed to have told the truth. If it is the truth clear and apparent, we shall never know for, like the fate of Richard II, it will be constantly shrouded in mystery.

In conclusion, it is interesting to note that when Richard's tomb was opened at the end of the nineteenth century the archaelogists and doctors found the skeleton of a man about six feet tall. Yet, according to one well informed chronicle, Richard was supposedly shorter than that. Perhaps even in this matter, Jankyn may not be too much of a liar.